CHRISS

RACE AGAINST DEATH

Inspector Narracott was the perfect model of a professional police inspector—calm, methodical, doing everything by the book.

Beautiful young Emily Trefusis was his perfect opposite—impulsive, intuitive, irreverent toward all rules and regulations.

Together, they entered into a competition to solve the baffling case of a man who had died at the very moment his murder was being forecast at a seance miles away.

And it was not long before even the Inspector had to admit Emily was as effective a sleuth as he could ever hope to be . . .

. . . unless, of course, she was a murderess, leading him on a merry chase . . .

Murder At Hazelmoor

AGATHA CHRISTIE

A DELL BOOK

Published by
DELL PUBLISHING CO., INC.
1 Dag Hammarskjold Plaza
New York, New York 10017
For information contact
Dodd, Mead & Company, Inc.,
New York, New York 10016.
Dell ® TM 681510, Dell Publishing Co., Inc.
Reprinted by arrangement with
Dodd, Mead & Company, Inc.
Printed in the United States of America
Previous Dell Edition #5940
New Dell Edition
First printing—July 1976

CONTENTS

CHAPTER ONE

SITTAFORD HOUSE

MAJOR BURNABY DREW ON HIS GUM BOOTS, buttoned his overcoat collar round his neck, took from a shelf near the door a hurricane lantern, and cautiously opened the front door of his little bungalow and peered out.

Everywhere was snow, deep drifts of it—no mere powdering an inch or two thick. Snow had fallen all over England for the last four days, and up here on the fringe of Dartmoor it had attained a depth of several feet. Up here, in the tiny village of Sittaford, at all times remote from the world, and now almost completely cut off, the rigors of winter were a very real problem.

Major Burnaby, however, was a hardy soul. He snorted twice, grunted once, and marched resolutely out into the snow. His destination was not far away. A few paces along a winding lane, then in at a gate, and so up a drive partially swept clear of snow to a house of some considerable size built of granite.

The door was opened by a neatly clad parlormaid. The Major was divested of his British warm, his gum boots, and his aged scarf. A door was flung open and he passed through it into a room which conveyed all the illusion of a transformation scene.

Although it was only half-past three, the curtains had been drawn, the electric lights were on, and a huge fire blazed cheerfully on the hearth. Two women in afternoon frocks rose to greet the stanch old warrior.

"Splendid of you to turn out, Major Burnaby," said the elder of the two.

"Not at all, Mrs. Willett, not at all. Very good of you to ask me." He shook hands with them both.

"Mr. Garfield is coming," went on Mrs. Willett, "and Mr. Duke, and Mr. Rycroft *said* he would come--but one can hardly expect him at his age in such weather. Really, it is *too* dreadful. One feels one *must* do something to keep oneself cheerful. Violet, put another log on the fire."

The Major rose gallantly to perform this task. "Allow me, Miss Violet."

He put the log expertly in the right place and returned once more to the armchair his hostess had indicated. He cast surreptitious glances round the room. Amazing how a couple of women could alter the whole character of a room—and without doing anything very outstanding that you could put your finger on.

Sittaford House had been built ten years ago by Captain Joseph Trevelyan, R.N., on the occasion of his retirement from the Navy. He was a man of substance, and he had always had a great hankering to live on Dartmoor. He had placed his choice on the tiny hamlet of Sittaford. It was not in a valley like most of the villages and farms, but perched right on the shoulder of the moor under the shadow of Sittaford Beacon. He had purchased a large tract of ground, had built a comfortable house with its own electric light plant and an electric pump to save labor in pumping water. Then, as a speculation, he had built six small bungalows, each in its quarter acre of ground, along the lane.

The first of these, the one at his very gates, had been allotted to his old friend and crony, John Burnaby—the others had by degrees been sold, there being still a few people who from choice or necessity like to live right out of the world. The village itself consisted of three picturesque but dilapidated cottages, a forge, and a combined post office and sweet shop. The nearest town was Exhampton, six miles away, a steady descent which necessitated the sign, *Motorists engage your lowest gear*, so familiar on the Dartmoor roads.

Captain Trevelyan, as has been said, was a man of substance. In spite of this—or perhaps because of it—he was a man who was inordinately fond of money. At the end of October a house-agent in Exhampton wrote to him asking if he would consider letting Sittaford House. A tenant had made inquiries concerning it, wishing to rent it for the winter.

Captain Trevelyan's first impulse was to refuse, his second to demand further information. The tenant in question proved to be a Mrs. Willett, a widow with one daughter. She had recently arrived from South Africa and wanted a house on Dartmoor for the winter.

"Damn it all, the woman must be mad," said Captain Trevelyan. "Eh, Burnaby, don't you think so?"

Burnaby did think so, and said so as forcibly as his friend. "Anyway, you don't want to let," he said. "Let the fool woman go somewhere else if she wants to freeze. Coming from South Africa too!"

But at this point Captain Trevelyan's money complex asserted itself. Not once in a hundred times would you get a chance of letting your house in midwinter. He demanded what rent the tenant was willing to pay.

An offer of twelve guineas a week clinched matters. Captain Trevelyan went into Exhampton, rented a small house on the outskirts at two guineas a week, and handed over Sittaford House to Mrs. Willett, half the rent to be paid in advance. "A fool and her money are soon parted," he growled.

But Burnaby was thinking this afternoon, as he scanned Mrs. Willett covertly, that she did not look a fool. She was a tall woman with a rather silly manner— but her physiognomy was shrewd rather than foolish. She was inclined to overdress, had a distinct Colonial accent, and seemed perfectly content with the transaction. She was clearly very well off and that, as Burnaby had reflected more than once, really made the whole affair more odd. She was not the kind of woman one would credit with a passion for solitude.

As a neighbor she had proved almost embarrassingly friendly. Invitations to Sittaford House were rained on everybody. Captain Trevelyan was constantly urged to "Treat the house as though we hadn't rented it." Trevelyan, however, was not fond of women. Report went that he had been jilted in his youth. He persistently refused all invitations. Two months had passed since the installation of the Willetts and the first wonder at their arrival had passed.

Burnaby, naturally a silent man, continued to study his hostess, oblivious to any need for small talk. Liked to make herself out a fool, but wasn't really. So he summed up the situation. His glance shifted to Violet Willett. Pretty girl—scraggy, of course—they all were nowadays.

He roused himself to the necessity of conversation.

"We were afraid at first that you wouldn't be able to come," said Mrs. Willett. "You said so, you remember. We were so pleased when you said that after all you would."

"Friday," said Major Burnaby, with an air of being explicit.

Mrs. Willett looked puzzled. "Friday?"

"Every Friday go to Trevelyan's. Tuesday he comes to me. Both of us done it for years."

"Oh! I see. Of course, living so near—"

"Kind of habit."

"But do you still keep it up? I mean now that he is living in Exhampton—"

"Pity to break a habit," said Major Burnaby. "We'd both of us miss those evenings."

"You go in for competitions, don't you?" asked Violet. "Acrostics and crosswords and all those things."

Burnaby nodded. "I do crosswords. Trevelyan does acrostics. We each stick to our own line of country. I won three books last month in a crossword competition," he volunteered.

"Oh! really. How nice. Were they interesting books?"

"Don't know. Haven't read them. Looked pretty hopeless."

"It's the winning them that matters, isn't it?" said Mrs. Willett vaguely.

"How do you get to Exhampton?" asked Violet. "You haven't got a car."

"Walk."

"What? Not really? Six miles."

"Good exercise. What's twelve miles? Keeps a man fit. Great thing to be fit."

"Fancy! Twelve miles. But both you and Captain Trevelyan were great athletes, weren't you?"

"Used to go to Switzerland together. Winter sports in winter, climbing in summer. Wonderful man on ice, Trevelyan. Both too old for that sort of thing now."

"You won the Army Racquets Championship, too, didn't you?" asked Violet.

The Major blushed like a girl. "Who told you that?" he mumbled.

"Captain Trevelyan."

"Joe should hold his tongue," said Burnaby. "He talks too much. What's the weather like now?"

Respecting his embarrassment, Violet followed him to the window. They drew the curtain aside and looked out. "More snow coming," said Burnaby. "A pretty heavy fall too, I should say."

"Oh! how thrilling," said Violet. "I do think snow is so romantic. I've never seen it before."

"It isn't romantic when the pipes freeze, you foolish child," said her mother.

"Have you lived all your life in South Africa, Miss Willett?" asked Major Burnaby.

Some of the girl's animation dropped away from her. She seemed almost constrained in her manner as she answered. "Yes—this is the first time I've ever been away. It's all most frightfully thrilling."

Thrilling to be shut away like this in a remote moorland village? Funny idea. He couldn't get the hang of these people.

The door opened and the parlormaid announced, "Mr. Rycroft and Mr. Garfield."

There entered a little, elderly, dried-up man and a fresh-colored, boyish young man. The latter spoke first. "I brought him along, Mrs. Willett. Said I wouldn't let him be buried in a snowdrift. Ha, ha. I say, this all looks simply marvelous. Yule logs burning."

"As he says, my young friend very kindly piloted me here," said Mr. Rycroft as he shook hands somewhat ceremoniously. "How do you do, Miss Violet? Very seasonable weather—rather too seasonable, I fear."

He moved to the fire talking to Mrs. Willett. Ronald Garfield buttonholed Violet.

"I say, can't we get up any skating anywhere? Aren't there some ponds about?"

"I think path digging will be your only sport."

"I've been at it all the morning."

"Oh! you he-man!"

"Don't laugh at me. I've got blisters all over my hands."

"How's your aunt?"

"Oh! she's always the same—sometimes she says she's better and sometimes she says she's worse, but I think it's all the same really. It's a ghastly life, you know. Each year, I wonder how I can stick it—but there it is. If one doesn't rally round the old bird for Xmas, why, she's quite capable of leaving her money to a cats' home. She's got five of them, you know. I'm always stroking the brutes and pretending I dote upon them."

"I like dogs much better than cats."

"So do I. Any day. What I mean is a dog is—well, a dog's a dog, you know."

"Has your aunt always been fond of cats?"

"I think it's just a kind of thing old maids grow into. Ugh! I hate the brutes."

"Your aunt's very nice, but rather frightening."

"I should think she was frightening. Snaps my head off sometimes. Thinks I've got no brains."

"Not really?"

"Oh! look here, don't say it like that. Lots of fellows look like fools and are laughing underneath."

"Mr. Duke," announced the parlormaid.

Mr. Duke was a recent arrival. He had bought the last of the six bungalows in September. He was a big man, very quiet and devoted to gardening. Mr. Rycroft, who was an enthusiast on birds, had taken him up, overruling the section of thought which voiced the opinion that of course Mr. Duke was a very nice man, quite unassuming, but was he, after all, quite—well, quite? Mightn't he, just possibly, be a retired tradesman?

But nobody liked to ask him—and indeed it was thought better not to know. Because if one did know, it might be awkward, and really in such a small community it was best to know everybody.

"Not walking to Exhampton in this weather?" he asked of Major Burnaby.

"No, I fancy Trevelyan will hardly expect me to-night."

"It's awful, isn't it?" said Mrs. Willett with a shudder. "To be buried up here, year after year—it must be ghastly."

Mr. Duke gave her a quick glance. Major Burnaby too stared at her curiously.

But at that moment tea was brought in.

CHAPTER TWO

THE MESSAGE

AFTER TEA, Mrs. Willett suggested bridge. "There are six of us. Two can cut in."

Ronnie's eyes brightened. "You four start," he suggested. "Miss Willett and I will cut in."

But Mr. Duke said that he did not play bridge. Ronnie's face fell.

"We might play a round game," said Mrs. Willett.

"Or table turning," suggested Ronnie. "It's a spooky evening. We spoke about it the other day, you remember. Mr. Rycroft and I were talking about it this evening as we came along here."

"I am a member of the Psychical Research Society," explained Mr. Rycroft in his precise way. "I was able to put my young friend right on one or two points."

"Tommyrot," said Major Burnaby distinctly.

"Oh! but it's great fun, don't you think?" said Violet Willett. "I mean, one doesn't believe in it or anything. It's just an amusement. What do you say, Mr. Duke?"

"Anything you like, Miss Willett."

"We must turn the lights out, and we must find a suitable table. No—not that one, Mother. I'm sure it's much too heavy."

Things were settled at last to everyone's satisfaction. A small round table with a polished top was brought from an adjoining room. It was set in front of the fire and everyone took his place round it with the lights switched off.

Major Burnaby was between his hostess and Violet. On the other side of the girl was Ronnie Garfield. A cynical smile creased the Major's lips. He thought to himself, *In my young days it was Up Jenkins.* And he tried to recall the name of a girl with fluffy fair hair whose hand he had held beneath the table at considerable length. A long time ago that was. But Up Jenkins had been a good game.

There were all the usual laughs, whispers, stereotyped remarks. "The spirits are a long time." "Got a long way to come." "Hush—nothing will happen unless we are serious." "Oh! do be quiet—everyone." "Nothing's happening." "Of course not—it never does at first." "If only you'd all be quiet."

At last, after some time, the murmur of talk died away. A silence.

"This table's dead as mutton," murmured Ronnie Garfield disgustedly.

"Hush."

A tremor ran through the polished surface. The table began to rock.

"Ask it questions. Who shall ask? You, Ronnie."

"Oh—er—I say—what do I ask it?"

"Is a spirit present?" prompted Violet.

"Oh! Hullo—is a spirit present?"

A sharp rock.

"That means yes," said Violet.

"Oh! er—who are you?"

No response.

"Ask it to spell its name."

"How can it?"

"We count the number of rocks."

"Oh! I see. Will you please spell your name."

The table started rocking violently.

"A B C D E F G H I—I say, was that I or J?"

"Ask it. Was that I?"

One rock.

"Yes. Next letter, please."

The spirit's name was Ida.

"Have you a message for anyone here?"

Yes.

"Who is it for? Miss Willett?"

No.

"Mrs. Willett?"

No.

"Mr. Rycroft?"

No.

"Me?"

Yes.

"It's for you, Ronnie. Go on. Make it spell it out."

The table spelled *Diana.*

"Who's Diana? Do you know anyone called Diana?"

"No, I don't. At least—"

"There you are. He does."

"Ask her if she's a widow?"

The fun went on. Mr. Rycroft smiled indulgently. Young people must have their jokes. He caught one glance of his hostess's face in a sudden flicker of the firelight. It looked worried and abstracted. Her thoughts were somewhere far away.

Major Burnaby was thinking of the snow. It was going to snow again this evening. Hardest winter he ever remembered.

Mr. Duke was playing very seriously. The spirits, alas, paid very little attention to him. All the messages seemed to be for Violet and Ronnie.

Violet was told she was going to Italy. Someone was going with her. A man. His name was Leonard.

More laughter. The table spelled the name of the town. A Russian jumble of letters—not in the least Italian.

The usual accusations were leveled.

"Look here, Violet. You are shoving."

"I'm not. Look, I take my hands right off the table and it rocks just the same."

"I like raps. I'm going to ask it to rap. Loud ones."

"There should be raps." Ronnie turned to Mr. Rycroft. "There ought to be raps, oughtn't there, sir?"

"Under the circumstances, I should hardly think it likely," said Mr. Rycroft dryly.

There was a pause. The table was inert. It returned no answer to questions.

"Has Ida gone away?"

One languid rock.

"Will another spirit come, please?"

Nothing. Suddenly the table began to quiver and rock violently.

"Hurrah. Are you a new spirit?"

Yes.

"Have you a message for someone?"

Yes.

"For me?"

No.

"For Violet?"

No.

"For Major Burnaby?"

Yes.

"It's for you, Major Burnaby. Will you spell it out, please."

The table started rocking slowly.

"T R E V—are you sure it's V? It can't be. T R E V—it doesn't make sense."

"Trevelyan, of course," said Mrs. Willett. "Captain Trevelyan."

"Do you mean Captain Trevelyan?"

Yes.

"You've got a message for Captain Trevelyan?"

No.

"Well, what is it then?"

The table began to rock—slowly, rhythmically. So slowly that it was easy to count the letters.

"D—" a pause "E—A D."

"Dead."

"Somebody is dead?"

Instead of *Yes* or *No,* the table began to rock again till it reached the letter T.

"T—do you mean Trevelyan?"

Yes.

"You don't mean Trevelyan is dead?"

A very sharp rock. *Yes.*

Somebody gasped. There was a faint stir all round the table. Ronnie's voice as he resumed his questions held a different note—an awed uneasy note.

"You mean—that Captain Trevelyan is dead?"

Yes.

There was a pause. It was as though no one knew what to ask next, or how to take this unexpected development. And in the pause, the table started rocking again.

Rhythmically and slowly. Ronnie spelled out the letters aloud, M-U-R-D-E-R.

Mrs. Willett gave a cry and took her hands off the table. "I won't go on with this. It's horrible. I don't like it."

Mr. Duke's voice rang out, resonant and clear. He was questioning the table. "Do you mean—that Captain Trevelyan has been murdered?"

The last word had hardly left his lips when the answer came. The table rocked so violently and assertively that it nearly fell over. One rock only. *Yes.*

"Look here," said Ronnie. He took his hands from the table. "I call this a rotten joke." His voice trembled.

"Turn up the lights," said Mr. Rycroft.

Major Burnaby rose and did so. The sudden glare revealed a company of pale, uneasy faces.

Everyone looked at each other. Somehow—nobody quite knew what to say.

"All rot, of course," said Ronnie, with an uneasy laugh.

"Silly nonsense," said Mrs. Willett. "Nobody ought to—to make jokes like that."

"Not about people dying," said Violet. "It's— Oh! I don't like it."

"I wasn't shoving," said Ronnie, feeling unspoken criticism leveled at him. "I swear I wasn't."

"I can say the same," said Mr. Duke. "And you, Mr. Rycroft?"

"Certainly not," said Mr. Rycroft warmly.

"You don't think I'd make a joke of that kind, do you?" growled Major Burnaby. "Rotten bad taste."

"Violet, dear—"

"I didn't, Mother. Indeed I didn't. I wouldn't do such a thing." The girl was almost tearful.

Everyone was embarrassed. A sudden blight had come over the cheerful party.

Major Burnaby pushed back his chair, went to the window, and pulled aside the curtain. He stood there looking out with his back to the room.

"Twenty-five minutes past five," said Mr. Rycroft glancing up at the clock. He compared it with his own watch and somehow everyone felt that the action was significant in some way.

"Let me see," said Mrs. Willett with forced cheerfulness. "I think we'd better have cocktails. Will you ring the bell, Mr. Garfield?"

Ronnie obeyed.

Ingredients for cocktails were brought and Ronnie was appointed mixer. The situation grew a little easier.

"Well," said Ronnie, raising his glass. "Here's how."

The others responded—all but the silent figure by the window.

"Major Burnaby. Here's your cocktail."

The Major roused himself with a start. He turned slowly. "Thank you, Mrs. Willett. Not for me." He looked once more out into the night then came slowly back to the group by the fire. "Many thanks for a very pleasant time. Good night."

"You're not going?"

"Afraid I must."

"Not so soon. And on a night like this."

"Sorry, Mrs. Willett—but it's got to be done. If there were only a telephone."

"A telephone?"

"Yes—to tell you the truth—I'm—well, I'd like to be sure that Joe Trevelyan's all right. Silly superstition and all that—but there it is. Naturally, I don't believe in this tommyrot—but—"

"But you can't telephone from anywhere. There's not such a thing in Sittaford."

"That's just it. As I can't telephone, I'll have to go."

"Go—but you couldn't get a car down that road! Elmer wouldn't take his car out on such a night."

Elmer was the proprietor of the sole car in the place, an aged Ford, hired at a handsome price by those who wished to go into Exhampton.

"No, no—car's out of the question. My two legs will take me there, Mrs. Willett."

There was a chorus of protest.

"Oh! Major Burnaby—it's *impossible*. You said yourself it was going to snow."

"Not for an hour—perhaps longer. I'll get there, never fear."

"Oh! you can't. We can't allow it." She was seriously disturbed and upset.

But argument and entreaty had no more effect on Major Burnaby than if he were a rock. He was an obstinate man. Once his mind was made up on any point, no power on earth could move him.

He had determined to walk to Exhampton and see for himself that all was well with his old friend, and he repeated that simple statement half a dozen times. In the end they were brought to realize that he meant it. He wrapped himself up in his overcoat, lighted the hurricane lantern, and stepped out into the night.

"I'll just drop into my place for a flask," he said cheerily, "and then push straight on. Trevelyan will put me up for the night when I get there. Ridiculous fuss, I know. Everything sure to be all right. Don't worry, Mrs. Willett. Snow or no snow—I'll get there in a couple of hours. Good night."

He strode away. The others returned to the fire.

Rycroft had looked up at the sky. "It *is* going to snow," he murmured to Mr. Duke. "And it will begin long before he gets to Exhampton. I—I hope he gets there all right."

Duke frowned. "I know. I feel I ought to have gone with him. One of us ought to have done so."

"Most distressing," Mrs. Willett was saying. "Most distressing. Violet, I will not have that silly game ever played again. Poor Major Burnaby will probably plunge into a snowdrift—or if he doesn't he'll die of the cold and exposure. At his age, too. Very foolish of him to go off like that. Of course, Captain Trevelyan is perfectly all right."

Everyone echoed, "Of course."

But even now they did not feel really too comfortable. Supposing something *had* happened to Captain Trevelyan. . . . Supposing. . . .

CHAPTER THREE

FIVE-AND-TWENTY PAST FIVE

TWO AND A HALF HOURS LATER, just before eight o'clock, Major Burnaby, hurricane lantern in hand, his head dropped forward so as not to meet the blinding drive of the snow, stumbled up the path to the door of "Hazelmoor," the small house tenanted by Captain Trevelyan.

The snow had begun to fall about an hour ago—great blinding flakes of it. Major Burnaby was gasping, emitting the loud sighing gasps of an utterly exhausted man. He was numbed with cold. He stamped his feet, blew, puffed, snorted, and applied a numbed finger to the bell push. The bell trilled shrilly.

Burnaby waited. After a pause of a few minutes, as nothing happened, he pushed the bell again.

Once more there was no stir of life.

Burnaby rang a third time. This time he kept his finger on the bell. It trilled on and on—but there was still no sign of life in the house.

There was a knocker on the door. Major Burnaby seized it and worked it vigorously, producing a noise like thunder. And still the little house remained silent as the dead.

The Major desisted. He stood for a moment as though perplexed—then he slowly went down the path and out at the gate, continuing on the road he had come toward Exhampton. A hundred yards brought him to the small police station. He hesitated again, then finally made up his mind and entered.

Constable Graves, who knew the Major well, rose in astonishment. "Well, I never, sir, fancy you being out on a night like this."

"Look here," said Burnaby curtly. "I've been ringing

and knocking at the Captain's house and I can't get any answer."

"Why, of course, it's Friday," said Graves, who knew the habits of the two pretty well. "But you don't mean to say you've actually come down from Sittaford on a night like this? Surely the Captain would never expect you."

"Whether he's expected me or not, I've come," said Burnaby testily. "And as I'm telling you, I can't get in. I've rung and knocked and nobody answers."

Some of his uneasiness seemed to communicate itself to the policeman. "That's odd," he said, frowning.

"Of course it's odd," said Burnaby.

"It's not as though he's likely to be out—on a night like this."

"Of course he's not likely to be out."

"It *is* odd," said Graves again.

Burnaby displayed impatience at the man's slowness. "Aren't you going to do something?" he snapped.

"Do something?"

"Yes, do something."

The policeman ruminated. "Think he might have been taken bad?" His face brightened. "I'll try the telephone." It stood at his elbow. He took it up and gave the number.

But to the telephone, as to the front door bell, Captain Trevelyan gave no reply.

"Looks as though he *had* been taken bad," said Graves as he replaced the receiver. "And all alone in the house, too. We'd best get hold of Dr. Warren and take him along with us."

Dr. Warren's house was almost next door to the police station. The doctor was just sitting down to dinner with his wife and was not pleased at the summons. However, he grudgingly agreed to accompany them, drawing on an aged British warm and a pair of rubber boots and muffling his neck with a knitted scarf.

The snow was still falling.

"Damnable night," murmured the doctor. "Hope you

haven't brought me out on a wild goose chase. Trevelyan's as strong as a horse. Never has anything the matter
with him."

Burnaby did not reply.

Arriving at Hazelmoor once more, they again rang
and knocked, but elicited no response.

The doctor then suggested going round the house to
one of the windows. "Easier to force than the door."

Graves agreeing, they went round to the back. There
was a side door which they tried on the way, but it too
was locked, and presently they emerged on the snow-
covered lawn that led up to the back windows. Suddenly
Warren uttered an exclamation.

"The window of the study—it's open."

True enough, the window, a French one, was standing ajar. They quickened their steps. On a night like
this, no one in his senses would open a window. There
was a light in the room that streamed out in a thin yel-
low band.

The three men arrived simultaneously at the window
—Burnaby was the first man to enter, the constable hard
on his heels. They both stopped dead inside and something like a muffled cry came from the ex-soldier. In
another moment Warren was beside them, and saw what
they had seen.

Captain Trevelyan lay on the floor, face downward.
His arms sprawled widely. The room was in confusion
—drawers of the bureau pulled out, papers lying about
the floor. The window beside them was splintered where
it had been forced near the lock. Beside Captain Trevelyan was a dark green baize tube about two inches in
diameter.

Warren sprang forward. He knelt down by the pros-
trate figure. One minute sufficed. He rose to his feet, his
face pale.

"He's dead?" asked Burnaby.

The doctor nodded. Then he turned to Graves.

"It's you to say what's to be done. I can do nothing
except examine the body and perhaps you'd rather I

didn't do that until the Inspector comes. I can tell you the cause of death now. Fracture of the base of the skull. And I think I can make a guess at the weapon."

He indicated the green baize tube.

"Trevelyan always had them along the bottom of the door—to keep the draft out," said Burnaby.

His voice was hoarse.

"Yes—a very efficient form of sandbag."

"My God!"

"But this here—" the constable broke in, his wits arriving at the point slowly. "You mean—this here is murder."

The policeman stepped to the table on which stood a telephone.

Major Burnaby approached the doctor. "Have you any idea," he said, breathing hard, "how long he's been dead?"

"About two hours, I should say, or possibly three. That's a rough estimate."

Burnaby passed his tongue over dry lips. "Would you say," he asked, "that he might have been killed at five twenty-five?"

The doctor looked at him curiously.

"If I had to give a time definitely, that's just about the time I would suggest."

"Oh! my God," said Burnaby.

Warren stared at him.

The Major felt his way blindly to a chair, collapsed on to it and muttered to himself while a kind of staring terror overspread his face.

"*Five-and-twenty past five*— Oh! my God, then it *was* true after all."

CHAPTER FOUR

INSPECTOR NARRACOTT

IT WAS THE MORNING AFTER THE TRAGEDY, and two men were standing in the little study of Hazelmoor.

Inspector Narracott looked round him. A little frown appeared upon his forehead. "Ye-es," he said thoughtfully. "Ye-es."

Inspector Narracott was a very efficient officer. He had a quiet persistence, a logical mind, and a keen attention to detail which brought him success where many another man might have failed.

He was a tall man with a quiet manner, rather faraway gray eyes, and a slow, soft Devonshire voice.

Summoned from Exeter to take charge of the case, he had arrived on the first train that morning. The roads had been impassable for cars, even with chains, otherwise he would have arrived the night before. He was standing now in Captain Trevelyan's study, having just completed his examination of the room. With him was Sergeant Pollock of the Exhampton police.

"Ye-es," said Inspector Narracott.

A ray of pale wintry sunshine came in through the window. Outside was the snowy landscape. There was a fence about a hundred yards from the window and beyond it the steep ascending slope of the hillside.

Inspector Narracott bent once more over the body which had been left for his inspection. An athletic man himself, he recognized the athlete's type, the broad shoulders, narrow flanks, and the good muscular development. The head was small and well set on the shoulders, and the pointed naval beard was carefully trimmed. Captain Trevelyan's age, he had ascertained, was sixty, but he looked not much more than fifty-one.

"It's a curious business," said Inspector Narracott.

"Ah!" said Sergeant Pollock.

The other turned on him. "What is your view of it?"

"Well—" Sergeant Pollock scratched his head. He was a cautious man, unwilling to advance further than necessary. "Well," he said, "as I see it, sir, I should say that the man came to the window, forced the lock, and started rifling the room. Captain Trevelyan, I suppose, must have been upstairs. Doubtless the burglar thought the house was empty—"

"Where is Captain Trevelyan's bedroom situated?"

"Upstairs, sir. Over this room."

"At the present time of year it is dark at four o'clock. If Captain Trevelyan was up in his bedroom, the electric light would have been on, the burglar would have seen it as he approached this window."

"You mean he'd have waited."

"No man in his senses would break into a house with a light in it. If anyone forced this window—he did it because he thought the house was empty."

Sergeant Pollock scratched his head.

"Seems a bit odd, I admit. But there it is."

"We'll let it pass for the moment. Go on."

"Well, suppose the Captain hears a noise downstairs. He comes down to investigate. The burglar hears him coming. He snatches up that bolster arrangement, gets behind the door, and as the Captain enters the room strikes him down from behind."

Inspector Narracott nodded. "Yes, that's true enough. He was struck down when he was facing the window. But all the same, Pollock, I don't like it."

"No, sir?"

"No, as I say, I don't believe in houses that are broken into at five o'clock in the afternoon."

"We-ell, he may have thought it a good opportunity—"

"It is not a question of opportunity—slipping in because he found a window unlatched. It was deliberate house-breaking—look at the confusion everywhere—what would a burglar go for first? The pantry where the silver is kept."

"That's true enough," admitted the Sergeant.

"And this confusion—this chaos," continued Narracott, "these drawers pulled out and their contents scattered. Pah! It's bunkum."

"Bunkum?"

"Look at the window, Sergeant. *That window was not locked and forced open!* It was merely shut and then splintered from the outside to give the appearance of forcing."

Pollock examined the latch of the window closely, uttering an ejaculation to himself as he did so.

"You are right, sir," he said with respect in his voice. "Who'd have thought of that now!"

"Someone who wishes to throw dust in our eyes—and hasn't succeeded."

Sergeant Pollock was grateful for the "our." In such small ways did Inspector Narracott endear himself to his subordinates. "Then it wasn't burglary? You mean, sir, it was an inside job?"

Inspector Narracott nodded. "Yes," he said. "The only curious thing is, though, that I think the murderer did actually enter by the window. As you and Graves reported, and as I can still see for myself, there are damp patches still visible where the snow melted and was trodden in by the murderer's boots. These damp patches are only in this room. Constable Graves was quite positive that there was nothing of the kind in the hall when he and Dr. Warren passed through it. In this room he noticed them immediately. In that case it seems clear that the murderer was admitted by Captain Trevelyan through the window. Therefore it must have been someone whom Captain Trevelyan knew. You are a local man, Sergeant, can you tell me if Captain Trevelyan was a man who made enemies easily?"

"No, sir, I should say he hadn't an enemy in the world. A bit keen on money, and a bit of a martinet—wouldn't stand for any slackness or incivility—but bless my soul, he was respected for that."

"No enemies," said Narracott thoughtfully.

"Not here, that is."

"Very true—we don't know what enemies he may have made during his naval career. It's my experience, Sergeant, that a man who makes enemies in one place will make them in another, but I agree that we can't put that possibility entirely aside. We come logically now to the next motive—the most common motive for every crime—gain. Captain Trevelyan was, I understand, a rich man?"

"Very warm indeed by all accounts. But close. Not an easy man to touch for a subscription."

"Ah!" said Narracott thoughtfully.

"Pity it snowed as it did," said the Sergeant. "But for that we'd have had his footprints as something to go on."

"There was no one else in the house?" asked the Inspector.

"No. For the last five years Captain Trevelyan has only had one servant—retired naval chap. Up at Sittaford House a woman came in daily, but this chap, Evans, cooked and looked after his master. About a month ago he got married—much to the Captain's annoyance. I believe that's one of the reasons he let Sittaford House to this South African lady. He wouldn't have any woman living in the house. Evans lives just round the corner here in Fore Street with his wife, and comes in daily to do for his master. I've got him here now for you to see. His statement is that he left here at half-past two yesterday afternoon, the Captain having no further need for him."

"Yes, I shall want to see him. He may be able to tell us something—useful."

Sergeant Pollock looked at his superior officer curiously. There was something so odd about his tone.

"You think—" he began.

"I think," said Inspector Narracott deliberately, "that there's a lot more in this case than meets the eye."

"In what way, sir?"

But the Inspector refused to be drawn. "You say this

man, Evans, is here now?"

"He's waiting in the dining-room."

"Good. I'll see him straight away. What sort of a fellow is he?"

Sergeant Pollock was better at reporting facts than at descriptive accuracy. "He's a retired naval chap. Ugly customer in a scrap, I should say."

"Does he drink?"

"Never been the worse for it that I know of."

"What about this wife of his? Not a fancy of the Captain's or anything of that sort?"

"Oh! no, sir, nothing of that kind about Captain Trevelyan. He wasn't that kind at all. He was known as a woman hater, if anything."

"And Evans was supposed to be devoted to his master?"

"That's the general idea, sir, and I think it would be known if he wasn't. Exhampton's a small place."

Inspector Narracott nodded. "Well," he said, "there's nothing more to be seen here. I'll interview Evans and I'll take a look at the rest of the house and after that we will go over to the Three Crowns and see this Major Burnaby. That remark of his about the time was curious. Twenty-five minutes past five, eh? He must know something he hasn't told, or why should he suggest the time of the crime so accurately."

The two men moved toward the door.

"It's a rum business," said Sergeant Pollock, his eye wandering to the littered floor. "All this burglary fake!"

"It's not that that strikes me as odd," said Narracott; "under the circumstances it was probably the natural thing to do. No—what strikes me as odd is the window."

"The window, sir?"

"Yes. Why should the murderer go to the window? Assuming it was someone Trevelyan knew and admitted without question, why not go to the front door? To get round to this window from the road on a night like last night would have been a difficult and unpleasant proceeding with the snow lying as thick as it does.

Yet there must have been some reason."

"Perhaps," suggested Pollock, "the man didn't want to be seen turning into the house from the road."

"There wouldn't be many people about yesterday afternoon to see him. Nobody who could help it was out of doors. No—there's some other reason. Well, perhaps it will come to light in due course."

CHAPTER FIVE

EVANS

THEY FOUND EVANS waiting in the dining-room. He rose respectfully on their entrance.

He was a short thickset man. He had very long arms and a habit of standing with his hands half clenched. He was clean shaven with small, rather piglike eyes, yet he had a look of cheerfulness and efficiency that redeemed his bulldog appearance.

Inspector Narracott mentally tabulated his impressions: *Intelligent. Shrewd and practical. Looks rattled.*

Then he spoke: "You're Evans, eh?"

"Yes, sir."

"Christian names?"

"Robert Henry."

"Ah! Now what do you know about this business?"

"Not a thing, sir. It's fair knocked me over. To think of the Capting being done in!"

"When did you last see your master?"

"Two o'clock I should say it was, sir. I cleared away the lunch things and laid the table here as you see for supper. The Capting, he told me I needn't come back."

"What do you usually do?"

"As a general rule, I come back about seven for a couple of hours. Not always—sometimes the Capting would say as I needn't."

"Then you weren't surprised when he told you that yesterday you wouldn't be wanted again?"

"No, sir. I didn't come back the evening before either —on account of the weather. Very considerate gentleman, the Capting was, as long as you didn't try to shirk things. I knew him and his ways pretty well."

"What exactly did he say?"

"Well, he looked out of the window and he says, 'Not

a hope of Burnaby today. Shouldn't wonder,' he says, 'if Sittaford isn't cut off altogether. Don't remember such a winter since I was a boy.' That was his friend Major Burnaby over to Sittaford that he was referring to. Always comes on a Friday, he does; he and the Capting play chess and do acrostics. And on Tuesdays the Capting would go to Major Burnaby's. Very regular in his habits was the Capting. Then he said to me, 'You can go now, Evans, and you needn't come till tomorrow morning.' "

"Apart from his reference to Major Burnaby, he didn't speak of expecting anyone that afternoon?"

"No, sir, not a word."

"There was nothing unusual or different in any way in his manner?"

"No, sir, not that I could see."

"Ah! Now I understand, Evans, that you have lately got married."

"Yes, sir. Mrs. Belling's daughter at the Three Crowns. Matter of two months ago, sir."

"And Captain Trevelyan was not overpleased."

A very faint grin appeared for a moment on Evans's face. "Cut up rough about it, he did, the Capting. My Rebecca is a fine girl, sir, and a very good cook. And I hoped we might have been able to do for the Capting together, but he—he wouldn't hear of it. Said he wouldn't have women servants about his house. In fact, sir, things were rather at a deadlock when this South African lady came along and wanted to take Sittaford House for the winter. The Capting he rented this place, I came in to do for him every day, and I don't mind telling you, sir, that I had been hoping that by the end of the winter the Capting would have come round to the idea; and that me and Rebecca would go back to Sittaford with him. Why, he would never even know she was in the house. She would keep to the kitchen, and she would manage so that he would never meet her on the stairs."

"Have you any idea what lay behind Captain Trevelyan's dislike of women?"

"Nothing to it, sir. Just an 'abit, sir, that's all. I have seen many a gentleman like it before. If you ask me, it's nothing more or less than shyness. Some young lady or other gives them a snub when they are young—and they gets the 'abit."

"Captain Trevelyan was not married?"

"No, indeed, sir."

"What relations had he? Do you know?"

"I believe he had a sister living at Exeter, sir, and I think I have heard him mention a nephew or nephews."

"None of them ever came to see him?"

"No, sir. I think he quarreled with his sister at Exeter."

"Do you know her name?"

"Gardner, I think, sir, but I wouldn't be sure."

"You don't know her address?"

"I'm afraid I don't, sir."

"Well, doubtless we shall come across that in looking through Captain Trevelyan's papers. Now, Evans, what were you yourself doing from four o'clock onward yesterday afternoon?"

"I was at home, sir."

"Where's home?"

"Just round the corner, sir, 85 Fore Street."

"You didn't go out at all?"

"Not likely, sir. Why, the snow was coming down a fair treat."

"Yes, yes. Is there anyone who can support your statement?"

"Beg pardon, sir."

"Is there anyone who knows that you were at home during that time?"

"My wife, sir."

"She and you were alone in the house?"

"Yes, sir."

"Well, well, I have no doubt that's all right. That will be all for the present, Evans."

The ex-sailor hesitated. He shifted from one foot to

the other. "Anything I can do here, sir—in the way of tidying up?"

"No—the whole place is to be left exactly as it is for the present."

"I see."

"You had better wait, though, until I have had a look around," said Narracott, "in case there might be any question I want to ask you."

"Very good, sir."

Inspector Narracott transferred his gaze from Evans to the room.

The interview had taken place in the dining-room. On the table an evening meal was set out. A cold tongue, pickles, a Stilton cheese and biscuits, and on a gas ring by the fire a saucepan containing soup. On the sideboard was a tantalus, a soda water siphon, and two bottles of beer. There was also an immense array of silver cups and with them—a rather incongruous item—three very new-looking novels.

Inspector Narracott examined one or two of the cups and read the inscriptions on them. "Bit of a sportsman, Captain Trevelyan," he observed.

"Yes, indeed, sir," said Evans. "Been an athlete all his life, he had."

Inspector Narracott read the titles of the novels: *Love Turns the Key, The Merry Men of Lincoln, Love's Prisoner.*

"H'm," he remarked. "The Captain's taste in literature seems somewhat incongruous."

"Oh! that, sir," Evans laughed. "That's not for reading, sir. That's the prizes he won in these Railway Pictures Names Competitions. Ten solutions the Capting sent in under different names, including mine, because he said 85 Fore Street was a likely address to give a prize to! The commoner your name and address the more likely you were to get a prize in the Capting's opinion. And sure enough a prize I got—but not the 2,000 pounds, only three new novels—and the kind of novels, in my opinion, that no one would ever pay money for."

Narracott smiled, then again mentioning that Evans was to wait, he proceeded on his tour of inspection. There was a large kind of cupboard in one corner of the room. It was almost a small room in itself. Here, packed in unceremoniously, were two pairs of skis, a pair of sculls mounted, ten or twelve hippopotamus tusks, rods and lines and various fishing tackle including a book of flies, a bag of golf clubs, a tennis racket, an elephant's foot stuffed and mounted, and a tiger skin. It was clear that, when Captain Trevelyan had let Sittaford House furnished, he had removed his most precious possessions, distrustful of female influence.

"Funny idea—to bring all this with him," said the Inspector. "The house was only let for a few months, wasn't it?"

"That's right, sir."

"Surely these things could have been locked up at Sittaford House?"

For the second time in the course of the interview, Evans grinned. "That would have been much the easiest way of doing it," he agreed. "Not that there *are* many cupboards at Sittaford House. The architect and the Capting planned it together, and it takes a female to understand the value of cupboard room. Still, as you say, sir, that would have been the common-sense thing to do. Carting them down here was a job—I should say it was a job! But there, the Capting couldn't bear the idea of anyone messing around with his things. And lock things up as you will, he says, a woman will always find a way of getting in. It's curiosity, he says. Better not lock them up at all if you don't want her to handle them, he says. But best of all, take them along, and then you're sure to be on the safe side. So take 'em along we did, and as I say, it was a job, and came expensive too. But there, those things of the Capting's was like his children."

Evans paused out of breath.

Inspector Narracott nodded thoughtfully. There was another point on which he wanted information, and it seemed to him that this was a good moment when the subject had arisen naturally.

"This Mrs. Willett," he said casually. "Was she an old friend or acquaintance of the Captain's?"

"Oh! no, sir, she was quite a stranger to him."

"You are sure of that?" said the Inspector, sharply.

"Well—" The sharpness took the old sailor aback. "The Capting never actually said so—but— Oh! yes, I'm sure of it."

"I ask," explained the Inspector, "because it is a very curious time of year for a let. On the other hand, if this Mrs. Willett was acquainted with Captain Trevelyan and knew the house, she might have written to him and suggested taking it."

Evans shook his head. " 'Twas the agents—Williamsons—that wrote, said they had an offer from a lady."

Inspector Narracott frowned. He found this business of the letting of Sittaford House distinctly odd. "Captain Trevelyan and Mrs. Willett met, I suppose?"

"Oh! yes. She came to see the house and he took her over it."

"And you're positive they hadn't met before?"

"Oh! quite, sir."

"Did they—er—" The Inspector paused, as he tried to frame the question naturally. "Did they get on well together? Were they friendly?"

"The lady was." A faint smile crossed Evans's lips. "All over him, as you might say. Admiring the house, and asking him if he'd planned the building of it. Altogether laying it on thick, as you might say."

"And the Captain?"

The smile broadened. "That sort of gushing lady wasn't likely to cut any ice with him. Polite he was, but nothing more. And declined her invitations."

"Invitations?"

"Yes, to consider the house as his own any time, and drop in, that's how she put it—drop in. You don't drop in to a place when you're living six miles away."

"She seemed anxious to—well—to see something of the Captain?"

Narracott was wondering. Was that the reason for the taking of the house? Was it only a prelude to the making of Captain Trevelyan's acquaintance? Was that the real game? It would probably not have occurred to her that the Captain would have gone as far as Exhampton to live. She might have calculated on his moving into one of the small bungalows, perhaps sharing Major Burnaby's.

Evans's answer was not very helpful. "She's a very hospitable lady, by all accounts. Someone in to lunch or dinner every day."

Narracott nodded. He could learn no more here. But he determined to seek an interview with this Mrs. Willett. Her abrupt arrival needed looking into.

"Come on, Pollock, we'll go upstairs now," he said. They left Evans in the dining-room and proceeded to the upper story.

"All right, do you think?" asked the Sergeant in a low voice, jerking his head over his shoulder in the direction of the closed dining-room door.

"He seems so," said the Inspector. "But one never knows. He's no fool, that fellow, whatever else he is."

"No, he's an intelligent sort of chap."

"His story seems straightforward enough," went on the Inspector. "Perfectly clear and aboveboard. Still, as I say, one never knows."

And with this pronouncement, very typical of his careful and suspicious mind, the Inspector proceeded to search the rooms. There were three bedrooms and a bathroom. Two of the bedrooms were empty and had clearly not been entered for some weeks. The third, Captain Trevelyan's own room, was in exquisite and apple-pie order. Inspector Narracott moved about in it, opening drawers and cupboards. Everything was in its right place. It was the room of a man almost fanatically tidy and neat in his habits. Narracott finished his inspection and glanced into the adjoining bathroom. Here, too, everything was in order.

Then he shook his head. "Nothing here," he said.

"No, everything seems in perfect order."

"There are the papers in the desk in the study. You had better go through those, Pollock. I'll tell Evans that he can go. I may call round and see him at his own place later."

"Very good, sir."

"The body can be removed. I shall want to see Warren, by the way. He lives near here, doesn't he?"

"Yes, sir."

"This side of the Three Crowns or the other?"

"The other, sir."

"Then I'll take the Three Crowns first. Carry on, Sergeant."

Pollock went to the dining-room to dismiss Evans. The Inspector passed out of the front door and walked rapidly in the direction of the Three Crowns.

CHAPTER SIX

AT THE THREE CROWNS

INSPECTOR NARRACOTT WAS NOT DESTINED to see Major Burnaby until he had had a protracted interview with Mrs. Belling—licensed proprietor of the Three Crowns. Mrs. Belling was fat and excitable, and so voluble that there was nothing to be done but to listen patiently until such time as the stream of conversation should dry up.

"And such a night as never was," she ended up. "And little did any of us think what was happening to the poor dear gentleman. Those nasty tramps—if I've said it once, I've said it a dozen times, I can't abide those nasty tramps. Do anybody in, they would. The Captain had not so much as a dog to protect him. Can't abide a dog, tramps can't. Ah, well, you never know what is happening within a stone's throw.

"Yes, Mr. Narracott," she proceeded in answer to his question, "the Major is having his breakfast now. You will find him in the coffee-room. And what kind of a night he has passed with no pajamas or anything, and me a widow woman with nothing to lend him, I can't say, I am sure. Said it made no matter, he did—all upset and queer he was—and no wonder with his best friend murdered. Very nice gentlemen the two of them, though the Captain had the reputation of being close with his money. Ah, well, well, I have always thought it dangerous to live up to Sittaford, miles away from anywhere, and here's the Captain struck down in Exhampton itself. It's always what you don't expect in this life that happens, isn't it, Mr. Narracott?"

The Inspector said that undoubtedly it was. Then he added, "Who did you have staying here yesterday, Mrs. Belling? Any strangers?"

"Now, let me see. There was Mr. Moresby and Mr. Jones—commercial gentlemen they are, and there was a young gentleman from London. Nobody else. It stands to reason there wouldn't be this time of year. Very quiet here in the winter. Oh, and there was another young gentleman—arrived by the last train. Nosy young fellow, I call him. He isn't up yet."

"The last train?" said the Inspector. "That gets in at ten o'clock, eh? I don't think we need trouble ourselves about him. What about the other—the one from London? Did you know him?"

"Never seen him before in my life. Not a commercial gentleman, oh, no—a cut above that. I can't remember his name for the moment—but you'll find it in the register. Left on the first train to Exeter this morning, he did. Six-ten. Rather curious. What did he want down here anyway, that's what I'd like to know."

"He didn't mention his business?"

"Not a word."

"Did he go out at all?"

"Arrived at lunch time, went out about half-past four and came in about twenty past six."

"Where did he go when he went out?"

"I haven't the remotest idea, sir. May have been just for a stroll like. That was before the snow came, but it wasn't what you might call a pleasant day for walking."

"Went out at half-past four and returned about twenty past six," said the Inspector thoughtfully. "That's rather odd. He didn't mention Captain Trevelyan?"

Mrs. Belling shook her head decisively. "No, Mr. Narracott, he didn't mention anybody at all. Kept himself to himself, he did. A nice-looking young fellow—but worried, I should say."

The Inspector nodded and stepped across to inspect the register. "James Pearson, London," said the Inspector. "Well—that doesn't tell us much. We'll have to make a few inquiries about Mr. James Pearson."

Then he strode off to the coffee-room in search of Major Burnaby.

The Major was the only occupant of the room. He was drinking some rather muddy-looking coffee and the *Times* was propped up in front of him.

"Major Burnaby?"

"That's my name."

"I am Inspector Narracott from Exeter."

"Good morning, Inspector. Any forrarder?"

"Yes, sir. I think we are a little forrarder. I think I can safely say that."

"Glad to hear it," said the Major dryly. His attitude was one of resigned disbelief.

"Now there are just one or two points I would like some information on, Major Burnaby," said the Inspector, "and I think you can probably tell me what I want to know."

"Do what I can," said Burnaby.

"Had Captain Trevelyan any enemies?"

"Not an enemy in the world." Burnaby was decisive.

"This man, Evans—do you yourself consider him trustworthy?"

"Should think so. Trevelyan trusted him, I know."

"There was no ill feeling about this marriage of his?"

"Not ill feeling, no. Trevelyan was annoyed—didn't like his habits upset. Old bachelor, you know."

"Talking of bachelors, that's another point. Captain Trevelyan was unmarried—do you know if he made a will? And in the event of there being no will, have you any idea who would inherit his estate?"

"Trevelyan made a will," said Burnaby promptly.

"Ah—you know that."

"Yes. Made me executor. Told me so."

"Do you know how he left his money?"

"That I can't say."

"I understand he was very comfortably off?"

"Trevelyan was a rich man," replied Burnaby. "I should say he was much better off than anyone round here suspected."

"What relations had he—do you know?"

"He'd a sister and some nephews and nieces, I believe.

Never saw much of any of them, but there was no quarrel."

"About this will, do you know where he kept it?"

"It's at Walters & Kirkwood—the solicitors here in Exhampton. They drew it up for him."

"Then, perhaps, Major Burnaby, as you are executor, I wonder if you would come round to Walters & Kirkwood with me now. I should like to have an idea of the contents of that will as soon as possible."

Burnaby looked up alertly. "What's in the wind?" he said. "What's the will got to do with it?"

Inspector Narracott was not disposed to show his hand too soon. "The case isn't such plain sailing as we thought," he said. "By the way, there's another question I want to ask you. I understand, Major Burnaby, that you asked Dr. Warren whether death had occurred at five-and-twenty minutes past five?"

"Well?" said the Major gruffly.

"What made you select that exact time, Major?"

"Why shouldn't I?" said Burnaby.

"Well—something must have put it into your head."

There was quite a pause before Major Burnaby replied. Inspector Narracott's interest was aroused. The Major had something which he quite patently wished to conceal. To watch him doing so was almost ludicrous.

"Why shouldn't I say twenty-five past five?" he demanded truculently, "or twenty-five to six—or twenty past four, for that matter?"

"Quite so, sir," said Inspector Narracott soothingly.

He did not wish to antagonize the Major just at this moment. He promised himself that he would get to the bottom of the matter before the day was out. "There's one thing that strikes me as curious, sir," he went on.

"Yes?"

"This business of the letting of Sittaford House. I don't know what you think about it, but it seems to me a curious thing to have happened."

"If you ask me," said Burnaby, "it's damned odd."

"That's your opinion?"

"It's everyone's opinion."

"In Sittaford?"

"In Sittaford and Exhampton too. The woman must be mad."

"Well, I suppose there's no accounting for tastes," said the Inspector.

"Damned odd taste for a woman of that kind."

"You know the lady?"

"I know her. Why, I was at her house when—"

"When what?" asked Narracott as the Major came to an abrupt halt.

"Nothing," said Burnaby.

Inspector Narracott looked at him keenly. There was something here he would have liked to get at. The Major's obvious confusion and embarrassment did not escape him. He had been on the point of saying—what?

All in good time, said Narracott to himself. *Now isn't the moment to rub him up the wrong way.*

Aloud he said innocently, "You were at Sittaford House, you say, sir. The lady has been there now—about how long?"

"A couple of months."

The Major was eager to escape the result of his imprudent words. It made him more loquacious than usual.

"A widow lady with her daughter?"

"That's it."

"Does she give any reason for her choice of residence?"

"Well—" The Major rubbed his nose dubiously. "She talks a lot, she's that kind of woman—beauties of nature —out of the world—that sort of thing. But—"

He paused rather helplessly. Inspector Narracott came to his rescue. "It didn't strike you as natural."

"Well, it's like this. She's a fashionable sort of woman. Dressed up to the nines—daughter's a smart, pretty girl. Natural thing would be for them to be staying at the Ritz or Claridges, or some other big hotel somewhere. You know the sort."

Narracott nodded. "They don't keep themselves to themselves, do they?" he asked. "You don't think they are—well—hiding?"

Major Burnaby shook his head positively. "Oh, no, nothing of that kind. They're very sociable—a bit too sociable. I mean, in a little place like Sittaford, you can't have previous engagements, and when invitations are showered on you it's a bit awkward. They're exceedingly kind, hospitable people, but a bit too hospitable for English ideas."

"The Colonial touch," said the Inspector.

"Yes, I suppose so."

"You've no reason to think they were previously acquainted with Captain Trevelyan?"

"Sure they weren't."

"You seem very positive?"

"Joe would have told me."

"And you don't think their motive could have been—well—to scrape acquaintance with the Captain?"

This was clearly a new idea to the Major. He pondered over it for some minutes. "Well, I never thought of that. They were very gushing to him, certainly. Not that they got any change out of Joe. But no, I think it was just their usual manner. Over friendly, you know, like Colonials are," added the Super Insular soldier.

"I see. Now, as to the house itself. Captain Trevelyan built that, I understand?"

"Yes."

"And nobody else has ever lived in it? I mean, it's not been let before?"

"Never."

"Then it doesn't seem as though it could be anything in the house itself that was the attraction. It's a puzzle. Ten to one it's got nothing to do with the case, but it just struck me as an odd coincidence. This house that Captain Trevelyan took, Hazelmoor, whose property was that?"

"Miss Larpent's. Middle-aged woman; she's gone to a boarding-house at Cheltenham for the winter. Does every year. Usually shuts the house up, but lets it if she can, which isn't often."

There seemed nothing promising there. The Inspector shook his head in a discouraged fashion. "Williamsons were the agents, I understand?" he said.

"Yes."

"Their office is in Exhampton?"

"Next door to Walters & Kirkwood."

"Ah! then, perhaps, if you don't mind, Major, we might just drop in on our way."

"Not at all. You won't find Kirkwood at his office before ten anyway. You know what lawyers are."

"Then, shall we go?"

The Major, who had finished his breakfast some time ago, nodded assent and rose.

CHAPTER SEVEN

THE WILL

AN ALERT-LOOKING YOUNG MAN rose to receive them in the office of Messrs. Williamson. "Good morning, Major Burnaby."

"Morning."

"Terrible business, this," said the young man chattily. "Not been such a thing in Exhampton for years."

He spoke with gusto and the Major winced. "This is Inspector Narracott," he said.

"Oh! yes," said the young man, pleasurably excited.

"I want some information that I think you can give me," said the Inspector. "I understand that you put through this let of Sittaford House."

"To Mrs. Willett? Yes, we did."

"Can you give me full details, please, of how that came about. Did the lady apply personally, or by letter?"

"By letter. She wrote, let me see—" He opened a drawer and turned up a file. "Yes, from the Carlton Hotel, London."

"Did she mention Sittaford House by name?"

"No, she merely said she wanted to rent a house for the winter; it must be right on Dartmoor and have at least eight bedrooms. Being near a railway station or a town was of no consequence."

"Was Sittaford House on your books?"

"No, it was not. But as a matter of fact it was the only house in the neighborhood that at all fulfilled the requirements. The lady mentioned in her letter that she would be willing to go to twelve guineas, and in these circumstances I thought it worth while writing to Captain Trevelyan and asking whether he would consider letting. He replied in the affirmative, and we fixed the thing up."

"Without Mrs. Willett seeing the house?"

"She agreed to take it without seeing it, and signed the agreement. Then she came down here for one day, drove up to Sittaford, saw Captain Trevelyan, arranged with him about plate and linen, and so on, and saw over the house."

"She was quite satisfied?"

"She came in and said she was delighted with it."

"And what did you think?" asked Inspector Narracott, eyeing him keenly.

The young man shrugged his shoulders. "You learn never to be surprised at anything in the house business," he said.

On this note of philosophy they left, the Inspector thanking the young man for his help.

"Not at all, a pleasure, I'm sure."

He accompanied them politely to the door.

The offices of Messrs. Walters & Kirkwood were, as Major Burnaby had said, next door to the estate agents. On reaching there, they were told that Mr. Kirkwood had just arrived and they were shown into his room.

Mr. Kirkwood was an elderly man with a benign expression. He was a native of Exhampton and had succeeded his father and grandfather in the firm.

He rose, put on his mourning face, and shook hands with the Major. "Good morning, Major Burnaby," he said. "This is a very shocking affair. Very shocking indeed. Poor Trevelyan."

He looked inquiringly at Narracott and Major Burnaby explained his presence in a few succinct words.

"You are in charge of the case, Inspector Narracott?"

"Yes, Mr. Kirkwood. In pursuance of my investigations, I have come to ask you for certain information."

"I shall be happy to give you any information if it is proper for me to do so," said the lawyer.

"It concerns the late Captain Trevelyan's will," said Narracott. "I understand the will is here in your office."

"That is so."

"It was made some time ago?"

"Five or six years ago. I cannot be sure of the exact date at the moment."

"Ah! I am anxious, Mr. Kirkwood, to know the contents of that will as soon as possible. It may have an important bearing on the case."

"Indeed?" said the lawyer. "Indeed! I should not have thought that, but naturally you know your own business best, Inspector. Well—" He glanced across at the other man. "Major Burnaby and myself are joint executors of the will. If he has no objection—"

"None."

"Then I see no reason why I should not accede to your request, Inspector."

Taking up a telephone that stood on his desk, he spoke a few words down it. In two or three minutes a clerk entered the room, laid a sealed envelope in front of the lawyer, and left the room. Mr. Kirkwood picked up the envelope, slit it open with a paper knife, drew out a large and important-looking document, cleared his throat, and began to read:

"I, Joseph Arthur Trevelyan, of Sittaford House, Sittaford, in the County of Devon, declare this to be my last will and testament.

" (1) I appoint John Edward Burnaby of 1 The Cottages, Sittaford, and Frederick Kirkwood of Exhampton, to be the executors and trustees of this, my will.

" (2) I give to Robert Henry Evans, who has served me long and faithfully, the sum of £100 (one hundred pounds) free of legacy duty for his own benefit absolutely, provided that he is my service at the time of my death and not under notice to leave whether given or received.

" (3) I give the said John Edward Burnaby, as a token of our friendship and of my affection and regard for him, all my trophies of sport, including my collection of heads and pelts of big game as well as any challenge cups and prizes awarded to me in any department of sport and any spoils of the chase in my possession.

" (4) I give all my real and personal property, not

otherwise disposed of by this, my will, or any codicil hereto to my trustees upon trust that my trustees shall sell, call in, and convert the same into money.

" (5) My trustees shall out of the moneys to arise out of such sale, calling in, and conversion pay any funeral and testamentary expenses and debts, and the legacies given by this, my will, or any codicil hereto and all death duties and other moneys.

" (6) My trustees shall hold the residue of such moneys or the investments for the time being, representing the same upon trust to divide the same into four equal parts, or shares.

" (7) Upon such division as aforesaid my trustees shall hold one such equal fourth part or share upon trust to pay the same to my sister Jennifer Gardner for her own use and enjoyment absolutely.

"And my trustees shall hold the remaining three such equal fourth parts or shares upon trust to pay one such equal fourth part or share to each of the three children of my deceased sister, Mary Pearson, for the benefit of each such child absolutely.

"In witness whereof I, the said Joseph Arthur Trevelyan, have hereunto set my hand the day and year first above written.

"Signed by the above named testator as his last will in the presence of us both present at the same time, who in his presence and at his request and in the presence of each other have hereunto subscribed our names as witness."

Mr. Kirkwood handed the document to the Inspector. "Witnessed by two of my clerks in this office."

The Inspector ran his eye over the will thoughtfully. "My deceased sister, Mary Pearson," he said. "Can you tell me anything about Mrs. Pearson, Mr. Kirkwood?"

"Very little. She died about ten years ago, I believe. Her husband, a stockbroker, had predeceased her. As far as I know, she never visited Captain Trevelyan here."

"Pearson," said the Inspector again. Then he added,

"One thing more. The amount of Captain Trevelyan's estate is not mentioned. To what sum do you think it will amount?"

"That is difficult to say exactly," said Mr. Kirkwood, enjoying, like all lawyers, making the reply to a simple question difficult. "It is a question of real or personal estate. Besides Sittaford House, Captain Trevelyan owns some property in the neighborhood of Plymouth, and various investments he made from time to time have fluctuated in value."

"I just want an approximate idea," said Inspector Narracott.

"I should not like to commit myself—"

"Just the roughest estimate as a guide. For instance, would twenty thousand pounds be out of the way?"

"Twenty thousand pounds! My dear sir! Captain Trevelyan's estate will be worth at least four times as much as that. Eighty or even ninety thousand pounds will be much nearer the mark."

"I told you Trevelyan was a rich man," said Burnaby.

Inspector Narracott rose. "Thank you very much, Mr. Kirkwood," he said, "for the information you have given me."

"You think you will find it helpful, eh?"

The lawyer very clearly was agog with curiosity, but Inspector Narracott was in no mood to satisfy it at present. "In a case like this we have to take everything into account," he said, noncommittally. "By the way, have you the names and addresses of this Jennifer Gardner and of the Pearson family?"

"I know nothing of the Pearson family. Mrs. Gardner's address is The Laurels, Waldon Road, Exeter."

The Inspector noted it down in his book. "That will do to get on with," he said.

The Inspector put away his notebook and thanked the lawyer once more and took his departure. When they had reached the street, he turned suddenly and faced his companion.

"And now, sir," he said, "we'll have the truth about

that twenty-five past five business."

Major Burnaby's face reddened with annoyance. "I have told you already—"

"That won't go down with me. Withholding information, that is what you are doing, Major Burnaby. You must have had some idea in mentioning that specific time to Dr. Warren—and I think I have a very good idea of what that something is."

"Well, if you know about it, why ask me?" growled the Major.

"I take it that you were aware that a certain person had an appointment with Captain Trevelyan somewhere about that time. Now, isn't that so?"

Major Burnaby stared at him in surprise.

"Nothing of the kind," he snarled.

"Be careful, Major Burnaby. What about Mr. James Pearson?"

"James Pearson? Who's he? Do you mean one of Trevelyan's nephews?"

"I presume it would be a nephew. He had one called James, hadn't he?"

"Not the least idea. Trevelyan had nephews—I know that. But what their names were, I haven't the vaguest idea."

"The young man in question was at the Three Crowns last night. You probably recognized him there."

"I didn't recognize anybody," growled the Major. "Shouldn't anyway—never saw any of Trevelyan's nephews in my life."

"But you knew that Captain Trevelyan was expecting a nephew to call upon him yesterday afternoon?"

"I did not," roared the Major.

Several people in the street turned round to stare.

"Damn it, won't you take plain truth? I knew nothing about any appointment. Trevelyan's nephews may have been in Timbuctoo for all I knew about them."

Inspector Narracott was a little taken aback. The Major's vehement denial bore the mark of truth too plainly for him to be deceived.

"Then why this twenty-five past five business?"

"Oh! well—I suppose I had better tell you." The Major coughed in an embarrassed fashion. "But mind you—the whole thing is damned foolishness! Tommyrot, sir. How any thinking man can believe such nonsense!"

Inspector Narracott looked more and more surprised. Major Burnaby was looking more uncomfortable and ashamed of himself every minute.

"You know what it is, Inspector. You have to join in these things to please a lady. Of course, I never thought there was anything in it."

"In what, Major Burnaby?"

"Table turning."

"*Table turning?*"

Whatever Narracott had expected he had not expected this. The Major proceeded to explain himself. Haltingly, and with many disclaimers of his own belief in the thing, he described the events of the previous afternoon and the message that had purported to come through.

"You mean, Major Burnaby, that the table spelled out the name of Trevelyan and informed you that he was dead—murdered?"

Major Burnaby wiped his forehead. "Yes, that's what happened. I didn't believe in it—naturally, I didn't believe in it." He looked ashamed. "Well—it was Friday and I thought after all I would make sure and go along and see if everything was all right."

The Inspector reflected on the difficulties of that six-mile walk, with the piled-up snowdrifts and the prospect of a heavy snowfall, and he realized that deny it as he would Major Burnaby must have been deeply impressed by the spirit message. Narracott turned it over in his mind. A queer thing to happen—a very queer thing to happen. The sort of thing you couldn't explain satisfactorily. There might be something in this spirit business after all. It was the first well-authenticated case he had come across.

A very queer business altogether but, as far as he

could see, though it explained Major Burnaby's attitude, it had no practical bearing on the case as far as he himself was concerned. He had to deal with the physical world and not the psychic.

It was his job to track down the murderer. And to do that he required no guidance from the spirit world.

CHAPTER EIGHT

MR. CHARLES ENDERBY

GLANCING AT HIS WATCH, the Inspector realized he could just catch the train for Exeter if he hurried off. He was anxious to interview the late Captain Trevelyan's sister as soon as possible and obtain from her the addresses of the other members of the family. So, with a hurried word of farewell to Major Burnaby, he raced off to the station. The Major retraced his steps to the Three Crowns. He had hardly put a foot across the doorstep when he was accosted by a bright young man with a very shiny head and a round, boyish face.

"Major Burnaby?" said the young man.

"Yes."

"Of No. 1 Sittaford Cottages?"

"Yes," said Major Burnaby.

"I represent the *Daily Wire*," said the young man, "and I—"

He got no further. In true military fashion of the old school, the Major exploded. "Not another word," he roared. "I know you and your kind. No decency. No reticence. Clustering round a murder like vultures round a carcass, but I can tell you, young man, you will get no information from me. Not a word. No story for your damned paper. If you want to know anything, go and ask the police, and have the decency to leave the friends of the dead man alone."

The young man seemed not a whit taken aback. He smiled more encouragingly than ever. "I say, sir, you know you have got hold of the wrong end of the stick. I know nothing about this murder business."

This was not, strictly speaking, the truth. No one in Exhampton could pretend ignorance of the event that had shaken the quiet moorland town to its core. "I am empowered on behalf of the *Daily Wire*," went on the young man, "to hand you this check for five thousand pounds and congratulate you on sending in the only correct solution of our football competition."

Major Burnaby was completely taken aback.

"I have no doubt," continued the young man, "that you have already received our letter yesterday morning informing you of the good news."

"Letter?" said Major Burnaby. "Do you realize, young man, that Sittaford is about ten feet deep in snow? What chance do you think we have had in the last few days of a regular delivery of letters?"

"But doubtless you saw your name announced as winner in the *Daily Wire*, this morning?"

"No," said Major Burnaby. "I haven't glanced at the paper this morning."

"Ah! of course not," said the young man. "This sad business. The murdered man was a friend of yours, I understand."

"My best friend," said the Major.

"Hard lines," said the young man, tactfully averting his eyes. Then he drew from his pocket a small folded piece of mauve paper and handed it to Major Burnaby with a bow. "With the compliments of the *Daily Wire*."

Major Burnaby took it and said the only thing possible under the circumstances. "Have a drink, Mr.—er—?"

"Enderby, Charles Enderby my name is. I got here last night," he explained. "Made inquiries about getting to Sittaford. We make it a point to hand checks to winners personally. Always publish a little interview. Interests our readers. Well, everyone told me it was out of the question—the snow was falling and it simply couldn't be done. And then with the greatest good luck I find you are actually here, staying at the Three Crowns." He smiled. "No difficulty about identification. Everybody seems to know everybody else in this part of the world."

"What will you have?" said the Major.

"Beer for me," said Enderby.

The Major ordered two beers.

"The whole place seems off its head with this murder," remarked Enderby. "Rather a mysterious business by all accounts."

The Major grunted. He was in something of a quandary. His sentiments toward journalists remained unchanged, but a man who has just handed you a check for 5,000 pounds is in a privileged position. You cannot very well tell him to go to the devil.

"No enemies, had he?" asked the young man.

"No," said the Major.

"But I hear the police don't think it is robbery," went on Enderby.

"How do you know that?" asked the Major.

Mr. Enderby, however, did not reveal the source of his information. "I hear it was you who actually discovered the body, sir," said the young man.

"Yes."

"It must have been an awful shock."

The conversation proceeded. Major Burnaby was still determined to give no information, but he was no match for the adroitness of Mr. Enderby. The latter made statements with which the Major was forced to agree or disagree, thereby providing the information the young man wanted. So pleasant was his manner, however, that the process was really not painful at all and the Major found himself taking quite a liking to the ingenuous young man.

Presently Mr. Enderby rose and observed that he must go along to the post office. "If you will just give me a receipt for that check, sir."

The Major went across to the writing-table, wrote a receipt, and handed it to him.

"I suppose," said Major Burnaby, "that you are off back to London today?"

"Oh! no," said the young man. "I want to take a few photographs, you know, of your cottage at Sittaford, and of you feeding the pigs, or hoeing up dandelions, or doing anything characteristic that you fancy. You have no idea how our readers appreciate that sort of thing. Then I would like to have a few words from you on *What I Intend to Do with the 5,000 Pounds.* Something snappy. You have no idea how disappointed our readers would be if they didn't get that sort of thing."

"Yes, but look here—it's impossible to get to Sittaford in this weather. The fall of snow was exceptionally heavy. No vehicle has been able to take the road for three days anyway, and it may be another three before the thaw sets in properly."

"I know," said the young man, "it *is* awkward. Well, well, one will just have to resign oneself to kicking up one's heels in Exhampton. They do you pretty well at the Three Crowns. So long, sir, see you later."

He emerged into the main street of Exhampton and made his way to the post office and wired his paper that by the greatest of good luck he would be able to supply them with tasty and exclusive information on the Exhampton Murder Case.

He reflected on his next course of action and decided on interviewing the late Captain Trevelyan's servant, Evans, whose name Major Burnaby had incautiously let slip during their conversation.

A few inquiries brought him to 85 Fore Street. The servant of the murdered man was a person of importance today. Everyone was willing and anxious to point out where he lived.

Enderby beat a smart rat-tat on the door. It was opened by a man so typically an ex-sailor that Enderby had no doubt of his identity.

"Evans, isn't it?" said Mr. Enderby cheerfully. "I have just come along from Major Burnaby."

"Oh!—" Evans hesitated a moment. "Will you come in, sir."

Enderby accepted the invitation. A buxom young woman with dark hair and red cheeks hovered in the background. Enderby judged her as the newly wed Mrs. Evans. "Bad thing this about your late master," said Enderby.

"It's shocking, sir, that's what it is."

"Who do you think did it?" demanded Enderby with an ingenuous air of seeking information.

"One of these low-down tramps, I suppose," said Evans.

"Oh! no, my dear man. That theory is quite exploded."

"Eh?"

"That's all a put-up job. The police saw through that at once."

"Who told you that, sir?"

Enderby's real informant had been the housemaid at the Three Crowns whose sister was the legal spouse of Constable Graves, but he replied, "Had a tip from headquarters. Yes, the burglary idea was all a put-up job."

"Who do they think did it then?" demanded Mrs. Evans, coming forward. Her eyes looked frightened.

"Now, Rebecca, don't you take on so," said her husband.

"Cruel stupid the police are," said Mrs. Evans. "Don't mind who they take up as long as they get hold of someone." She cast a quick glance at Enderby.

"Are you connected with the police, sir?"

"Me? Oh! no. I am from a newspaper, the *Daily Wire*. I came down to see Major Burnaby. He has just won our Free Football Competition for five thousand pounds."

"What?" cried Evans. "Damn it all, then these things are square after all."

"Didn't you think they were?" asked Enderby.

"Well, it's a wicked world, sir." Evans was a little confused, feeling that his exclamation had been wanting in tact. "I have heard there's a lot of trickery concerned. The late Capting used to say that a prize never went to a good address. That's why he used mine time and again."

With a certain naïveté he described the Captain's winning of three new novels.

Enderby encouraged him to talk. He saw a very good story being made out of Evans. The faithful servant—old-sea-dog touch. He wondered just a little why Mrs. Evans seemed so nervous, and put it down to the suspicious ignorance of her class.

"You find the skunk what done it," said Evans. "Newspapers can do a lot, they say, in hunting down criminals."

"It was a burglar," said Mrs. Evans. "That's what it was."

"Of course it was a burglar," said Evans. "Why, there's no one in Exhampton would want to harm the Capting."

Enderby rose. "Well," he said. "I must be going. I will run in now and then and have a little chat, if I may. If the Captain won three new novels in a *Daily Wire* Competition, the *Daily Wire* ought to make it a personal matter to hunt down his murderer."

"You can't say fairer than that, sir. No, you can't say fairer than that."

Wishing them a cheery good day, Charles Enderby took his leave.

I wonder who really did the beggar in? he murmured to himself. *I don't think our friend Evans. Perhaps it was a burglar! Very disappointing, if so. Doesn't seem any woman in the case, which is a pity. We've got to have some sensational development soon or the case will fade into insignificance. Just my luck, if so. First time I have ever been on the spot in a matter of this kind. I must make good. Charles, my boy, your chance in life has come. Make the most of it. Our military friend will, I see, soon be eating out of my hand if I remember to be sufficiently respectful and call him "sir" often enough. Wonder if he was in the Indian Mutiny. No, of course not, not old enough for that. The South African War, that's it. Ask him about the South African War, that will tame him.*

And pondering these good resolutions in his mind, Mr. Enderby sauntered back to the Three Crowns.

CHAPTER NINE

THE LAURELS

IT TAKES ABOUT HALF AN HOUR from Exhampton to Exeter by train. At five minutes to twelve Inspector Narracott was ringing the front door bell of the Laurels.

The Laurels was a somewhat dilapidated house, badly in need of a new coat of paint. The garden round it was unkempt and weedy and the gate hung askew.

Not too much money about here, thought Inspector Narracott to himself. *Evidently hard up.*

He was a very fair-minded man, but inquiries seemed to indicate that there was very little possibility of the Captain's having been done to death by an enemy. On the other hand, four people, as far as he could make out, stood to gain a considerable sum by the old man's death. The movements of each of these four people had to be inquired into. The entry in the hotel register was suggestive, but after all Pearson was quite a common name. Inspector Narracott was anxious not to come to any decision too rapidly and to keep a perfectly open mind while covering the preliminary ground as rapidly as possible.

A somewhat slatternly looking maid answered the bell. "Good afternoon," said Inspector Narracott. "I want to see Mrs. Gardner, please. It is in connection with the death of her brother, Captain Trevelyan, at Exhampton."

He purposely did not hand his official card to the maid. The mere fact of his being a police officer, as he knew by experience, would render her awkward and tongue-tied. "She's heard of her brother's death?" asked the Inspector casually as the maid drew back to let him into the hall.

"Yes, got a telegram she did. From the lawyer, Mr. Kirkwood."

"Just so," said Inspector Narracott.

The maid ushered him into the drawing-room—a room which, like the outside of the house, was badly in need of a little money spent upon it, but had with all that an air of charm which the Inspector felt without being able to particularize.

"Must have been a shock to your mistress."

The girl seemed a little vague about that, he noticed. "She didn't see much of him," was her answer.

"Shut the door and come here," said Inspector Narracott. He was anxious to try the effect of a surprise attack. "Did the telegram say that it was murder?" he asked.

"Murder!" The girl's eyes opened wide, a mixture of horror and intense enjoyment in them. "Murdered, was he?"

"Ah!" said Inspector Narracott, "I thought you hadn't heard that. Mr. Kirkwood didn't want to break the news too abruptly to your mistress, but you see, my dear—what is your name, by the way?"

"Beatrice, sir."

"Well, you see, Beatrice, it will be in the evening papers tonight."

"Well, I never," said Beatrice. "Murdered. 'Orrible, isn't it? Did they bash his head in or shoot him or what?"

The Inspector satisfied her passion for detail, then added casually, "I believe there was some idea of your mistress going over to Exhampton yesterday afternoon. But I suppose the weather was too bad for her."

"I never heard anything about it, sir," said Beatrice. "I think you must have made a mistake. The mistress went out in the afternoon to do some shopping and then she went to the pictures."

"What time did she get in?"

"About six o'clock."

So that let Mrs. Gardner out.

"I don't know much about the family," he went on

in a casual tone. "Is Mrs. Gardner a widow?"

"Oh, no, sir, there's master."

"What does he do?"

"He doesn't do anything," said Beatrice staring. "He can't. He's an invalid."

"An invalid, is he? Oh, I'm sorry. I hadn't heard."

"He can't walk. He lies in bed all day. Got a nurse always in the house, we have. It isn't every girl what stays on with an 'ospital nurse in the house the whole time. Always wanting trays carried up and pots of tea made."

"Must be very trying," said the Inspector soothingly. "Now, will you go and tell your mistress please, that I am here from Mr. Kirkwood of Exhampton?"

Beatrice withdrew and a few minutes later the door opened and a tall, rather commanding woman came into the room. She had an unusual-looking face, broad about the brows, and black hair with a touch of gray at the temples, which she wore combed straight back from her forehead. She looked at the Inspector inquiringly. "You have come from Mr. Kirkwood at Exhampton?"

"Not exactly, Mrs. Gardner. I put it that way to your maid. Your brother, Captain Trevelyan, was murdered yesterday afternoon and I am Divisional Inspector Narracott in charge of the case."

Whatever else Mrs. Gardner might be she was certainly a woman of iron nerve. Her eyes narrowed and she drew in her breath sharply, then motioning the Inspector to a chair and sitting down herself she said, "Murdered! How extraordinary! Who in the world would want to murder Joe?"

"That is what I'm anxious to find out, Mrs. Gardner."

"Of course. I hope I shall be able to help you in some way, but I doubt it. My brother and I have seen very little of each other in the last ten years. I know nothing of his friends or of any ties he has formed."

"You'll excuse me, Mrs. Gardner, but had you and your brother quarreled?"

"No—not quarreled. I think estranged would be a

better word to describe the position between us. I don't want to go into family details, but my brother rather resented my marriage. Brothers, I think, seldom approve of their sisters' choice, but usually, I fancy, they conceal it better than my brother did. My brother, as perhaps you know, had a large fortune left him by an aunt. Both my sister and myself married poor men. When my husband was invalided out of the army after the war, a little financial assistance would have been a wonderful relief—would have enabled me to give him an expensive course of treatment which was otherwise denied to him. I asked my brother for a loan, which he refused. That, of course, he was perfectly entitled to do. But since then we have met at very rare intervals, and hardly corresponded at all."

It was a clear, succinct statement.

An intriguing personality, this Mrs. Gardner's, the Inspector thought. Somehow, he couldn't quite make her out. She seemed unnaturally calm, unnaturally ready with her recital of facts. He also noticed that, with all her surprise, she asked for no details of her brother's death. That struck him as extraordinary.

"I don't know if you want to hear what exactly occurred—at Exhampton," he began.

She frowned. "Must I hear it? My brother was killed, painlessly—I hope."

"Quite painlessly, I should say."

"Then please spare me any revolting details."

Unnatural, thought the Inspector, *decidedly unnatural.*

As though she had read his mind she used the very word that he had spoken to himself. "I suppose you think that very unnatural, Inspector, but—I have heard a good many horrors. My husband has told me things when he has had one of his bad turns—" She shivered. "I think you would understand if you knew my circumstances better."

"Oh! quite so, quite so, Mrs. Gardner. What I really came for was to get a few family details from you."

"Yes?"

"Do you know how many relatives living your brother has besides yourself?"

"Of near relations, only the Pearsons. My sister Mary's children."

"And they are?"

"James, Sylvia, and Brian."

"James?"

"He is the eldest. He works in an insurance office."

"What age is he?"

"Twenty-eight."

"Is he married?"

"No, but he is engaged—to a very nice girl, I believe. I've not yet met her."

"And his address?"

"21 Cromwell Street, S.W. 3."

The Inspector noted it down. "Yes, Mrs. Gardner?"

"Then there's Sylvia. She's married to Martin Dering —you may have read his books. He's a moderately successful author."

"Thank you, and their address?"

"The Nook, Surrey Road, Wimbledon."

"Yes?"

"And the youngest is Brian—but he is out in Australia. I am afraid I don't know his address, but either his brother or sister would know."

"Thank you, Mrs. Gardner. Just as a matter of form, do you mind my asking you how you spent yesterday afternoon?"

She looked surprised. "Let me see. I did some shopping—yes—then I went to the pictures. I came home about six and lay down on my bed until dinner, as the pictures had given me rather a headache."

"Thank you, Mrs. Gardner."

"Is there anything else?"

"No, I don't think I have anything further to ask you. I will now get into communication with your nephew and niece. I don't know if Mr. Kirkwood has informed you of the fact yet, but you and the three young Pearsons are the joint inheritors of Captain Trevelyan's money."

The color came into her face in a slow, rich blush. "That will be wonderful," she said quietly. "It has been so difficult—so terribly difficult—always skimping and saving and wishing."

She started up as a man's rather querulous voice came floating down the stairs: "Jennifer, I want you."

"Excuse me," she said.

As she opened the door the call came again, louder and more imperiously: "Jennifer, where are you? I want you, Jennifer."

The Inspector had followed her to the door. He stood in the hall looking after her as she ran up the stairs.

"I am coming, dear," she called.

A hospital nurse who was coming down the stairs stood aside to let her pass up. "Please go to Mr. Gardner, he is getting excited. You always manage to calm him."

Inspector Narracott stood deliberately in the nurse's way as she reached the bottom of the stairs.

"May I speak to you for a moment?" he said. "My conversation with Mrs. Gardner was interrupted."

The nurse came with alacrity into the drawing-room. "The news of the murder has upset my patient," she explained, adjusting a well-starched cuff. "That foolish girl, Beatrice, came running up and blurted it all out."

"I am sorry," said the Inspector. "I am afraid that was my fault."

"Oh, of course, you couldn't be expected to know," said the nurse graciously.

"Is Mr. Gardner dangerously ill?" inquired the Inspector.

"It's a sad case," said the nurse. "Of course, in a manner of speaking, there's nothing the matter with him really. He's lost the use of his limbs entirely through nervous shock. There's no visible disability."

"He had no extra strain or shock yesterday afternoon?" inquired the Inspector.

"Not that I know of." The nurse looked surprised.

"You were with him all the afternoon?"

"I intended to be, but, well—as a matter of fact, Captain Gardner was very anxious for me to change two books for him at the library. He had forgotten to ask his wife before she went out. So, to oblige him, I went out with them, and he asked me at the same time to get one or two other little things for him—presents for his wife as a matter of fact. Very nice about it he was, and told me I was to have tea at his expense at Boots. He said nurses never liked missing their tea. His little joke, you know. I didn't get out until past four, and what with the shops being so full just before Christmas, and one thing and another, I didn't get back until after six, but the poor fellow had been quite comfortable. In fact, he told me he had been asleep most of the time."

"Mrs. Gardner was back by then?"

"Yes, I believe she was lying down."

"She's very devoted to her husband, isn't she?"

"She worships him. I really do believe that woman would do anything in the world for him. Quite touching, and very different from some of the cases I have attended. Why, only last month—"

But Inspector Narracott fended off the impending scandal of last month with considerable skill. He glanced at his watch and gave a loud exclamation. "Goodness gracious," he cried, "I shall miss my train. The station is not far away, is it?"

"St. David's is only three minutes' walk, if it's St. David's you want, or did you mean Queen Street?"

"I must run," said the Inspector. "Tell Mrs. Gardner I am sorry not to have seen her to say good-by. Very pleased to have had this little chat with you, nurse."

The nurse bridled ever so slightly. *Rather a good-looking man,* she said to herself as the front door shut after the Inspector. *Really quite good-looking. Such a nice sympathetic manner.* And with a slight sigh she went upstairs to her patient.

CHAPTER TEN

THE PEARSON FAMILY

INSPECTOR NARRACOTT'S NEXT MOVE was to report to his superior, Superintendent Maxwell. The latter listened with interest to the Inspector's narrative. "It's going to be a big case," he said thoughtfully. "There'll be headlines in the papers over this."

"I agree with you, sir."

"We've got to be careful. We don't want to make any mistake. But I think you're on the right tack. You must get after this James Pearson as soon as possible—find out where he was yesterday afternoon. As you say, it's a common enough name, but there's the Christian name as well. Of course, his signing his own name openly like that shows there wasn't any premeditation about it. He'd hardly have been such a fool otherwise. It looks to me like a quarrel and a sudden blow. If it is the man, he must have heard of his uncle's death that night. And if so, why did he sneak off by the six train in the morning without a word to anyone? No, it looks bad. Always granting that the whole thing's not a coincidence. You must clear that up as quickly as possible."

"That's what I thought, sir. I'd better take the one forty-five to town. Some time or other I want to have a word with this Willett woman who rented the Captain's house. There's something fishy there. But I can't get to Sittaford at present; the roads are impassable with snow. And anyway, she can't have any direct connection with the crime. She and her daughter were actually—well—table turning at the time the crime was committed. And, by the way, rather a queer thing happened—" The Inspector narrated the story he had heard from Major Burnaby.

"That's a rum go," ejaculated the Superintendent.

"Think this old fellow was telling the truth? That's the sort of story that gets cooked up afterward by those believers in spooks and things of that kind."

"I fancy it's true all right," said Narracott with a grin. "I had a lot of difficulty getting it out of him. *He's* not a believer—just the opposite—old soldier, all damned nonsense attitude."

The Superintendent nodded his comprehension. "Well, it's odd, but it doesn't get us anywhere," was his conclusion.

"Then I'll take the one forty-five to London."

The other nodded.

On arrival in town Narracott went straight to 21 Cromwell Street. Mr. Pearson, he was told, was at the office. He would be back for certain about seven o'clock.

Narracott nodded carelessly as though the information were of no value to him. "I'll call back if I can," he said. "It's nothing of importance," and departed quickly without leaving a name.

He decided not to go to the insurance office, but to visit Wimbledon and have an interview with Mrs. Martin Dering, formerly Miss Sylvia Pearson.

Mrs. Dering was at home. A rather pert-looking maid dressed in lilac color showed him into a rather over-crowded drawing-room. He gave her his official card to take to her mistress.

Mrs. Dering came to him almost immediately, his card in her hand. "I suppose you have come about poor Uncle Joseph," was her greeting. "It's shocking—really shocking! I am so dreadfully nervous of burglars myself. I had two extra bolts put on the back door last week, and new patent catches on the windows."

Sylvia Dering, the Inspector knew from Mrs. Gardner, was only twenty-five, but she looked considerably over thirty. She was small and fair and anemic-looking, with a worried and harassed expression. Her voice had that faintly complaining note in it which is about the most annoying sound a human voice can contain. Still, not allowing the Inspector to speak, she went on: "If there's anything I can do to help you in any way, of course, I shall be only too glad to do so, but one hardly ever saw Uncle Joseph. He wasn't a very nice man—I am sure he couldn't have been. Not the sort of person one could go to in trouble, always carping and criticizing. Not the sort of man who had any knowledge of what literature meant. Success, true success, is not always measured in terms of money, Inspector."

At last she paused and the Inspector, to whom those remarks had opened certain fields of conjecture, was given his turn to speak. "You've heard of the tragedy very quickly, Mrs. Dering."

"Aunt Jennifer wired it to me."

"I see."

"But I suppose it will be in the evening papers. Dreadful, isn't it?"

"I gather you've not seen your uncle of late years."

"I have only seen him twice since my marriage. On the second occasion he was really very rude to Martin. Of course, he was a regular philistine in every way—devoted to sport. No appreciation, as I said just now, of literature."

Husband applied to him for a loan and got refused, was Inspector Narracott's private comment.

"Just as a matter of form, Mrs. Dering, will you tell me what your movements were yesterday afternoon?"

"My movements? What a very queer way of putting it, Inspector. I played bridge most of the afternoon and a friend came in and spent the evening with me, as my husband was out."

"Out, was he? Away from home altogether?"

"A literary dinner," explained Mrs. Dering with importance. "He lunched with an American publisher and had this dinner in the evening."

"I see." That seemed quite fair and above board. He went on: "Your younger brother is in Australia, I believe, Mrs. Dering?"

"Yes."

"You have his address?"

"Oh, yes, I can find it for you if you wish—rather a peculiar name—I've forgotten it for the minute. Somewhere in New South Wales."

"And now, Mrs. Dering, your elder brother?"

"Jim?"

"Yes. I shall want to get in touch with him."

Mrs. Dering hastened to supply him with the address —the same as that which Mrs. Gardner had already given him.

Then, feeling there was no more to be said on either side, he cut the interview short. Glancing at his watch, he noted that by the time he had returned to town it would be seven o'clock—a likely time, he hoped, for finding Mr. James Pearson at home.

The same superior-looking, middle-aged woman opened the door of No. 21. Yes, Mr. Pearson was at home now. It was on the second floor, if the gentleman would walk up. She preceded him, tapped at a door, and in a murmured and apologetic voice said, "The gentleman to see you, sir."

A young man in evening dress was standing in the middle of the room. He was good-looking, indeed handsome, if you took no account of the rather weak mouth and the irresolute slant of the eyes. He had a haggard, worried look and an air of not having had much sleep of late. He looked inquiringly at the Inspector.

"I am Detective Inspector Narracott," the latter began —but got no further.

With a hoarse cry the young man dropped onto a chair, flung his arms out in front of him on the table, bowing his head on them and muttering, "Oh! my God! It's come."

After a minute or two he lifted his head and said, "Well, why don't you get on with it, man?"

Inspector Narracott looked exceedingly stolid and unintelligent. "I am investigating the death of your uncle, Captain Joseph Trevelyan. May I ask you, sir, if you have anything to say?"

The young man rose slowly to his feet and said in a

low, strained voice, "Are you—arresting me?"

"No, sir, I am not. If I was arresting you, I would give you the customary caution. I am simply asking you to account for your movements yesterday afternoon. You may reply to my questions or not as you see fit."

"And if I don't reply to them—it will tell against me. Oh, yes, I know your little ways. You've found out then that I was down there yesterday?"

"You signed your name in the hotel register."

"Oh, I suppose there's no use denying it. I *was* there —why shouldn't I be?"

"Why indeed?" said the Inspector mildly.

"I went down there to see my uncle."

"By appointment?"

"What do you mean, by appointment?"

"Did your uncle know you were coming?"

"I—no—he didn't. It—it was a sudden impulse."

"No reason for it?"

"I—reason? No—no, why should there be? I—I just wanted to see my uncle."

"Quite so, sir. And you did see him?"

There was a pause—a very long pause. Indecision was written on every feature of the young man's face. Inspector Narracott felt a kind of pity as he watched him. Couldn't the boy see that his palpable indecision was as good as an admission of the fact?

At last Jim Pearson drew a deep breath. "I—I suppose I had better make a clean breast of it. Yes—I did see him. I asked at the station how I could get to Sittaford. They told me it was out of the question. The roads were impassable for any vehicle. I said it was urgent."

"Urgent?" murmured the Inspector.

"I—I wanted to see my uncle very much."

"So it seems, sir."

"The porter continued to shake his head and say that it was impossible. I mentioned my uncle's name and at once his face cleared up, and he told me my uncle was actually in Exhampton, and gave me full directions as to how to find the house he had rented."

"This was at what time, sir?"

"About one o'clock, I think. I went to the inn—the Three Crowns—booked a room, and had some lunch there. Then afterward I—I went out to see my uncle."

"Immediately afterward?"

"No, not immediately."

"What time was it?"

"Well, I couldn't say for certain."

"Half-past three? Four o'clock? Half-past four?"

"I—I—" he stammered worse than ever— "I don't think it could have been as late as that."

"Mrs. Belling, the proprietress, said you went out at half-past four."

"Did I? I—I think she's wrong. It couldn't have been as late as that."

"What happened next?"

"I found my uncle's house, had a talk with him, and came back to the Inn."

"How did you get into your uncle's house?"

"I rang the bell and he opened the door himself."

"Wasn't he surprised to see you?"

"Yes—yes—he was rather surprised."

"How long did you remain with him, Mr. Pearson?"

"A quarter of an hour—twenty minutes. But look here, he was perfectly all right when I left him. Perfectly all right. I swear it."

"And what time *did* you leave him?"

The young man lowered his eyes. Again the hesitation was palpable in his tone, "I don't know exactly."

"I think you do, Mr. Pearson."

The assured tone had its effect. The boy replied in a low tone, "It was a quarter-past five."

"You returned to the Three Crowns at a quarter to six. At most it could only take you seven or eight minutes to walk over from your uncle's house."

"I didn't go straight back. I walked about the town."

"In that icy weather—in the snow!"

"It wasn't actually snowing then. It came on to snow later."

"I see. And what was the nature of your conversation with your uncle?"

"Oh! nothing in particular. I—I just wanted to talk to the old boy, look him up, that sort of thing."

He's a poor liar, thought Inspector Narracott. *Why, I could manage better than that myself.*

Aloud he said, "Very good, sir. Now, may I ask you why, on hearing of your uncle's murder, you left Exhampton without disclosing your relationship to the murdered man?"

"I was scared," said the young man frankly. "I heard he had been murdered round about the time I left him. Now, dash it all, that's enough to scare anyone, isn't it? I got the wind up and left the place by the first available train. Oh, I dare say I was a fool to do anything of the sort. But you know what it is when you are rattled. And anyone might have been rattled under these circumstances."

"And that's all you have to say, sir?"

"Yes—yes, of course."

"Then perhaps you'll have no objection, sir, to coming round with me and having this statement taken down in writing, after which you will have it read over to you, and you will sign it."

"Is—is that all?"

"I think it possible, Mr. Pearson, that it may be necessary to detain you until after the inquest."

"Oh! my God," said Jim Pearson. "Can nobody help me?"

At that moment the door opened and a young woman walked into the room. She was, as the observant Inspector Narracott noted at once, a very exceptional kind of young woman. She was not strikingly beautiful, but she had a face which was arresting and unusual, a face that having once seen you could not forget. There was about her an atmosphere of common sense, *savoir faire*, invincible determination, and a most tantalizing fascination.

"Oh! Jim," she exclaimed, "what's happened?"

"It's all over, Emily," said the young man. "They think I murdered my uncle."

"Who thinks so?" demanded Emily.

The young man indicated his visitor by a gesture. "This is Inspector Narracott," he said, and he added with a dismal attempt at introduction, "Miss Emily Trefusis."

"Oh!" said Emily Trefusis.

She studied Inspector Narracott with keen hazel eyes. "Jim," she said, "is a frightful idiot. But he doesn't murder people."

The Inspector said nothing.

"I expect," said Emily, turning to Jim, "that you've been saying the most frightfully imprudent things. If you read the papers a little better than you do, Jim, you would know that you must never talk to policemen unless you have a strong solicitor sitting beside you making objections to every word. What's happened? Are you arresting him, Inspector Narracott?"

Inspector Narracott explained technically and clearly exactly what he was doing.

"Emily," cried the young man, "you won't believe I did it? You never will believe it, will you?"

"No, darling," said Emily kindly. "Of course not." And she added in a gentle, meditative tone, "You haven't got the guts."

"I don't feel as if I had a friend in the world," groaned Jim.

"Yes, you have," said Emily. "You've got me. Cheer up, Jim; look at the winking diamonds on the third finger of my left hand. Here stands the faithful fiancée. Go with the Inspector and leave everything to me."

Jim Pearson rose, still with a dazed expression on his face. His overcoat was lying over a chair and he put it on. Inspector Narracott handed him a hat which was lying on a bureau near by. They moved toward the door and the Inspector said politely, "Good evening, Miss Trefusis."

"Au revoir, Inspector," said Emily sweetly.

And if he had known Miss Emily Trefusis better he would have known that in these three words lay a challenge.

CHAPTER ELEVEN

EMILY SETS TO WORK

THE INQUEST ON THE BODY of Captain Trevelyan was held on Monday morning. From the point of view of sensation it was a tame affair, for it was almost immediately adjourned for a week, thus disappointing large numbers of people. Between Saturday and Monday, Exhampton had sprung into fame. The knowledge that the dead man's nephew had been detained in connection with the murder made the whole affair spring from a mere paragraph in the back pages of the newspapers to gigantic headlines. On the Monday, reporters had arrived at Exhampton in large numbers. Mr. Charles Enderby had reason once more to congratulate himself on the superior position he had obtained from the purely fortuitous chance of the football competition prize.

It was the journalist's intention to stick to Major Burnaby like a leech and, under the pretext of photographing the latter's cottage, to obtain exclusive information of the inhabitants of Sittaford and their relations with the dead man.

It did not escape Mr. Enderby's notice that at lunch time a small table near the door was occupied by a very attractive girl. Mr. Enderby wondered what she was doing in Exhampton. She was well dressed in a demure and provocative style, and did not appear to be a relation of the deceased, and still less could be labeled as one of the idle curious.

I wonder how long she's staying? thought Mr. Enderby. *Rather a pity I am going up to Sittaford this afternoon. Just my luck. Well, you can't have it both ways.*

But shortly after lunch, Mr. Enderby received an agreeable surprise. He was standing on the steps of the Three Crowns observing the fast melting snow, and enjoying the sluggish rays of wintry sunshine, when he was aware of a voice, an extremely charming voice, addressing him. "I beg your pardon—but could you tell me—if there is anything to see in Exhampton?"

Charles Enderby rose to the occasion promptly. "There's a castle, I believe," he said. "Not much to it—but there it is. Perhaps you would allow me to show you the way to it."

"That would be frightfully kind of you," said the girl. "If you are sure you are not too busy—"

Charles Enderby disclaimed immediately the notion of being busy. They set out together.

"You are Mr. Enderby, aren't you?" said the girl.

"Yes. How did you know?"

"Mrs. Belling pointed you out to me."

"Oh, I see."

"My name is Emily Trefusis. Mr. Enderby—I want you to help me."

"To help you?" said Enderby. "Why, certainly—but—"

"You see, I am engaged to Jim Pearson."

"Oh!" said Mr. Enderby, journalistic possibilities rising before his mind.

"And the police are going to arrest him. I know they are. Mr. Enderby, I *know* that Jim didn't do this thing. I am down here to prove he didn't. But I must have someone to help me. One can't do anything without a man. Men know so much, and are able to get information in so many ways that are simply impossible to women."

"Well—I—yes, I suppose that is true," said Mr. Enderby complacently.

"I was looking at all these journalists this morning," said Emily. "Such a lot of them I thought had such stupid faces. I picked you out as the one really clever one among them."

"Oh! I say. I don't think that's true, you know," said Mr. Enderby still more complacently.

"What I want to propose," said Emily Trefusis, "is a

kind of partnership. There would, I think, be advantages on both sides. There are certain things I want to investigate—to find out about. There you in your character of journalist can help me. I want—"

Emily paused. What she really wanted was to engage Mr. Enderby as a kind of private sleuth of her own. To go where she told him, to ask the questions she wanted asked, and in general to be a kind of bond slave. But she was aware of the necessity of couching these proposals in terms at once flattering and agreeable. The whole point was that she was to be the boss, but the matter needed managing tactfully. "I want," said Emily, "to feel that I can *depend* upon you."

She had a lovely voice, liquid and alluring. As she uttered the last sentence a feeling rose in Mr. Enderby's bosom that this lovely, helpless girl could depend upon him to the last ditch. "It must be ghastly," said Mr. Enderby, and taking her hand he squeezed it with fervor.

"But you know," he went on with a journalistic reaction, "my time is not entirely my own. I mean, I have to go where I am sent, and all that."

"Yes," said Emily. "I have thought of that, and that is where I come in. Surely I am what you call a 'scoop,' aren't I? You can do an interview with me every day, you can make me say anything that you think your readers will like. *Jim Pearson's fiancée. Girl who believes passionately in his innocence. Reminiscences of his childhood which she supplies.* I don't really know about his childhood, you know," she added, "but that doesn't matter."

"I think," said Mr. Enderby, "that you are marvelous. You really are marvelous."

"And then," said Emily, pursuing her advantage, "I have access naturally to Jim's relations. I can get you in there as a friend of mine, where quite possibly you might have the door shut in your face any other way."

"Don't I know that only too well," said Mr. Enderby with feeling, recalling various rebuffs of the past.

A glorious prospect opened out before him. He had been in luck over this affair all round. First the lucky chance of the football competition, and now this. "It's a deal," he said fervently.

"Good," said Emily, becoming brisk and businesslike. "Now, what's the first move?"

"I'm going up to Sittaford this afternoon."

He explained the fortunate circumstance that had put him in such an advantageous position with regard to Major Burnaby. "Because, mind you, he is the kind of old buffer that hates newspaper men like poison. But you can't exactly push a chap in the face who has just handed you 5,000 pounds, can you?"

"It would be awkward," said Emily. "Well, if you are going to Sittaford, I am coming with you."

"Splendid," said Mr. Enderby. "I don't know, though, if there's anywhere to stay up there. As far as I know, there's only Sittaford House and a few odd cottages belonging to people like Burnaby."

"We shall find something," said Emily. "I always find something."

Mr. Enderby could well believe that. Emily had the kind of personality that soars over all obstacles.

They had arrived by now at the ruined castle, but paying no attention to it, they sat down on a piece of wall in the so-called sunshine and Emily proceeded to develop her ideas. "I am looking at this, Mr. Enderby, in an absolutely unsentimental and businesslike way. You've got to take it from me to begin with that Jim didn't do the murder. I'm not saying that simply because I am in love with him, or believe in his beautiful character or anything like that. It's just—well—knowledge. You see, I have been on my own pretty well since I was sixteen. I have never come into contact with many women and I know very little about them, but I know really a lot about men. And unless a girl can size up a man pretty accurately, and know what she's got to deal with, she will never get on. I have got on. I work as a mannequin at Lucie's, and I can tell you, Mr. Enderby, that to arrive there is a feat.

"Well, as I was saying, I can size up men pretty accurately. Jim is rather a weak character in many ways. I am not sure," said Emily, forgetting for a moment her role of admirer of strong men, "that that's not why I like him. The feeling that I can run him and make something of him. There are quite a lot of—well—even criminal things that I can imagine him doing if pushed to it—but not murder. He simply couldn't pick up a sandbag and hit an old man on the back of the neck with it. He would make a bosh shot and hit him in the wrong place if he did. He is a—he is a *gentle* creature, Mr. Enderby. He doesn't even like killing wasps. He always tries to put them out of a window without hurting them and usually gets stung. However, it's no good my going on like this. You've got to take my word for it and start on the assumption that Jim is innocent."

"Do you think that somebody is deliberately trying to fasten the crime on him?" asked Charles Enderby in his best journalistic manner.

"I don't think so. You see, nobody knew about Jim coming down to see his uncle. Of course, one can't be certain, but I should put that down as just a coincidence and bad luck. What we have to find is someone else with a motive for killing Captain Trevelyan. The police are quite certain that this is not what they call an 'outside job'—I mean, it wasn't a burglar. The broken window was faked."

"Did the police tell you all this?"

"Practically," said Emily.

"What do you mean by 'practically'?"

"The chambermaid told me, and her sister is married to Constable Graves, so, of course, she knows everything the police think."

"Very well," said Mr. Enderby, "it wasn't an outside job. It was an inside one."

"Exactly," said Emily. "The police—that is, Inspector Narracott, who by the way I should think is an awfully sound man—have started investigating to find who bene-

fits by Captain Trevelyan's death, and with Jim sticking
out a mile, so to speak, they won't bother to go on with
other investigations much. Well, that's got to be our
job."

"What a scoop it would be," said Mr. Enderby, "if
you and I discovered the real murderer. The crime expert of the *Daily Wire*—that's the way I should be described. But it's too good to be true," he added despond-
ently. "That sort of thing only happens in books."

"Nonsense," said Emily, "it happens with me."

"You're simply marvelous," said Enderby again.

Emily brought out a little notebook. "Now let's put
things down methodically. Jim himself, his brother and
sister, and his Aunt Jennifer benefit equally by Captain
Trevelyan's death. Of course Sylvia—that's Jim's sister—
wouldn't hurt a fly, but I wouldn't put it past her husband; he's what I call a nasty sort of brute. You know—
the artistic nasty kind; has affairs with women—all that
sort of thing. Very likely to be in a hole financially. The
money they'd come into would actually be Sylvia's, but
that wouldn't matter to him. He would soon manage to
get it out of her."

"He sounds a most unpleasant person," said Mr. Enderby.

"Oh! yes. Good-looking in a bold sort of way. Women
talk about sex with him in corners. Real men hate him."

"Well, that's suspect Number One," said Mr. Enderby, also writing in a little book. "Investigate his movements on Friday—easily done under the guise of interview with popular novelist connected with the crime.
Is that all right?"

"Splendid," said Emily. "Then there's Brian, Jim's
younger brother. He's supposed to be in Australia, but
he might quite easily have come back. I mean, people do
sometimes without saying."

"We could send him a cable."

"We will. I suppose Aunt Jennifer is out of it. From
all I've heard she's rather a wonderful person. She's got
character. Still, after all, she wasn't very far away; she

was only at Exeter. She *might* have come over to see her
brother, and he *might* have said something nasty about
her husband whom she adores, and she *might* have seen
red and snatched up a sandbag and biffed him one."

"Do you really think so?" said Mr. Enderby.

"No, not really. But one never *knows*. Then, of
course, there's the batman. He only gets 100 pounds under the will and he seems all right. But there again, one
never knows. His wife is Mrs. Belling's daughter. You
know Mrs. Belling, who keeps the Three Crowns. I
think I shall weep on her shoulder when I get back. She
looks rather a motherly and romantic soul. I think she
would be terribly sorry for me with my young man
probably going to prison, and she might let slip something useful. And then, of course, there's Sittaford
House. Do you know what struck me as queer?"

"No, what?"

"These people, the Willetts. The ones that took Captain Trevelyan's house furnished in the middle of winter. It's an awfully queer thing to do."

"Yes, it is odd," agreed Mr. Enderby. "There might
be something at the bottom of that—something to do
with Captain Trevelyan's past life.

"That séance business was queer too," he added. "I'm
thinking of writing that up for the paper."

"What séance business?"

Mr. Enderby recounted it with gusto. There was nothing connected with the murder that he had not managed somehow or other to hear. "Bit odd, isn't it?" he
finished. "I mean, it makes you think and all that. May
be something in these things. First time I've really ever
come across anything authentic."

Emily gave a slight shiver. "I hate supernatural
things," she said. "Just for once, as you say, it does look
as though there was something in it. But how—how
gruesome!"

"This séance business never seems very practical, does
it? If the old boy could get through and say he was dead,

why couldn't he say who murdered him? It ought to be all so simple."

"I feel there may be a clue in Sittaford," said Emily thoughtfully.

"Yes, I think we ought to investigate there thoroughly," said Enderby. "I've hired a car and I'm starting there in about half an hour's time. You had better come along with me."

"I will," said Emily. "What about Major Burnaby?"

"He's going to tramp it," said Enderby. "Started immediately after the inquest. If you ask me, he wanted to get out of having my company on the way there. Nobody could like trudging there through all this slush."

"Will the car be able to get up all right?"

"Oh! yes. First day a car has been able to get through."

"Well," said Emily, rising to her feet. "It's about time we went back to the Three Crowns and I will pack my suitcase and do a short weeping act on Mrs. Belling's shoulder."

"Don't you worry," said Mr. Enderby rather fatuously. "You leave everything to me."

"That's just what I mean to do," said Emily with a complete lack of truth. "It's so wonderful to have someone you can really rely on."

Emily Trefusis was really a very accomplished young woman.

CHAPTER TWELVE

THE ARREST

ON HER RETURN TO THE THREE CROWNS, Emily had the good fortune to run right into Mrs. Belling, who was standing in the hallway. "Oh! Mrs. Belling," she exclaimed. "I am leaving this afternoon."

"Yes, Miss. By the four-ten train to Exeter, Miss?"

"No, I am going up to Sittaford."

"To Sittaford?"

Mrs. Belling's countenance showed lively curiosity.

"Yes, and I wanted to ask you if you knew of anywhere there where I could stay."

"You want to stay up there?" The curiosity was heightened.

"Yes, that is— Oh! Mrs. Belling, is there somewhere I could speak to you privately for a moment?"

With something like alacrity, Mrs. Belling led the way to her own private sanctum. A small, comfortable room with a large fire burning.

"You won't tell anyone, will you?" began Emily, knowing well that of all openings on earth this one is the most certain to provoke interest and sympathy.

"No, indeed, Miss, that I won't," said Mrs. Belling, her dark eyes aglitter with interest.

"You see, Mr. Pearson—you know—"

"The young gentleman that stayed here on Friday? And that the police have arrested?"

"Arrested? Do you mean really arrested?"

"Yes, Miss. Not half an hour ago."

Emily had gone very white. "You—you're sure?"

"Oh! yes, Miss. Our Amy had it from the Sergeant."

"It's too awful!" said Emily. She had been expecting this but it was none the better for that. "You see, Mrs. Belling, I—I'm engaged to him. And he didn't do it, and, oh dear, it's all too dreadful!"

And here Emily began to cry. She had announced her intentions to Charles Enderby of doing so, but what appalled her so was with what ease the tears came. To cry at will is not an easy accomplishment. There was something much too real about these tears. It frightened her. She mustn't really give way. Giving way wasn't the least use to Jim. To be resolute, logical, and clear-sighted—these were the qualities that were going to count in this game. Sloppy crying had never helped anyone yet.

But it was a relief all the same, to let yourself go. After all, she had meant to cry. Crying would be an undeniable passport to Mrs. Belling's sympathy and help. So why not have a good cry while she was about it. A real orgy of weeping in which all her troubles, doubts, and unacknowledged fears might be swept away.

"There, there, my dear, don't ee take on so," said Mrs. Belling. She put a large motherly arm round Emily's shoulders and patted her consolingly. "Said from the start I have that he didn't do it. A regular nice young gentleman. A lot of chuckleheads the police are, and so I've said before now. Some thieving tramp is a great deal more likely. Now, don't ee fret, my dear, it'll all come right, you see if it don't."

"I am so dreadfully fond of him," wailed Emily.

Dear Jim, dear, sweet, boyish, helpless, impractical Jim. So utterly to be depended on to do the wrong thing at the wrong moment. What possible chance had he got against that steady, resolute Inspector Narracott? "We *must* save him," she wailed.

"Of course we will. Of course we will," Mrs. Belling consoled her.

Emily dabbed her eyes vigorously, gave one last sniff and gulp, and raising her head demanded fiercely, "Where can I stay at Sittaford?"

"Up to Sittaford? You're set on going there?"

"Yes," Emily nodded vigorously.

"Well, now." Mrs. Belling cogitated the matter. "There's only one place for ee to stay. There's not much to Sittaford. There's the big house, Sittaford House, which Captain Trevelyan built, and that's let now to a South African lady. And there's the six cottages he built, and Number Five of them cottages has got Curtis, what used to be gardener at Sittaford House, in it, and Mrs. Curtis. She lets rooms in the summer time, the Captain allowing her to do so. There's nowhere else you could stay and that's a fact. There's the blacksmith's and the post office, but Mary Hibbert, she's got six children and her sister-in-law living with her, and the blacksmith's wife she's expecting her eighth, so there won't be so much a corner there. But how are you going to get up to Sittaford, Miss? Have you hired a car?"

"I am going to share Mr. Enderby's."

"Ah, and where will he be staying, I wonder?"

"I suppose he will have to be put up at Mrs. Curtis's too. Will she have room for both of us?"

"I don't know that that will look quite right for a young lady like you," said Mrs. Belling.

"He's my cousin," said Emily. On no account, she felt, must a sense of propriety intervene to work against her in Mrs. Belling's mind.

The landlady's brow cleared. "Well, that may be all right then," she allowed grudgingly, "and likely as not if you're not comfortable with Mrs. Curtis they would put you up at the big house."

"I'm sorry I've been such an idiot," said Emily, mopping once more at her eyes.

"It's only natural, my dear. And you feel better for it."

"I do," said Emily truthfully. "I feel much better."

"A good cry and a good cup of tea—there's nothing to beat them, and a nice cup of tea you shall have at once, my dear, before you start off on that cold drive."

"Oh, thank you, but I don't think I really want—"

"Never mind what you want, it's what you're going to have," said Mrs. Belling, rising with determination and moving toward the door. "And you tell Amelia Curtis from me that she's to look after you and see you take your food proper and see you don't fret."

"You *are* kind," said Emily.

"And what's more I shall keep my eyes and ears open down here," said Mrs. Belling, entering with relish into her part of the romance. "There's many a little thing that I hear that never goes to the police. And anything I do hear I'll pass on to you, Miss."

"Will you really?"

"That I will. Don't ee worry, my dear, we'll have your young gentleman out of his trouble in no time."

"I must go and pack," said Emily, rising.

"I'll send the tea up to you," said Mrs. Belling.

Emily went upstairs, packed her few belongings into her suitcase, sponged her eyes with cold water, and applied a liberal allowance of powder.

"You *have* made yourself look a sight," she apostrophized herself in the glass. She added more powder and a touch of rouge. "Curious," said Emily, "how much better I feel. It's worth the puffy look."

She rang the bell. The chambermaid (the sympathetic sister-in-law of Constable Graves) came promptly. Emily presented her with a pound note and begged her earnestly to pass on any information she might acquire in roundabout ways from police circles. The girl promised readily.

"Mrs. Curtis's up to Sittaford? I will indeed, Miss. Do anything, that I will. We all feel for you, Miss, more than I can say. All the time I keep saying to myself, 'Just fancy if it was you and Fred,' I keep saying. I would be distracted—that I would. The least thing I hears I'll pass it on to you, Miss."

"You angel," said Emily.

"Just like a sixpenny I got at Woolworth's the other day, *The Syringa Murders* it was called. And do you know what led them to find the real murderer, Miss? Just a bit of common sealing wax. Your gentleman *is* good-looking, Miss, isn't he? Quite unlike his picture in the papers. I'm sure I'll do anything I can, Miss, for you and for him."

Thus the center of romantic attention, Emily left the

Three Crowns, having duly gulped down the cup of tea prescribed by Mrs. Belling.

"By the way," she said to Enderby as the aged Ford sprang forward, "you are my cousin, don't forget."

"Why?"

"They've got such pure minds in the country," said Emily. "I thought it would be better."

"Splendid. In that case," said Mr. Enderby, rising to his opportunities, "I had better call you Emily."

"All right, cousin—what's your name?"

"Charles."

"All right, Charles."

The car went upward on the Sittaford road.

CHAPTER THIRTEEN

SITTAFORD

EMILY WAS RATHER FASCINATED by her first view of Sittaford. Turning off the main road about two miles from Exhampton, they went upward over a rough moorland road until they reached a village that was situated right on the edge of the moor. It consisted of a smithy, and a combined post office and sweet shop. From there they followed a lane and came to a row of newly built small granite bungalows. At the second of these the car stopped and the driver volunteered the information that this was Mrs. Curtis's.

Mrs. Curtis was a small, thin, gray-haired woman, energetic, and shrewish in disposition. She was all agog with the news of the murder which had only penetrated to Sittaford that morning. "Yes, of course I can take you in, Miss, and your cousin too, if he can just wait until I shift a few duds. You won't mind having your meals along of us, I don't suppose? Well, who would have believed it! Captain Trevelyan murdered and an inquest and all! Cut off from the world we've been since Friday morning, and this morning when the news came you could have knocked me down with a feather. 'The Captain's dead,' I said to Curtis, 'that *shows* you the wickedness there is in the world nowadays.' But I'm keeping you talking here, Miss. Come away in and the gentleman too. I have got the kettle on and you shall have a cup of tea immediately, for you must be perished by the drive up, though of course, it's warmer today after what it's been. Eight and ten feet the snow has been."

Drowned in this sea of talk, Emily and Charles Enderby were shown their new quarters. Emily had a small square room, scrupulously clean, looking out and up to the slope of Sittaford Beacon. Charles's room was a small slit facing the front of the house and the lane, containing a bed and a microscopic chest of drawers and washstand.

"The great thing is," he observed after the driver of the car had disposed his suitcase upon the bed, and had been duly paid and thanked, "that we are here. If we don't know all there is to be known about everyone living in Sittaford within the next quarter of an hour, I'll eat my hat."

Ten minutes later, they were sitting downstairs in the comfortable kitchen being introduced to Curtis, a rather gruff-looking gray-haired old man, and being regaled with strong tea, bread and butter, Devonshire cream, and hard boiled eggs. While they ate and drank they listened. Within half an hour they knew everything there was to be known about the inhabitants of the small community.

First there was Miss Percehouse, who lived in No. 4 The Cottages, a spinster of uncertain years and temper who had come down here to die, according to Mrs. Curtis, six years ago.

"But believe it or not, Miss, the air of Sittaford is that healthy that she picked up from the day she came. Wonderfully pure air for lungs it is. Miss Percehouse has a nephew who occasionally comes down to see her, and indeed he's staying with her at the present time. Seeing to it that the money doesn't go out of the family, that's what he's doing. Very dull for a young gentleman at this time of year. But there, there's more ways than one of amusing yourself, and his coming has been a providence for the young lady at Sittaford House. Poor young thing, the idea of bringing her to that great barrack of a house in the winter time. Selfish is what some mothers are. A very pretty young lady, too. Mr. Ronald Garfield is up there as often as he can be without neglecting Miss Percehouse."

Charles Enderby and Emily exchanged glances. Charles remembered that Ronald Garfield had been mentioned as present at the table turning.

"The cottage this side of mine, Number Six," continued Mrs. Curtis, "has only just been took. Gentleman of the name of Duke. That is, if you would call him a gentleman. Of course, he may be and he may not. There's no saying—folks aren't so particular nowadays as they used to be. He's been made free of the place in the heartiest manner. A bashful sort of gentleman he is —might be a military gentleman from the look of him, but somehow he hasn't got the manner. Not like Major Burnaby, that you would know as a military gentleman the first time you clapped eyes on him.

"Number Three, that's Mr. Rycroft's, little elderly gentleman. They do say that he used to go after birds to outlandish parts for the British Museum. What they call a naturalist he is. Always out and roaming over the moor when the weather permits. And he has a very fine library of books. His cottage is nearly all bookcases.

"Number Two is an invalid gentleman's, a Captain Wyatt with an Indian servant. And poor fellow he does feel the cold, he does. The servant I mean, not the Captain. Coming from warm outlandish parts, it's no wonder. The heat they keep up inside the house would frighten you. It's like walking into an oven.

"Number One is Major Burnaby's cottage. Lives by himself he does, and I go in to do for him early mornings. He is a very neat gentleman, he is, and very particular. He and Captain Trevelyan were as thick as thieves. Friends of a lifetime they were. And they both have the same kind of outlandish heads on the walls.

"As for Mrs. Willett and Miss Willett, that's what no one can make out. Plenty of money there. Amos Parker at Exhampton they deal with, and he tells me their weekly book comes to well over eight pounds or nine pounds. You wouldn't believe the eggs that goes into that house! Brought their maid servants from Exeter with them, they did, but they don't like it and want to leave, and I'm sure I don't blame them. Mrs. Willett, she sends them into Exeter twice a week in her car, and what with that and the living being so good, they agreed to stop on, but if you ask me it's a queer business, burying yourself in the country like this, a smart lady like that. Well, well, I suppose I had better be clearing away these tea things."

She drew a deep breath and so did Charles and Emily. The flow of information loosened with so little difficulty had almost overwhelmed them. Charles ventured to put a question. "Has Major Burnaby got back yet?"

Mrs. Curtis paused at once, tray in hand. "Yes, indeed, sir, came tramping in just the same as ever about half an hour before you arrived. 'Why, sir,' I cried to him. 'You've never walked all the way from Exhampton?' And he says in his stern way, 'Why not? If a man has got two legs he doesn't need four wheels. I do it once a week anyway as you know, Mrs. Curtis.' 'Oh, yes, sir,' I says, 'but this is different. What with the shock and the murder and the inquest it's wonderful you've got the strength to do it.' But he only grunted like and walked on. He looks bad, though. It's a miracle he ever got through on Friday night. Brave I call it at his age. Tramping off like that and three miles of it in a snowstorm. You may say what you like, but nowadays the young gentlemen aren't a patch on the old ones. That Mr. Ronald Garfield he would never have done it, and it's my opinion, and it's the opinion of Mrs. Hibbert at the post office, and it's the opinion of Mr. Pound, the blacksmith, that Mr. Garfield ought never to have let him go off alone the way he did. He should have gone with him. If Major Burnaby had been lost in a snowdrift, everybody would have blamed Mr. Garfield. And that's a fact."

She disappeared triumphantly into the scullery amid a clatter of tea things. Mr. Curtis thoughtfully removed an aged pipe from the right side of his mouth to the left side. "Women," he said, "talk a lot." He paused and then murmured, "And half the time they don't know the truth of what they are talking about."

Emily and Charles received this announcement in

silence. Seeing that no more was coming, however, Charles murmured approvingly, "That's very true."

"Ah!" said Mr. Curtis, and relapsed into a pleasant and contemplative silence.

Charles rose. "I think I'll go round and see old Burnaby," he said, "tell him the camera parade will be tomorrow morning."

"I'll come with you," said Emily. "I want to know what he really thinks about Jim and what ideas he has about the crime in general."

"Have you got any rubber boots or anything? It's awfully slushy."

"I bought some Wellingtons in Exhampton," said Emily.

"What a practical girl you are. You think of everything."

"Unfortunately," said Emily, "that's not much help to you in finding out who's done a murder. It might help one to do a murder," she added reflectively.

"Well, don't murder me," said Mr. Enderby.

They went out together. Mrs. Curtis immediately returned. "They be gone round to the Major's," said Mr. Curtis.

"Ah!" said Mrs. Curtis. "Now, what do you think? Are they sweethearting, or are they not? A lot of harm comes of cousins marrying, so they say. Deaf and dumbs and halfwits and a lot of other evils. He's sweet on her, that you can see easily enough. As for her, she's a deep one like my Great Aunt Sarah's Belinda, she is. Got a way with her and with the men. I wonder what she's after now? Do you know what I think, Curtis?"

Mr. Curtis grunted.

"This young gentleman that the police are holding on account of the murder, it's my belief that he's the one she's set on. And she's come up here to nose about and see what she can find out. And mark my words," said Mrs. Curtis, rattling china, "if there's anything *to* find out she will find it!"

CHAPTER FOURTEEN

THE WILLETTS

AT THE SAME MOMENT that Charles and Emily started out to visit Major Burnaby, Inspector Narracott was seated in the drawing-room of Sittaford House, trying to formulate an impression of Mrs. Willett.

He had not been able to interview her sooner as the roads had been impassable until this morning. He had hardly known what he had expected to find, but certainly not what he had found. It was Mrs. Willett who had taken charge of the situation, not he.

She had come rushing into the room, thoroughly businesslike and efficient. He saw a tall woman, thin-faced and keen-eyed. She was wearing rather an elaborate knitted silk jumper suit that was just over the border line of unsuitability for country wear. She wore several valuable rings and rather a large quantity of very good and expensive imitation pearls.

"Inspector Narracott?" said Mrs. Willett. "Naturally you want to come over the house. What a shocking tragedy! I could hardly believe it. We only heard about it this morning, you know. We were terribly shocked. Sit down, won't you, Inspector? This is my daughter, Violet."

He had hardly noticed the girl who had followed her in, and yet she was a very pretty girl, tall and fair with big blue eyes.

Mrs. Willett herself took a seat. "Is there any way in which I can help you, Inspector? I knew very little of poor Captain Trevelyan, but if there is anything you can think of—"

The Inspector said slowly, "Thank you, madam. Of course, one never knows what may be useful."

"I quite understand. There may possibly be something in the house that may throw light upon this sad business, but I rather doubt it. Captain Trevelyan removed all his personal belongings. He even feared I should tamper with his fishing-rods, poor, dear man." She laughed a little.

"You were not acquainted with him?"

"Before I took the house, you mean? Oh, no! I've asked him here several times since, but he never came. Terribly shy, poor dear. That was what was the matter with him. I've known dozens of men like it. They are called women haters and all sorts of silly things, and really all the time it's only shyness. If I could have got at him," said Mrs. Willett with determination, "I'd soon have got over all that nonsense. That sort of man only wants bringing out."

Inspector Narracott began to understand Captain Trevelyan's strongly defensive attitude toward his tenants.

"We both asked him," continued Mrs. Willett. "Didn't we, Violet?"

"Oh, yes, mother."

"A real simple sailor at heart," said Mrs. Willett. "Every woman loves a sailor, Inspector Narracott."

It occurred to Inspector Narracott at this juncture that the interview so far had been run entirely by Mrs. Willett. He was convinced that she was an exceedingly clever woman. She might be as innocent as she appeared. On the other hand she might not. "The point I am anxious to get information about is this," he said and paused.

"Yes, Inspector?"

"Major Burnaby, as you doubtless know, discovered the body. He was led to do so by an incident that occurred in this house."

"You mean?"

"I mean the table turning. I beg your pardon—" He turned sharply. A faint sound had come from the girl.

"Poor Violet," said her mother. "She was terribly upset—indeed we all were! Most unaccountable. I'm not superstitious, but really it was the most unaccountable thing."

"It did occur, then?"

Mrs. Willett opened her eyes very wide. "Occur? Of course it occurred. At the time I thought it was a joke—a most unfeeling joke and one in very bad taste. I suspected young Ronald Garfield—"

"Oh, no, mother! I'm sure he didn't. He absolutely swore he didn't."

"I'm saying what I thought at the time, Violet. What could one think it but a joke?"

"It was curious," said the Inspector slowly. "You were very upset, Mrs. Willett?"

"We all were. Up to then it had been, oh, just light-hearted fooling. You know the sort of thing. Good fun on a winter's evening. And then suddenly—this! I was very angry."

"Angry?"

"Well, naturally, I thought someone was doing it deliberately—for a joke, as I say."

"And now?"

"Now?"

"Yes, what do you think now?"

Mrs. Willett spread her hands out expressively. "I don't know what to think. It—it's uncanny."

"And you, Miss Willett?"

"I?" The girl started. "I—I don't know. I shall never forget it. I *dream* of it. I shall never dare to do table turning again."

"Mr. Rycroft would say it was genuine, I suppose," said her mother. "He believes in all that sort of thing. Really, I'm inclined to believe in it myself. What other explanation is there except that it was a genuine message from a spirit?"

The Inspector shook his head. The table turning had been his red herring. His next remark was most casual sounding. "Don't you find it very bleak here in winter, Mrs. Willett?"

"Oh, we love it! Such a change. We're South Africans,

you know." Her tone was brisk and ordinary.

"Really? What part of South Africa?"

"Oh! the Cape. Violet has never been in England before. She is enchanted with it—finds the snow most romantic. This house is really most comfortable."

"What led you to come to this part of the world?" There was just gentle curiosity in his voice.

"We've read so many books on Devonshire, and especially on Dartmoor. We were reading one on the boat —all about Widdecombe Fair. I've always had a hankering to see Dartmoor."

"What made you fix on Exhampton? It's not a very well known little town."

"Well—we were reading these books as I told you, and there was a boy on board who talked about Exhampton—he was so enthusiastic about it."

"What was his name?" asked the Inspector. "Did he come from this part of the world?"

"Now, what was his name? Cullen—I think. No—it was Smythe. How stupid of me. I really can't remember. You know how it is on board ship, Inspector, you get to know people so well and plan to meet again—and a week after you've landed, you can't even be sure of their names!" She laughed. "But he was such a nice boy—not good-looking, reddish hair, but a delightful smile."

"And on the strength of that you decided to take a house in these parts?" said the Inspector, smiling.

"Yes, wasn't it mad of us?"

Clever, thought Narracott. *Distinctly clever.* He began to realize Mrs. Willett's methods. She always carried the war into the enemy's country. "So you wrote to the house agents and inquired about a house?"

"Yes—and they sent us particulars of Sittaford. It sounded just what we wanted."

"It wouldn't be my taste at this time of year," said the Inspector with a laugh.

"I dare say it wouldn't be ours if we lived in England," said Mrs. Willett brightly.

The Inspector rose. "How did you know the name of a house agent to write to in Exhampton?" he asked. "That must have presented a difficulty."

There was a pause. The first pause in the conversation. He thought he caught a glimpse of vexation, more, of anger in Mrs. Willett's eyes. He had hit upon something to which she had not thought out the answer. She turned toward her daughter. "How did we, Violet? I can't remember."

There was a different look in the girl's eyes. She looked frightened.

"Why, of course," said Mrs. Willett. "Delfridges. Their information bureau. It's too wonderful. I always go and inquire there about everything. I asked them the name of the best agent here and they told me."

Quick, thought the Inspector. *Very quick. But not quite quick enough. I had you there, madam.*

He made a cursory examination of the house. There was nothing there. No papers, no locked drawers or cupboards. Mrs. Willett accompanied him, talking brightly. He took his leave, thanking her politely.

As he departed he caught a glimpse of the girl's face over her shoulder. There was no mistaking the expression on her face. It was fear he saw on her countenance. Fear written there plainly at this moment when she thought herself unobserved.

Mrs. Willett was still talking. "Alas. We have one grave drawback here. The domestic problem, Inspector. Servants will not stand these country places. All of mine have been threatening to leave us for some time, and the news of the murder seems to have unsettled them utterly. I don't know what I shall do. Perhaps men servants would answer the case. That is what the Registery Office in Exeter advised."

The Inspector answered mechanically. He was not listening to her flow of talk. He was thinking of the expression he had surprised on the girl's face. Mrs. Willett had been clever—but not quite clever enough. If the Willetts had nothing to do with Captain Trevelyan's death, why was Violet Willett afraid? He fired his last shot. With his foot actually over the threshold of the front door he turned back. "By the way," he said, "you know young Pearson, don't you?"

There was no doubt of the pause this time. A dead silence of about a second. Then Mrs. Willett spoke: "Pearson?" she said. "I don't think—"

She was interrupted. A queer sighing breath came from the room behind her and then the sound of a fall. The Inspector was over the threshold and into the room in a flash. Violet Willett had fainted.

"Poor child," cried Mrs. Willett. "All this strain and shock. That dreadful table-turning business and the murder on the top of it. She isn't strong. Thank you so much, Inspector. Yes, on the sofa please. If you would ring the bell. No, I don't think there is anything more you can do. Thank you so much."

The Inspector went down the drive with his lips set in a grim line. Jim Pearson was engaged, he knew, to that extremely charming-looking girl he had seen in London. Why then should Violet Willett faint at the mention of his name? What was the connection between Jim Pearson and the Willetts?

He paused indecisively as he emerged from the front gate. Then he took from his pocket a small notebook. In it was entered a list of the inhabitants of the six bungalows built by Captain Trevelyan with a few brief remarks against each name. Inspector Narracott's stubby forefinger paused at the entry against No. 6 The Cottages. *Yes,* he said to himself. *I'd better see him*.

He strode briskly down the lane and beat a firm rat-tat on the knocker of No. 6—the bungalow inhabited by Mr. Duke.

CHAPTER FIFTEEN

VISIT TO MAJOR BURNABY

LEADING THE WAY UP THE PATH to the Major's front door, Mr. Enderby rapped upon it in a cheery fashion. The door was flung open almost immediately and Major Burnaby, red in the face, appeared on the threshold. "It's you, is it?" he observed with no very great fervor in his voice, and was about to go on in the same strain when he caught sight of Emily and his expression altered.

"This is Miss Trefusis," said Charles with the air of one producing the ace of trumps. "She was very anxious to see you."

"May I come in?" said Emily with her sweetest smile.

"Oh, yes! Certainly. Of course— Oh, yes, of course." Stumbling in his speech, the Major backed into the living-room of his cottage and began pulling forward chairs and pushing aside tables.

Emily, as was her fashion, came straight to the point. "You, see, Major Burnaby, I am engaged to Jim—Jim Pearson, you know. And naturally I am terribly anxious about him."

In the act of pushing a table the Major paused with his mouth open. "Oh, dear," he said, "that's a bad business. My dear young lady, I am more sorry about it than I can say."

"Major Burnaby, tell me honestly. Do you yourself believe he is guilty? Oh, you needn't mind saying if you do. I would a hundred times rather people didn't lie to me."

"No, I do *not* think him guilty," said the Major in a loud, assertive voice. He hit a cushion once or twice vigorously, and then sat down facing Emily. "The chap is a nice young chap. Mind you, he might be a bit weak.

Don't be offended if I say that he's the kind of young fellow that might easily go wrong if temptation came in his way. But murder—no. And mind you, I know what I am talking about—a lot of subalterns have passed through my hands in my time. It's the fashion to poke fun at retired army officers nowadays, but we know a thing or two all the same, Miss Trefusis."

"I'm sure you do," said Emily. "I'm awfully grateful to you for saying what you've done."

"Have—have a whisky and soda?" said the Major. "I'm afraid there's nothing else," he said apologetically.

"No, thank you, Major Burnaby."

"Some plain soda then?"

"No, thank you," said Emily.

"I ought to be able to produce tea," said the Major with a touch of wistfulness.

"We've had it," said Charles. "At Mrs. Curtis's."

"Major Burnaby," said Emily, "who do you think did it—have you any idea at all?"

"No. I am damned—er—bother—if I have," said the Major. "Took it for granted it was some chap that broke in, but now the police say that can't be so. Well, it's their job, and I suppose they know best. They say nobody broke in, so I suppose nobody did break in. But all the same it beats me, Miss Trefusis. Trevelyan hadn't an enemy in the world as far as I know."

"And *you* would know if anybody did," said Emily.

"Yes, I suppose I knew more of Trevelyan than many of his relations did."

"And you can't think of anything—anything that would help, in any way?" asked Emily.

The Major pulled at his short mustache. "I know what you're thinking. Like in books there ought to be some little incident that I should remember that would be a clue. Well, I'm sorry, but there isn't any such thing. Trevelyan just led an ordinary, normal life. Got very few letters and wrote less. There were no female complications in his life, I am sure of that. No, it beats me."

All three were silent.

"What about that servant of his?" asked Charles.

"Been with him for years. Absolutely faithful."

"He had married lately," said Charles.

"Married a perfectly decent, respectable girl."

"Major Burnaby," said Emily, "forgive me putting it this way—but didn't you get the wind up rather easily about him?"

The Major rubbed his nose with the embarrassed air that always came over him when the table turning was mentioned. "Yes, there's no denying it, I did. I knew the whole thing was tommyrot and yet—"

"You felt somehow it wasn't," said Emily helpfully.

The Major nodded.

"That's why I wonder—" said Emily.

The two men looked at her.

"I can't quite put what I mean in the way I want," said Emily. "What I mean is this: You say that you don't believe in all this table-turning business—and yet, in spite of the awful weather and what must have seemed to you the absurdity of the whole thing—you felt so uneasy that you had to set out, no matter what the weather conditions, and see for yourself that Captain Trevelyan was all right. Well, don't you think that may have been because—because there was something in the atmosphere?

"I mean," she continued desperately as she saw no trace of comprehension in the Major's face, "that there was something in someone else's mind as well as yours. And that somehow or other you felt it."

"Well, I don't know," said the Major. He rubbed his nose again. "Of course," he added hopefully, "women do take these things seriously."

"Women!" said Emily. *Yes,* she murmured to herself, *I believe somehow or other that's it.* She turned abruptly to Major Burnaby. "What are they like, these Willetts?"

"Oh, well—" Major Burnaby cast about in his mind, he was clearly no good at personal descriptions. "Well—they are very kind, you know—very helpful and all that."

"Why do they want to take a house like Sittaford

House at this time of year?"

"I can't imagine," said the Major. "Nobody does," he added.

"Don't you think it's very queer?" persisted Emily.

"Of course it's queer. However, there's no accounting for tastes. That's what the Inspector said."

"That's nonsense," said Emily. "People don't do things without a reason."

"Well, I don't know," said Major Burnaby cautiously. "Some people don't. You wouldn't, Miss Trefusis. But some people—" He sighed and shook his head.

"You are sure they hadn't met Captain Trevelyan before?"

The Major scouted the idea. Trevelyan would have said something to him. No, he was as astonished himself as anyone could be.

"So *he* thought it queer?"

"Of course. I've told you we all did."

"What was Mrs. Willett's attitude toward Captain Trevelyan?" asked Emily. "Did she try and avoid him?"

A faint chuckle came from the Major. "No, indeed she didn't. Pestered the life out of him—always asking him to come and see them."

"Oh!" said Emily thoughtfully. She paused and then said, "So she might—just possibly she might have taken Sittaford House just on purpose to get acquainted with Captain Trevelyan."

"Well—" the Major seemed to turn it over in his mind. "Yes, I suppose she might have. Rather an expensive way of doing things."

"I don't know," said Emily. "Captain Trevelyan wouldn't have been an easy person to get to know otherwise."

"No, he wouldn't," agreed the late Captain Trevelyan's friend.

"I wonder," said Emily.

"The Inspector thought of that too," said Burnaby.

Emily felt a sudden irritation against Inspector Narracott. Everything that she thought of seemed to have already been thought of by the Inspector. It was galling to a young woman who prided herself on being sharper than other people.

She rose and held out her hand. "Thank you very much," she said simply.

"I wish I could help you more," said the Major. "I'm rather an obvious sort of person—always have been. If I were a clever chap I might be able to hit upon something that might be a clue. At any rate count on me for anything you want."

"Thank you," said Emily. "I will."

"Good-by, sir," said Enderby. "I shall be along in the morning with my camera, you know."

Burnaby grunted.

Emily and Charles retraced their steps to Mrs. Curtis's. "Come into my room, I want to talk to you," said Emily.

She sat on the one chair and Charles sat on the bed. Emily plucked off her hat and sent it spinning into a corner of the room. "Now, listen," she said. "I think I've got a kind of starting point. I may be wrong and I may be right, at any rate it's an idea. I think a lot hinges on this table-turning business. You've done table turning, haven't you?"

"Oh, yes, now and then. Not serious, you know."

"No, of course not. It's the kind of thing one does on a wet afternoon, and everyone accuses everyone else of shoving. Well, if you've played it you know what happens. The table starts spelling out, say, a name. Well, it's a name somebody knows. Very often they recognize it at once and hope it isn't going to be that, and all the time unconsciously they are what one calls shoving. I mean sort of recognizing things makes one give an involuntary jerk when the next letter comes and stops the thing. And the less you want to do that sometimes the more it happens."

"Yes, that's true," agreed Mr. Enderby.

"I don't believe for a moment in spirits or anything

like that. But supposing that one of those people who were playing knew that Captain Trevelyan was being murdered at that minute—"

"Oh, I say," protested Charles, "that's awfully far-fetched."

"Well, it needn't be quite so crude as that. Yes, I think it must be. We are just taking a hypothesis—that's all. We are asserting that somebody knew that Captain Trevelyan was dead and absolutely couldn't hide their knowledge. The table betrayed them."

"It's awfully ingenious," said Charles, "but I don't believe for a minute it's true."

"We'll assume that it is true," said Emily firmly. "I am sure that in detection of crime you mustn't be afraid to assume things."

"Oh, I'm quite agreeable," said Mr. Enderby. "We'll assume that it is true—anything you like."

"So what we have to do," said Emily, "is to consider very carefully the people who were playing. To begin with, there's Major Burnaby and Mr. Rycroft; well, it seems wildly unlikely that either of them should have an accomplice who was the murderer. Then there is this Mr. Duke. Well, for the moment we know nothing about him. He has only just arrived here lately and of course, he might be a sinister stranger—part of a gang or something. We will put X against his name. And now we come to the Willetts. Charles, there is something awfully mysterious about the Willetts."

"What on earth have they got to gain from Captain Trevelyan's death?"

"Well, on the face of it, nothing. But if my theory is correct there must be a connection somewhere. We've got to find what is the connection."

"Right," said Mr. Enderby. "And supposing it's all a mare's nest?"

"Well, we'll have to start all over again," said Emily.

"Hark!" cried Charles suddenly. He held up his hand. Then he went over to the window and opened it, and Emily too heard the sound that had aroused his attention. It was the far-off booming of a great bell.

As they stood listening, Mrs. Curtis's voice called excitedly from below, "Do you hear the bell, Miss—do you hear it?"

Emily opened the door.

"D'you hear it? Plain as plain, isn't it? Well, now, to think of that!"

"What is it?" asked Emily.

"It's the bell at Princetown, Miss, near to twelve mile away. It means that a convict's escaped. George, George, where is that man? D'you hear the bell? There's a convict loose." Her voice died away as she went through the kitchen.

Charles shut the window and sat down on the bed again. "It's a pity that things happen all wrong," he said dispassionately. "If only this convict had escaped on Friday, why, there would be our murderer nicely accounted for. No farther to look. Hungry man, desperate criminal breaks in. Trevelyan defends his Englishman's castle—and desperate criminal biffs him one. All so simple."

"It would have been," said Emily with a sigh.

"Instead of which," said Charles, "he escapes three days too late. It's—it's hopelessly inartistic."

He shook his head sadly.

CHAPTER SIXTEEN

MR. RYCROFT

EMILY WOKE EARLY THE NEXT MORNING. Being a sensible young woman, she realized there was little possibility of Mr. Enderby's collaboration until the morning was well advanced. So, feeling restless and unable to lie still, she set out for a brisk walk along the lane in the opposite direction from which they had come last night.

She passed the gates of Sittaford House on her right and shortly after that the lane took a sharp turn to the right and ran steeply up hill and came out on the open moor where it degenerated into a grass track and soon petered out altogether. The morning was a fine one, cold and crisp and the view was lovely. Emily ascended to the very top of Sittaford Tor, a pile of gray rock of a fantastic shape. From this height she looked down over an expanse of moorland, unbroken as far as she could see, without any habitation or any road. Below her, on the opposite side of the Tor, were gray masses of granite boulders and rocks. After considering the scene for a minute or two, she turned to view the prospect to the north from which she had come. Just below her lay Sittaford, clustering on the flank of the hill, the square gray blob of Sittaford House, and the dotted cottages beyond it. In the valley below she could see Exhampton.

One ought, thought Emily confusedly, *to see things better when you are high up like this. It ought to be like lifting off the top of a doll's house and peering in.*

She wished with all her heart that she had met the dead man even if only once. It was so hard to get an idea of people you had never seen. You had to rely on other people's judgment, and Emily had never yet acknowledged that any other person's judgment was superior to her own. Other people's impressions were no good to

you. They might be just as true as yours but you
couldn't act on them. You couldn't, as it were, use another person's angle of attack.

Meditating vexedly on these questions, Emily sighed
impatiently and shifted her position. She had been so
lost in her own thoughts that she had been oblivious to
her immediate surroundings. It was with a shock of
surprise that she realized that a small, elderly gentleman
was standing a few feet away from her, his hat held
courteously in his hand, while he breathed rather fast.

"Excuse me," he said. "Miss Trefusis, I believe?"

"Yes," said Emily.

"My name is Rycroft. You must forgive me speaking
to you, but in this little community of ours the smallest
detail is known, and your arrival here yesterday has
naturally gone the round. I can assure you that everyone
feels a deep sympathy with your position, Miss Trefusis.
We are all, one and all, anxious to assist you in any way
we can."

"That's very kind of you," said Emily.

"Not at all, not at all," said Mr. Rycroft. "Beauty in
distress, you will pardon my old-fashioned manner of
putting it. But seriously, my dear young lady, do count
on me if there is any way in which I can possibly assist
you. Beautiful view from up here, is it not?"

"Wonderful," agreed Emily. "The moor is a wonderful place."

"You know that a prisoner must have escaped last
night from Princetown."

"Yes. Has he been recaptured?"

"Not yet, I believe. Ah, well, poor fellow, he will no
doubt be recaptured soon enough. I believe I am right
in saying that no one has escaped successfully from
Princetown for the last twenty years."

"Which direction is Princetown?"

Mr. Rycroft stretched out his arm and pointed south-
ward over the moor. "It lies over there, about twelve
miles as the crow flies over unbroken moorland. It's sixteen miles by road."

Emily gave a faint shiver. The idea of the desperate hunted man impressed her powerfully. Mr. Rycroft was watching her and gave a little nod.

"Yes," he said. "I feel the same myself. It's curious how one's instincts rebel at the thought of a man being hunted down, and yet these men at Princetown are all dangerous and violent criminals, the kind of men whom probably you and I would do our utmost to put there in the first place."

He gave a little apologetic laugh. "You must forgive me, Miss Trefusis, I am deeply interested in the study of crime. A fascinating study. Ornithology and criminology are my two subjects." He paused and then went on: "That's the reason why, if you will allow me to do so, I should like to associate myself with you in this matter. To study a crime at first hand has long been an unrealized dream of mine. Will you place your confidence in me, Miss Trefusis, and allow me to place my experience at your disposal? I have read and studied this subject deeply."

Emily was silent for a minute. She was congratulating herself on the way events were playing into her hand. Here was first-hand knowledge being offered her of life as it had been lived at Sittaford. *Angle of attack,* Emily repeated the phrase that had crept into her mind so short a time before. She had had Major Burnaby's angle —matter of fact—simple—direct. Taking cognizance of facts and completely oblivious of subtleties. Now she was being offered another angle which she suspected might open up a very different field of vision. This little, shriveled, dried-up gentleman had read and studied deeply, was well versed in human nature, had that devouring interested curiosity in life displayed by the man of reflection as opposed to the man of action.

"Please help me," she said simply. "I am so very worried and unhappy."

"You must be, my dear, you must be. Now, as I understand the position, Trevelyan's eldest nephew has been arrested or detained—the evidence against him being of a somewhat simple and obvious nature. I, of course, have an open mind. You must allow me that."

"Of course," said Emily. "Why should you believe in his innocence when you know nothing about him?"

"Most reasonable," said Mr. Rycroft. "Really, Miss Trefusis, you yourself are a most interesting study. By the way, your name—is it Cornish like our poor friend Trevelyan?"

"Yes," said Emily. "My father was Cornish, my mother was Scottish."

"Ah!" said Mr. Rycroft, "very interesting. Now to approach our little problem. On the one hand we assume that young Jim—the name is Jim, is it not? We assume that young Jim had a pressing need of money, that he came down to see his uncle, that he asked for money, that his uncle refused, that in a moment of passion he picked up a sandbag that was lying at the door and that he hit his uncle over the head. The crime was unpremeditated—was in fact a foolish irrational affair most deplorably conducted. Now, all that may be so. On the other hand he may have parted with his uncle in anger and some other person may have stepped in shortly afterward and committed the crime. That is what you believe—and to put it a little differently, that is what I hope. I do not want your fiancé to have committed the crime, for from my point of view it is so uninteresting that he should have done so. I am therefore backing the other horse. The crime was committed by someone else. We will assume that and go at once to a most important point. Was that someone else aware of the quarrel that had just taken place? Did that quarrel, in fact, actually precipitate the murder? You see my point? Someone is meditating doing away with Captain Trevelyan and seizes this opportunity, realizing that suspicion is bound to fall on young Jim."

Emily considered the matter from this angle. "In that case," she said slowly—

Mr. Rycroft took the words out of her mouth. "In that case," he said briskly, "the murderer would have to be a person in close association with Captain Trevelyan. He would have to be domiciled in Exhampton. In all probability he would have to be in the house, either during or after the quarrel. And since we are not in a court of law and can bandy about names freely, the name of the servant, Evans, leaps to our minds as a person who could satisfy our conditions. A man who quite possibly might have been in the house. Have overheard the quarrel and seized the opportunity. Our next point is to discover whether Evans benefits in any way from his master's death."

"I believe he gets a small legacy," said Emily.

"That may or may not constitute a sufficient motive. We shall have to discover whether or not Evans had a pressing need of money. We must also consider Mrs. Evans—there is a Mrs. Evans of recent date, I understand. If you had studied criminology, Miss Trefusis, you would realize the curious effect caused by inbreeding, especially in country districts. There are at least four young women in Broadmoor, pleasant in manner, but with a curious kink in their dispositions that makes human life of little or no account to them. No—we must not leave Mrs. Evans out of account."

"What do you think about this table-turning business, Mr. Rycroft?"

"Now, that is very strange. Most strange. I confess, Miss Trefusis, that I am powerfully impressed by it. I am, as perhaps you may have heard, a believer in psychic things. To a certain degree I am a believer in spiritualism. I have already written out a full account and sent it up to the Society of Psychical Research. A well authenticated and amazing case. Five people present, none of whom could have the least idea or suspicion that Captain Trevelyan was murdered."

"You don't think—"

Emily stopped. It was not so easy to suggest her own idea to Mr. Rycroft that one of the five people might have guilty foreknowledge, as he himself had been one of them. Not that she suspected for a moment that there was anything whatever to connect Mr. Rycroft with the tragedy. Still she felt that the suggestion might not be wholly tactful. She pursued her object in a more round-about manner.

"It all interested me very much, Mr. Rycroft. It is, as you say, an amazing occurrence. You don't think that any of the people present, with the exception of yourself of course, were in any way psychic?"

"My dear young lady, I myself am not psychic. I have no powers in that direction. I am only a very deeply interested observer."

"What about this Mr. Garfield?"

"A nice lad," said Mr. Rycroft, "but not remarkable in any way."

"Well off, I suppose," said Emily.

"Stony broke, I believe," said Mr. Rycroft. "I hope I am using that idiom correctly. He comes down here to dance attendance on an aunt, from whom he has what I call 'expectations.' Miss Percehouse is a very sharp lady and I think she knows what these attentions are worth. But as she has a sardonic form of humor of her own she keeps him dancing."

"I should like to meet her," said Emily.

"Yes, you must certainly meet her. She will no doubt insist on meeting you. Curiosity—alas, my dear Miss Trefusis—curiosity."

"Tell me about the Willetts," said Emily.

"Charming," said Mr. Rycroft, "quite charming. Co-lonial, of course. No real poise, if you understand me. A little too lavish in their hospitality. Everything a shade on the ornate side. Miss Violet is a charming girl."

"A funny place to come for the winter," said Emily.

"Yes, very odd, is it not? But after all, it is only logical. We ourselves living in this country long for the sun-shine, hot climates, waving palm trees. People who live in Australia or South Africa are enchanted with the idea of an old-fashioned Christmas with snow and ice."

I wonder which of them, said Emily to herself, *told him that.* She reflected that it was not necessary to bury yourself in a moorland village in order to obtain an old-fashioned Christmas with snow and ice. Clearly, Mr. Rycroft did not see anything suspicious in the Willetts' choice of a winter resort. But that, she reflected, was perhaps natural in one who was an ornithologist and a criminologist. Sittaford clearly appeared an ideal residence to Mr. Rycroft, and he could not conceive of it as an unsuitable environment to someone else.

They had been slowly descending the slope of the hillside and were now wending their way down the lane. "Who lives in that cottage?" asked Emily abruptly.

"Captain Wyatt—he is an invalid. Rather unsociable, I fear."

"Was he a friend of Captain Trevelyan's?"

"Not an intimate friend in any way. Trevelyan merely made a formal visit to him every now and then. As a matter of fact Wyatt doesn't encourage visitors. A surly man."

Emily was silent. She was reviewing the possibility of how she herself might become a visitor. She had no intention of allowing any angle of attack to remain unexplored. She suddenly remembered the hitherto unmentioned member of the séance. "What about Mr. Duke?" she asked brightly.

"What about him?"

"Well, who is he?"

"Well," said Mr. Rycroft slowly, "that is what nobody knows."

"How extraordinary," said Emily.

"As a matter of fact," said Mr. Rycroft, "it isn't. You see, Duke is an entirely unmysterious individual. I should imagine that the only mystery about him was his social origin. Not—not quite, if you understand me. But a very solid good fellow."

Emily was silent.

"This is my cottage," said Mr. Rycroft, pausing, "perhaps you will do me the honor of coming in and inspecting it."

"I should love to," said Emily.

They went up the small path and entered the cottage. The interior was charming. Bookcases lined the walls. Emily went from one to the other, glancing curiously at the titles of the books. One section dealt with occult phenomena, another with modern detective fiction, but by far the greater part of the bookcases was given up to criminology and to the world's famous trials. Books on ornithology held a comparatively small position.

"I think it's all delightful," said Emily. "I must get back now. I expect Mr. Enderby will be up and waiting for me. As a matter of fact I haven't had breakfast yet. We told Mrs. Curtis half-past nine, and I see it's ten o'clock. I shall be dreadfully late—that's because you've been so interesting—and so very helpful."

"Anything I can do," burbled Mr. Rycroft as Emily turned a bewitching glance on him. "You can count on me. We are collaborators."

Emily gave him her hand and squeezed his warmly. "It's so wonderful," she said, using the phrase that in the course of her short life she had found so effectual, "to feel that there's someone on whom one can really rely."

CHAPTER SEVENTEEN

MISS PERCEHOUSE

EMILY RETURNED TO FIND EGGS AND BACON, and Charles, waiting for her. Mrs. Curtis was still agog with excitement over the escape of the convict. "Two years it is since last one escaped," she said, "and three days it was before they found him. Near to Moretonhampstead he was."

"Do you think he'll come this way?" asked Charles.

Local knowledge vetoed this suggestion. "They never comes this way, all bare moorland it is, and only small towns when you do come off the moor. He'll make for Plymouth, that's the most likely. But they'll catch him long before that."

"You could find a good hiding-place among these rocks on the other side of the Tor," said Emily.

"You're right, Miss, and there *is* a hiding-place there, the Pixie's Cave they call it. As narrow an opening between two rocks as you could find, but it widens out inside. They say one of King Charles's men hid there once for a fortnight with a serving maid from a farm bringing him food."

"I must take a look at that Pixie's Cave," said Charles.

"You'll be surprised how hard it is to find, sir. Many a picnic party in summer looks for it the whole afternoon and doesn't find it, but if you do find it, be sure you leave a pin inside it for luck."

"I wonder," said Charles when breakfast was over and he and Emily had strolled out into the small bit of garden, "if I ought to go off to Princetown? Amazing how things pile up once you have a bit of luck. Here I am—I start with a simple football competition prize, and before I know where I am I run straight into an escaped convict and a murderer. Marvelous!"

"What about this photographing of Major Burnaby's cottage?"

Charles looked up at the sky. "H'm," he said. "I think I shall say the weather is wrong. I have got to hang on to my *raison d'être* of being in Sittaford as long as possible, and it's coming over misty. Er—I hope you don't mind, I have just posted off an interview with you?"

"Oh, that's all right," said Emily mechanically. "What have you made me say?"

"Oh, the usual sort of things people like to hear," said Mr. Enderby. "Our special representative records his interview with Miss Emily Trefusis, the fiancée of Mr. James Pearson who has been arrested by the police and charged with the murder of Captain Trevelyan— Then my impression of you as a high-spirited, beautiful girl."

"Thank you," said Emily.

"It was a splendid interview. You've no idea what fine, womanly, touching things you said about standing by your man, no matter if the whole world was against him."

"Did I really say that?" said Emily, wincing slightly.

"Do you mind?" said Mr. Enderby anxiously.

"Oh, no!" said Emily. "Enjoy yourself, darling."

Mr. Enderby looked slightly taken aback.

"It's all right," said Emily. "That's a quotation. I had it on my bib when I was small—my Sunday bib. The weekday one had *Don't be a glutton* on it."

"Oh! I see. I put in a very good bit about Captain Trevelyan's sea career and just a hint at foreign idols looted and a possibility of a strange priest's revenge— only a hint, you know."

"Well, you seem to have done your day's good deed," said Emily.

"What have you been up to? You were up early enough, heaven knows."

Emily described her meeting with Mr. Rycroft.

She broke off suddenly and Enderby, glancing over his shoulder and following the direction of her eyes, became aware of a pink, healthy-looking young man lean-

ing over the gate and making various apologetic noises
to attract attention. "I say," said the young man, "frightfully sorry to butt in and all that. I mean, it is awfully
awkward, but my aunt sent me along."

Emily and Charles both said, "Oh?" in an inquiring
tone.

"Yes," said the young man. "To tell the truth, my
aunt's rather a Tartar. What she says *goes*, if you know
what I mean. Of course, I think it's frightfully bad form
coming along at a time like this but if you knew my
aunt—and if you do as she wants, you will know her in
a few minutes—"

"Is your aunt Miss Percehouse?" broke in Emily.

"That's right," said the young man, much relieved.
"So you know all about her? Old Mother Curtis has
been talking, I suppose. She can wag a tongue, can't
she? Not that she's a bad sort, mind you. Well, the fact
is, my aunt said she wanted to see you, and I was to
come along and tell you so. Compliments, and all that,
and would it be troubling you too much—she was an
invalid and quite unable to get out and it would be a
great kindness—well, you know the sort of thing. I
needn't say it all. It's curiosity really, of course, and if
you say you've got a headache, or have got letters to
write it will be quite all right and you needn't bother."

"Oh, but I should like to bother," said Emily. "I'll
come with you at once. Mr. Enderby has got to go along
and see Major Burnaby."

"Have I?" said Enderby in a low voice.

"You have," said Emily firmly.

She dismissed him with a brief nod and joined her
new friend. "I suppose you're Mr. Garfield," she said.

"That's right. I ought to have told you."

"Oh, well," said Emily, "it wasn't very difficult to
guess."

"Splendid of you coming along like this," said Mr.
Garfield. "Lots of girls would have been awfully offended. But you know what old ladies are."

"You don't live down here, do you, Mr. Garfield?"

"You bet your life I don't," said Ronnie Garfield with fervor. "Did you ever see such a god-forsaken spot? Not so much as the pictures to go to. I wonder someone doesn't commit a murder to—"

He paused, appalled by what he had said. "I say, I *am* sorry. I am the most unlucky devil that ever lived. Always coming out with the wrong thing. I never meant it for a moment."

"I'm sure you didn't," said Emily soothingly.

"Here we are," said Mr. Garfield. He pushed open a gate and Emily passed through and went up the path leading to a small cottage identical with the rest. In the living-room giving on the garden was a couch and on it was lying an elderly lady with a thin wrinkled face and with one of the sharpest and most interrogative noses that Emily had ever seen. She raised herself on an elbow with a little difficulty.

"So you've brought her," she said. "Very kind of you, my dear, to come along to see an old woman. But you know what it is when you are an invalid. You must have a finger in every pie going and if you can't go to the pie, then the pie has got to come to you. And you needn't think it's all curiosity—it's more than that. Ronnie, go out and paint the garden furniture. In the shed at the end of the garden. Two basket chairs and a bench. You'll find the paint there all ready."

"Right oh, Aunt Caroline." The obedient nephew disappeared.

"Sit down," said Miss Percehouse.

Emily sat on the chair indicated. Strange to say, she had immediately felt conscious of a distinct liking and sympathy for this rather sharp-tongued, middle-aged invalid. She felt indeed a kind of kinship.

Here is someone, thought Emily, *who goes straight to the point and means to have her own way and bosses everybody she can. Just like me only I happen to be rather good-looking and she has to do it all by force of character.*

"I understand you are the girl who is engaged to

Trevelyan's nephew," said Miss Percehouse. "I've heard all about you and now I have seen you I understand exactly what you are up to. And I wish you good luck."

"Thank you," said Emily.

"I hate a slobbering female," said Miss Percehouse. "I like one who gets up and does things."

She looked at Emily sharply. "I suppose you pity me—lying here never able to get up and walk about?"

"No," said Emily thoughtfully, "I don't know that I do. I suppose that one can, if one has the determination, always get something out of life. If you can't get it one way you get it in another."

"Quite right," said Miss Percehouse. "You've got to take life from a different angle, that's all."

"Angle of attack," murmured Emily.

"What's that you say?"

As clearly as she was able, Emily outlined the theory that she had evolved that morning and the application of it she had made to the matter in hand.

"Not bad," said Miss Percehouse, nodding her head. "Now, my dear—we will get down to business. Not being a born fool, I suppose you've come up to this village to find out what you can about the people here, and to see if what you find out has any bearing on the murder. Well, if there's anything you want to know about the people here, I can tell it to you."

Emily wasted no time. Concise and businesslike, she came to the point. "Major Burnaby?" she asked.

"Typical retired army officer, narrow-minded and limited in outlook, jealous disposition. Credulous in money matters. Kind of man who invests in a South Sea Bubble because he can't see a yard in front of his own nose. Likes to pay his debts promptly and dislikes people who don't wipe their feet on the mat."

"Mr. Rycroft?" said Emily.

"Queer little man, enormous egoist. Cranky. Likes to think himself a wonderful fellow. I suppose he has offered to help you solve the case aright owing to his wonderful knowledge of criminology."

Emily admitted that that was the case.

"Mr. Duke?" she asked.

"Don't know a thing about the man—and yet I ought to. Most ordinary type. I ought to know—and yet I don't. It's queer. It's like a name on the tip of your tongue and yet for the life of you, you can't remember it."

"The Willetts?" asked Emily.

"Ah! the Willetts!" Miss Percehouse hoisted herself up on an elbow again in some excitement. "What about the Willetts indeed? Now, I'll tell you something about them, my dear. It may be useful to you, or it may not. Go over to my writing-table there and pull out the little top drawer. Bring me the blank envelope that's there."

Emily brought the envelope as directed.

"I don't say it's important—it probably isn't," said Miss Percehouse. "Everybody tells lies one way or another and Mrs. Willett is perfectly entitled to do the same as everybody else."

She took the envelope and slipped her hand inside.

"I will tell you all about it. When the Willetts arrived here, with their smart clothes and their maids and their trunks, she and Violet came up in Forder's car and the maids and the trunks came by the station bus. And naturally, the whole thing being an event as you might say, I was looking out as they passed and I saw a colored label blow off from one of the trunks and dive down onto one of my borders. Now, if there is one thing I hate more than another it is a litter of paper or mess of any kind, so I sent Ronnie out to pick it up, and I was going to throw it away when it struck me it was a bright, pretty thing, and I might as well keep it for the scrap-books I make for the children's hospital. Well, I wouldn't have thought about it again except for Mrs. Willett deliberately mentioning on two or three occasions that Violet had never been out of South Africa and that she herself had only been to South Africa, England, and the Riviera."

"Yes?" said Emily.

"Exactly. Now—look at this."

Miss Percehouse thrust a luggage label into Emily's hand. It bore the inscription: *Mendle's Hotel, Melbourne.*

"Australia," said Miss Percehouse, "isn't South Africa —or it wasn't in my young days. I dare say it isn't important but there it is for what it is worth. And I'll tell you another thing, I have heard Mrs. Willett calling to her daughter and she called *Coo-ee* and that again is more typical of Australia than South Africa. And what I say is, it is queer. Why shouldn't you wish to admit that you come from Australia if you do?"

"It's certainly curious," said Emily. "And it's curious that they should come to live here in winter time as they have."

"That leaps to the eye," said Miss Percehouse. "Have you met them yet?"

"No. I thought of going there this morning. Only I didn't know quite what to say."

"I'll provide you with an excuse," said Miss Percehouse briskly. "Fetch me my fountain pen and some notepaper and an envelope. That's right. Now, let me see." She paused deliberately, then without the least warning raised her voice in a hideous scream.

"Ronnie, Ronnie, Ronnie! Is the boy deaf? Why can't he come when he's called? Ronnie! Ronnie!"

Ronnie arrived at a brisk trot, paint brush in hand.

"Is there anything the matter, Aunt Caroline?"

"What should be the matter? I was calling you, that was all. Did you have any particular cake for tea when you were at the Willetts yesterday?"

"Cake?"

"Cake, sandwiches—anything. How slow you are, boy. What did you have to eat for tea?"

"There was a coffee cake," said Ronnie very much puzzled, "and some *pâté* sandwiches—"

"Coffee cake," said Miss Percehouse. "That'll do." She began to write briskly. "You can go back to your painting, Ronnie. Don't hang about, and don't stand there with your mouth open. You had your adenoids out when you were eight years old."

She continued to write:

DEAR MRS. WILLETT: *I hear you had the most delicious coffee cake for tea yesterday afternoon. Will you be so very kind as to give me the recipe for it. I know you'll not mind my asking you this—an invalid has so little variety except in her diet. Miss Trefusis has kindly promised to take this note for me as Ronnie is busy this morning. Is not this news about the convict too dreadful? Yours very sincerely,* CAROLINE PERCEHOUSE.

She put it in an envelope, sealed it down, and addressed it. "There you are, young woman. You will probably find the doorstep littered with reporters. A lot of them passed along the lane in Forder's charabanc. I saw them. But you ask for Mrs. Willett and say you have brought a note from me and you'll sail in. I needn't tell you to keep your eyes open and make the most you can of your visit. You will do that anyway."

"You are kind," said Emily. "You really are."

"I help those who can help themselves," said Miss Percehouse. "By the way, you haven't asked me what I think of Ronnie yet. I presume he is on your list of the village. He is a good lad in his way, but pitifully weak. I am sorry to say he would do almost anything for money. Look at what he stands from me! And he hasn't got the brains to see that I would like him just ten times better if he stood up to me now and again, and told me to go to the devil."

"The only other person in the village is Captain Wyatt. He smokes opium, I believe. And he's easily the worst-tempered man in England. Anything more you want to know?"

"I don't think so," said Emily. "What you have told me seems pretty comprehensive."

CHAPTER EIGHTEEN

EMILY VISITS SITTAFORD HOUSE

As EMILY WALKED BRISKLY ALONG THE LANE she noticed once more how the character of the morning was changing. The mist was closing up and round.

What an awful place to live in England is, thought Emily. *If it isn't snowing or raining or blowing, it's misty. And if the sun does shine it's so cold that you can't feel your fingers or toes.*

She was interrupted in these reflections by a rather hoarse voice speaking rather close to her right ear. "Excuse me," it said, "but do you happen to have seen a bull terrier?"

Emily started and turned. Leaning over a gate was a tall, thin man with a very brown complexion, bloodshot eyes, and gray hair. He was propped up with a crutch on one side, and was eyeing Emily with enormous interest. She had no difficulty in identifying him as Captain Wyatt, the invalid owner of No. 3 The Cottages.

"No, I haven't," said Emily.

"She's got out," said Captain Wyatt. "An affectionate creature, but an absolute fool. With all these cars—"

"I shouldn't think many motors come up this lane," said Emily.

"Charabancs do in the summer time," said Captain Wyatt grimly. "It's the three and sixpenny morning run from Exhampton. Ascent of Sittaford Beacon with a halt halfway up from Exhampton for light refreshments."

"Yes, but this isn't summer time," said Emily.

"All the same a charabanc came along just now. Reporters, I suppose, going to have a look at Sittaford House."

"Did you know Captain Trevelyan well?" asked Emily. She was of opinion that the incident of the bull terrier had been a mere subterfuge on Captain Wyatt's part dictated by a very natural curiosity. She was, she was well aware, the principal object of attention in Sittaford at present, and it was only natural that Captain Wyatt should wish to have a look at her as well as everyone else.

"I don't know about well," said Captain Wyatt. "He sold me this cottage."

"Yes," said Emily encouragingly.

"A skinflint, that's what he was," said Captain Wyatt. "The arrangement was that he was to do the place up to suit the purchaser's taste, and just because I had the window sashes in chocolate picked out in lemon, he wanted me to pay half. Said the arrangement was for a uniform color."

"You didn't like him," said Emily.

"I was always having rows with him," said Captain Wyatt. "But I always have rows with everyone," he added as an afterthought. "In a place like this you have to teach people to leave a man alone. Always knocking at the door and dropping in and chattering. I don't mind seeing people when I am in the mood—but it has got to be my mood, not theirs. No good Trevelyan giving me his lord of the manor airs and dropping in whenever he felt like it. There's not a soul in the place comes near me now," he added with satisfaction.

"Oh!" said Emily.

"That's the best of having a native servant," said Captain Wyatt. "They understand orders. Abdul," he roared.

A tall Indian in a turban came out of the cottage and waited attentively.

"Come in and have something," said Captain Wyatt. "And see my little cottage."

"I'm sorry," said Emily, "but I have to hurry on."

"Oh, no, you haven't," said Captain Wyatt.

"Yes, I have," said Emily. "I've got an appointment."

"Nobody understands the art of living nowadays,"

said Captain Wyatt. "Catching trains, making appointments, fixing times for everything—all nonsense. Get up with the sun I say, have your meals when you feel like it, and never tie yourself to a time or a date. I could teach people how to live if they would listen to me."

The results of this exalted idea of living were not too hopeful, Emily reflected. Anything more like a battered wreck of a man than Captain Wyatt she had never seen. However, feeling that his curiosity had been sufficiently satisfied for the time being, she insisted on her appointment and went on her way.

Sittaford House had a solid oak front door, a neat bell pull, an immense wire mat, and a brilliantly polished brass letter box. It represented, as Emily could not fail to see, comfort and decorum. A neat and conventional parlormaid answered the bell.

Emily deduced the journalist evil had been before her as the parlormaid said at once in a distant tone, "Mrs. Willett is not seeing anyone this morning."

"I have brought a note from Miss Percehouse," said Emily, and handed the paper to the maid.

This clearly altered matters. The parlormaid's face expressed indecision, then she shifted her ground. "Will you come inside, please."

Emily was ushered into what house agents describe as "a well-appointed hall," and from there into a large drawing-room. A fire was burning brightly and there were traces of feminine occupation in the room.

Having taken in all there was to see, Emily was warming her hands in front of the fire when the door opened and a girl about her own age came in. She was a very pretty girl, Emily noticed, smartly and expensively dressed, and she also thought that she had never seen a girl in a greater state of nervous apprehension. Not that this was apparent on the surface, however. Miss Willett was making a gallant appearance of being at her ease. "Good morning," she said, adavncing and shaking hands. "I'm so sorry mother isn't down, but she's spending the morning in bed."

"Oh, I am so sorry. I'm afraid I have come at an unfortunate time."

"No, of course not. The cook is writing out the recipe for that cake now. We are only too delighted for Miss Percehouse to have it. Are you staying with her?"

Emily reflected with an inward smile that this was perhaps the only house in Sittaford whose members were not exactly aware of who she was and why she was there. Sittaford House had a definite regime of employers and employed. The employed might know about her —the employers clearly did not.

"I am not exactly staying with her," said Emily. "In fact, I'm at Mrs. Curtis's."

"Of course the cottage is terribly small and she has her nephew, Ronnie, with her, hasn't she? I suppose there wouldn't be room for you too. She's a wonderful person, isn't she? So much character, I always think, but I am rather afraid of her really."

"She's a bully, isn't she?" agreed Emily cheerfully. "But it's an awful temptation to be a bully, especially if people won't stand up to you."

Miss Willett sighed. "I wish I could stand up to people," she said. "We've had the most awful morning, absolutely pestered by reporters."

"Oh, of course," said Emily. "This is Captain Trevelyan's house really, isn't it?—the man who was murdered at Exhampton."

She was trying to determine the exact cause of Violet Willett's nervousness. The girl was clearly on the jump. Something was frightening her—and frightening her badly. She mentioned Captain Trevelyan's name bluntly on purpose. The girl didn't noticeably react to it in any way, but then she was probably expecting some such reference.

"Yes, wasn't it dreadful?"

"Do tell me—that's if you don't mind talking about it?"

"No—no—of course not—why should I?"

There's something very wrong with this girl, thought

Emily. *She hardly knows what she's saying. What has made her get the wind up this morning particularly?*

"About that table turning," went on Emily. "I heard about it in a casual sort of way and it seemed to me so frightfully interesting—I mean so absolutely gruesome." *Girlish thrills,* she thought to herself, *that's my line.*

"Oh, it was horrid," said Violet. "That evening—I shall never forget it! We thought, of course, that it was somebody just fooling—only it seemed a very nasty kind of joke."

"Yes?"

"I shall never forget when we turned the lights on—everybody looked so queer. Not Mr. Duke and Major Burnaby—they are the stolid kind, they would never like to admit that they were impressed by anything of that kind. But you could see that Major Burnaby was really awfully rattled by it. I think that actually he believed in it more than anybody else. But I thought poor little Mr. Rycroft was going to have a heart attack or something, yet he must be used to that kind of thing because he does a lot of psychic research, and as for Ronnie, Ronnie Garfield you know—he looked as though he had seen a ghost—actually seen one. Even mother was awfully upset—more than I have ever seen her before."

"It must have been most spooky," said Emily. "I wish I had been there to see."

"It was rather horrid really. We all pretended that it was—just fun, you know, but it didn't seem like that. And then Major Burnaby suddenly made up his mind to go over to Exhampton and we all tried to stop him, and said he would be buried in a snowdrift, but he would go. And there we sat, after he had gone, all feeling dreadful and worried. And then, last night—no, yesterday morning—we got the news."

"You think it was Captain Trevelyan's spirit?" said Emily in an awed voice. "Or do you think it was clairvoyance or telepathy?"

"Oh, I don't know. But I shall never, never laugh at these things again."

The parlormaid entered with a folded piece of paper on a salver which she handed to Violet. She withdrew and Violet unfolded the paper, glanced over it, and handed it to Emily.

"There you are," she said. "As a matter of fact you are just in time. This murder business has upset the servants. They think it's dangerous to live in this out-of-the-way part. Mother lost her temper with them yesterday evening and has sent them all packing. They are going after lunch. We are going to get two men instead—a house-parlorman and a kind of butler-chauffeur. I think it will answer much better."

"Servants are silly, aren't they?" said Emily.

"It isn't even as if Captain Trevelyan had been killed in this house."

"What made you think of coming to live here?" asked Emily, trying to make the question sound artless and girlishly natural.

"Oh, we thought it would be rather fun," said Violet.

"Don't you find it rather dull?"

"Oh, no, I love the country." But her eyes avoided Emily's. Just for a moment she looked suspicious and afraid.

She stirred uneasily in her chair and Emily rose rather reluctantly to her feet. "I must be going now," she said. "Thank you so much, Miss Willett. I do hope your mother will be all right."

"Oh, she's quite well really. It's only the servants—and all the worry."

"Of course."

Adroitly, unperceived by the other, Emily managed to discard her gloves on a small table. Violet Willett accompanied her to the front door and they took leave of each other with a few pleasant remarks.

The parlormaid who had opened the door to Emily had unlocked it, but as Violet Willett closed it behind her retreating guest Emily caught no sound of the key being turned. When she reached the gate, therefore, she retraced her steps slowly.

Her visit had more than confirmed the theories she held about Sittaford House. There was something queer going on here. She didn't think Violet Willett was directly implicated—that is, unless she was a very clever actress indeed. But there was something wrong, and that something *must* have a connection with the tragedy. There *must* be some link between the Willetts and Captain Trevelyan, and in that link there might lie the clue to the mystery.

She came up to the front door, turned the handle very gently, and passed across the threshold. The hall was deserted. Emily paused, uncertain what to do next. She had her excuse—the gloves left thoughtfully behind in the drawing-room. She stood stock still, listening. There was no sound anywhere except a very faint murmur of voices from upstairs. As quietly as possible, Emily crept to the foot of the stairs and stood looking up. Then, very gingerly, she ascended a step at a time. This was rather more risky. She could hardly pretend that her gloves had walked upstairs of their own accord, but she had a burning desire to overhear something of the conversation that was going on above. Modern builders never made their doors fit well, in Emily's opinion. You could hear a murmur of voices down here. Therefore, if you reached the door itself you would hear plainly the conversation that was going on inside the room. Another step—one more again. . . . Two women's voices—Violet and her mother without doubt.

Suddenly there was a break in the conversation—a sound of a footstep. Emily retreated rapidly.

When Violet Willett opened her mother's door and came down the stairs she was surprised to find her late guest standing in the hall peering about her in a lost dog kind of way.

"My gloves," Emily explained. "I must have left them. I came back for them."

"I expect they are in here," said Violet.

They went into the drawing-room and there, sure enough, on a little table near where Emily had been sitting lay the missing gloves.

"Oh, thank you," said Emily. "It's so stupid of me. I am always leaving things."

"And you want gloves in this weather," said Violet. "It's so cold." Once again they parted at the hall door, and this time Emily heard the key being turned in the lock.

She went down the drive with plenty to think about for, as that door on the upper landing had opened, she had heard distinctly one sentence spoken in an older woman's fretful and plaintive voice:

"My God," the voice had wailed, *"I can't bear it. Will tonight never come?"*

CHAPTER NINETEEN

THEORIES

EMILY ARRIVED BACK AT THE COTTAGE to find her boy friend absent. He had, Mrs. Curtis explained, gone off with several other young gentlemen, but two telegrams had come for the young lady. Emily took them, opened them, and put them in the pocket of her sweater, Mrs. Curtis eyeing them hungrily the while. "Not bad news, I hope?" said Mrs. Curtis.

"Oh, no," said Emily.

"Always gives me a turn a telegram does," said Mrs. Curtis.

"I know," said Emily. "Very disturbing."

At the moment she felt disinclined for anything but solitude. She wanted to sort out and arrange her own ideas. She went up to her own room, and taking pencil and notepaper she set to work on a system of her own. After twenty minutes of this exercise she was interrupted by Mr. Enderby.

"Hullo, hullo, hullo, there you are. Fleet Street has been hard on your tracks all morning but they have just missed you everywhere. Anyway they have had it from me that you are not to be worried. As far as you're concerned, I am the big noise."

He chuckled. "Envy and malice aren't in it!" he said. "I have been handing them out the goods. I know everyone and I am right in it. It's too good to be true. I keep pinching myself and feeling I will wake up in a minute. I say, have you noticed the fog?"

"It won't stop me going to Exeter this afternoon, will it?" said Emily.

"Do you want to go to Exeter?"

"Yes. I have to meet Mr. Dacres there. My solicitor, you know—the one who is undertaking Jim's defense.

He wants to see me. And I think I shall pay a visit to
Jim's Aunt Jennifer, while I am there. After all, Exeter
is only half an hour away."

"Meaning she might have nipped over by train and
batted her brother over the head and nobody would
have noticed her absence."

"Oh, I know it sounds rather improbable but one has
to go into everything. Not that I want it to be Aunt
Jennifer—I don't. I would much rather it was Martin
Dering. I hate the sort of man who presumes on going
to be a brother-in-law and does things in public that you
can't smack his face for."

"Is he that kind?"

"Very much that kind. He's an ideal person for a
murderer—always getting telegrams from bookmakers
and losing money on horses. It's annoying that he's got
such a good alibi. Mr. Dacres told me about it. A publisher and a literary dinner seems so very unbreakable
and respectacle."

"A literary dinner," said Enderby. "Friday night.
Martin Dering—let me see—Martin Dering—why, yes—
I am almost sure of it. Dash it all, I am quite sure of it,
but I can clinch things by wiring to Carruthers."

"What are you talking about?" said Emily.

"Listen. You know I came down to Exhampton on
Friday evening. Well, there was a bit of information I
was going to get from a pal of mine, another newspaper
man, Carruthers his name is. He was coming round to
see me about half-past six if he could—before he went
on to some literary dinner—he is rather a big bug, Carruthers, and if he couldn't make it he would send me a
line to Exhampton. Well, he didn't make it and he did
send me a line."

"What *has* all this got to do with it?" said Emily.

"Don't be so impatient, I am coming to the point. The
old chap was rather screwed when he wrote it—done
himself well at the dinner—after giving me the item I
wanted, he went on to waste a good bit of juicy description on me. You know—about the speeches, and what

asses so and so, a famous novelist and a famous play-
wright, were. And he said he had been rottenly placed
at the dinner. There was an empty seat on one side of
him where Ruby McAlmott, that awful best-seller
woman, ought to have sat and an empty place on the
other side of him where the sex specialist, Martin Dering, ought to have been, but he moved up near to a poet,
who is very well known in Blackheath, and tried to
make the best of things. Now, do you see the point?"

"Charles! Darling!" Emily became lyrical with excitement. "How marvelous. Then the brute wasn't at
the dinner at all?"

"Exactly."

"You are sure you've remembered the name right?"

"I'm positive. I have torn up the letter, worse luck,
but I can always wire to Carruthers to make sure. But I
absolutely know that I'm not mistaken."

"There's the publisher still, of course," said Emily.
"The one he spent the afternoon with. But I rather
think it was a publisher who was just going back to
America, and if so, that looks fishy. I mean it looks as
though he had selected someone who couldn't be asked
without rather a lot of trouble."

"Do you really think we have hit it?"

"Well, it looks like it. I think the best thing to be
done is—to go straight to that nice Inspector Narracott
and just tell him these new facts. I mean, we can't tackle
an American publisher who is on the sea or somewhere.
That's a job for the police."

"My word, if this comes off. What a scoop!" said Mr.
Enderby. "If it does, I should think the *Daily Wire*
couldn't offer me less than—"

Emily broke ruthlessly into his dreams of advance-
ment. "But we mustn't lose our heads," she said, "and
throw everything else to the wind. I must go to Exeter.
I don't suppose I shall be able to be back here until tomorrow. But I've got a job for you."

"What kind of a job?"

Emily described her visit to the Willetts and the

strange sentence she had overheard. "We have got absolutely and positively to find out what is going to happen tonight. There's something in the wind."

"What an extraordinary thing!"

"Wasn't it? But of course it may be a coincidence. Or it may not—but you observe that the servants are being cleared out of the way. Something queer is going to happen there tonight, and *you* have to be on the spot to see what it is."

"You mean I have to spend the whole night shivering under a bush in the garden?"

"Well, you don't mind that, do you? Journalists don't mind what they do in a good cause."

"Who told you that?"

"Never mind who told me, I know it. You will do it, won't you?"

"Oh, rather," said Charles. "I am not going to miss anything. If anything queer goes on at Sittaford House tonight, I shall be in it."

Emily then told him about the luggage label.

"It's odd," said Mr. Enderby. "Australia is where the third Pearson is, isn't it?—the youngest one. Not, of course, that that means anything, but still it—well, there might be a connection."

"H'm," said Emily. "I think that's all. Have you anything to report on your side?"

"Well," said Charles, "I've got an idea."

"Yes?"

"The only thing is I don't know how you'll like it."

"What do you mean—how I'll like it?"

"You won't fly out over it, will you?"

"I don't suppose so. I mean I hope I can listen sensibly and quietly to anything."

"Well, the point is," said Charles Enderby, eyeing her doubtfully, "don't think I mean to be offensive or anything like that, but do you think that lad of yours is to be depended on for the strict truth?"

"Do you mean," said Emily, "that he did murder Captain Trevelyan after all? You are quite welcome to that view if you like. I said to you at the beginning that that was the natural view to take, but I said we had to work on the assumption that he didn't."

"I don't mean that," said Enderby. "I am with you in assuming that he didn't do the old boy in. What I mean is, how far is his own story of what happened true? He says that he went there, had a chat with the old fellow, and came away leaving him alive and well."

"Yes."

"Well, it just occurred to me, you don't think it's possible that he went there and actually found the old man dead? I mean, he might have got the wind up and been scared and not liked to say so."

Charles had propounded this theory rather dubiously but he was relieved to find that Emily showed no signs of flying out at him over it. Instead, she frowned and creased her brow in thought. "I am not going to pretend," she said. "It *is* possible. I hadn't thought of it before. I know Jim wouldn't murder anyone, but he might quite well get rattled and tell a silly lie and then, of course, he would have to stick to it."

"The awkward thing is that you can't go and ask him about it now. I mean they wouldn't let you see him alone, would they?"

"I can put Mr. Dacres on to him," said Emily. "You see your solicitor alone, I believe. The worst of Jim is that he is frightfully obstinate; if he has once said a thing he sticks to it."

"That's my story and I'm going to stick to it," said Mr. Enderby comprehendingly.

"Yes. I am glad you mentioned that possibility to me, Charles; it hadn't occurred to me. We have been looking for someone who came in *after* Jim had left—but if it was *before*—"

She paused, lost in thought. Two very different theories stretched out in opposite directions. There was the one suggested by Mr. Rycroft, in which Jim's quarrel with his uncle was the determining point. The other theory, however, took no cognizance of Jim whatsoever.

The first thing to do, Emily felt, was to see the doctor who had first examined the body. If it were possible that Captain Trevelyan had been murdered at—say—four o'clock, it might make a considerable difference to the question of alibis. And the other thing to do was to make Mr. Dacres urge most strongly on his client the absolute necessity of speaking the truth.

She rose from the bed. "Well," she said, "you had better find out how I can get to Exhampton. The man at the smithy has a car of a kind, I believe. Will you go and settle with him about it? I'll start immediately after lunch. There's a train at three-ten to Exeter. That will give me time to see the doctor first. What's the time?"

"Half-past twelve," said Mr. Enderby, consulting his watch.

"Then we will both go up and fix up about that car," said Emily. "And there's just one other thing I want to do before leaving Sittaford."

"What's that?"

"I am going to pay a call on Mr. Duke. He's the only person in Sittaford I haven't seen. And he was one of the people at the table turning."

"Oh, we'll pass his cottage on the way to the smithy."

Mr. Duke's cottage was the last of the row. Emily and Charles unlatched the gate and walked up the path. And then something rather surprising occurred. For the door opened and a man came out. And that man was Inspector Narracott. He, too, looked surprised and, Emily fancied, embarrassed.

Emily abandoned her original intention. "I am so glad to have met you, Inspector," she said. "There are one or two things I want to talk to you about."

"Delighted, Miss Trefusis." He drew out a watch. "I'm afraid you will have to look sharp, I've a car waiting. I've got to go back to Exhampton almost immediately."

"How extraordinarily fortunate," said Emily; "you might give me a lift, will you, Inspector?"

The Inspector said rather woodenly that he would be

very pleased to do so.

"You might go and get my suitcase, Charles," said Emily. "It's packed up and ready."

Charles departed immediately.

"It's a great surprise meeting you here, Miss Trefusis," said Inspector Narracott.

"I said *au revoir*," Emily reminded him.

"I didn't notice it at the time."

"You've not seen the last of me by a long way," said Emily candidly. "You know, Inspector Narracott, you've made a mistake. Jim's not the man you're after."

"Indeed!"

"And what's more," said Emily, "I believe in your heart that you agree with me."

"What makes you think that, Miss Trefusis?"

"What were you doing in Mr. Duke's cottage?"

Narracott looked embarrassed and she was quick to follow it up. "You're doubtful, Inspector—that's what you are—doubtful. You thought you had got the right man and now you are not so sure, and so you are making a few investigations. Well, I have got something to tell you that may help. I'll tell it to you on the way to Exhampton."

Footsteps sounded down the road, and Ronnie Garfield appeared. He had the air of a truant, breathless and guilty. "I say, Miss Trefusis," he began. "What about a walk this afternoon? While my aunt has a nap."

"Impossible," said Emily. "I'm going away. To Exeter."

"What, not really! For good, you mean?"

"Oh, no," said Emily. "I shall be back again tomorrow."

"Oh, that's splendid."

Emily took something from the pocket of her sweater and handed it to him. "Give that to your aunt, will you? It's a recipe for coffee cake, and tell her that she was just in time; the cook is leaving today and so are the other servants. Be sure you tell her, she will be interested."

A far-off scream was borne on the breeze. "Ronnie," it said, "Ronnie, Ronnie."

"There's my aunt," said Ronnie, starting nervously. "I had better go."

"I think you had," said Emily. "You've got green paint on your left cheek," she called after him. Ronnie Garfield disappeared through his aunt's gate.

"Here's my boy friend with my suitcase," said Emily. "Come on, Inspector. I'll tell you everything in the car."

CHAPTER TWENTY

VISIT TO AUNT JENNIFER

AT HALF-PAST TWO Dr. Warren received a call from Emily. He took an immediate fancy to this businesslike and attractive girl. Her questions were blunt and to the point.

"Yes, Miss Trefusis, I see exactly what you mean. You'll understand that contrary to the popular belief in novels it is extremely difficult to fix the time of death accurately. I saw the body at eight o'clock. I can say decidedly that Captain Trevelyan had been dead at least two hours. How much longer than that would be difficult to say. If you were to tell me that he was killed at four o'clock, I should say that it was possible, though my own opinion inclines to a later time. On the other hand he could certainly not have been dead for much longer than that. Four and a half hours would be the outside limit."

"Thank you," said Emily, "that's all that I wanted to know."

She caught the three-ten train at the station and drove straight to the hotel where Mr. Dacres was staying. Their interview was businesslike and unemotional. Mr. Dacres had known Emily since she was a small child, and had managed her affairs for her since she came of age.

"You must prepare yourself for a shock, Emily," he said. "Things are much worse for Jim Pearson than we imagined."

"Worse?"

"Yes. It's no good beating about the bush. Certain facts have come to light which are bound to show him up in a most unfavorable light. It is those facts which led the police actually to charge him with the crime.

I should not be acting in your interests if I withheld these facts from you."

"Please tell me," said Emily.

Her voice was perfectly calm and composed. Whatever the inward shock she might have felt, she had no intention of making an outward display of her feelings. It was not feelings that were going to help Jim Pearson, it was brains. She must keep all her wits about her.

"There is no doubt that he was in urgent and immediate need of money. I am not going to enter into the ethics of the situation at the moment. Pearson had apparently before now occasionally borrowed money—to use a euphemism—from his firm—I may say without their knowledge. He was fond of speculating in shares, and on one occasion previously, knowing that certain dividends were to be paid into his account in a week's time, he anticipated them by using the firm's money to buy certain shares which he had pretty certain knowledge were bound to go up. The transaction was quite satisfactory, the money was replaced, and Pearson really doesn't seem to have had any doubts as to the honesty of the transaction. Apparently he repeated this just over a week ago. This time an unforeseen thing occurred. The books of the firm are examined at certain stated times, but for some reason or other this date was advanced and Pearson was faced with a very unpleasant dilemma. He was quite aware of the construction that would be put on his action and he was quite unable to raise the sum of money involved. He admits himself that he had tried in various quarters and failed when as a last resource he rushed down to Devonshire to lay the matter before his uncle and persuade him to help him. This Captain Trevelyan absolutely refused to do.

"Now, my dear Emily, we shall be quite unable to prevent these facts from being brought to light. The police have already unearthed the matter. And you see, don't you, that we have here a very pressing and urgent motive for the crime? The moment Captain Trevelyan was dead Pearson could easily have obtained the necessary sum as an advance from Mr. Kirkwood and saved himself from disaster and possibly criminal prosecution."

"Oh, the idiot," said Emily helplessly.

"Quite so," said Mr. Dacres dryly. "It seems to me that our only chance lies in proving that Jim Pearson was quite unaware of the provisions of his uncle's will."

There was a pause while Emily considered the matter. Then she said quietly, "I'm afraid that's impossible. All three of them knew—Sylvia, Jim, and Brian. They often discussed it and laughed and joked about the rich uncle in Devonshire."

"Dear, dear," said Mr. Dacres. "That's unfortunate."

"You don't think him guilty, Mr. Dacres?"

"Curiously enough, I do not," replied the lawyer. "In some ways Jim Pearson is a most transparent young man. He hasn't, if you will allow me to say so, Emily, a very high standard of commercial honesty, but I do not believe for one minute that his hand sandbagged his uncle."

"Well, that's a good thing," said Emily. "I wish the police thought the same."

"Quite so. Our own impressions and ideas are of no practical use. The case against him is unfortunately strong. I am not going to disguise from you, my dear child, that the outlook is bad. I should suggest Lorimer, K.C., as the defense. Forlorn-hope man they call him," he added cheerfully.

"There is one thing I should like to know," said Emily. "You have, of course, seen Jim?"

"Certainly."

"I want you to tell me honestly if you think he has told the truth in other respects." She outlined to him the idea that Enderby had suggested to her.

The lawyer considered the matter carefully before replying. "It's my impression," he said, "that he is speaking the truth when he describes his interview with his uncle. But there is little doubt that he has got the wind up badly, and if he went round to the window, entered that way, and came across his uncle's dead body—he might just possibly be too scared to admit the fact and have concocted this other story."

"That's what I thought," said Emily. "Next time you see him, Mr. Dacres, will you urge him to speak the truth? It may make the most tremendous difference,"

"I will do so. All the same," he said after a moment or two's pause, "I think you are mistaken in this idea. The news of Captain Trevelyan's death was bandied around in Exhampton about eight-thirty. At that time the last train had left for Exeter but Jim Pearson got the first train available in the morning—a thoroughly unwise proceeding, by the way, as it called attention to his movements which would not have been aroused if he had left by a train at a more conventional hour. Now if, as you suggest, he discovered his uncle's dead body some time after half-past four, I think he would have left Exhampton straight away. There's a train which leaves shortly after six and another at a quarter to eight."

"That's a point," admitted Emily.

"I have questioned him narrowly about his method of entering his uncle's house," went on Mr. Dacres. "He says that Captain Trevelyan made him remove his boots and leave them on the doorstep. That accounts for no wet marks being discovered in the hall."

"He doesn't speak of having heard any sound—anything at all—that gives him the idea that there might have been someone else in the house?"

"He didn't mention it to me. But I will ask him."

"Thank you," said Emily. "If I write a note can you take it to him?"

"Subject to its being read, of course."

"Oh, it will be a very discreet one."

She crossed to the writing-table and scribbled a few words:

DEAREST JIM: *Everything's going to be all right, so cheer up. I am working like fury to find out the truth. What an idiot you've been, darling. Love from* EMILY.

"There," she said.

Mr. Dacres read it but made no comment.

"I have taken pains with my handwriting," said Emily, "so that the prison authorities can read it easily. Now, I must be off."

"You will allow me to offer you a cup of tea."

"No, thank you, Mr. Dacres. I have no time to lose. I am going to see Jim's Aunt Jennifer."

At the Laurels, Emily was informed that Mrs. Gardner was out but would be home shortly.

Emily smiled upon the parlormaid. "I'll come in and wait then."

"Would you like to see Nurse Davis?"

Emily was always ready to see anybody. "Yes," she said promptly.

A few minutes later Nurse Davis, starched and curious, arrived.

"How do you do," said Emily. "I am Emily Trefusis— a kind of niece of Mrs. Gardner's. That is, I am going to be a niece but my fiancé, Jim Pearson, has been arrested as I expect you know."

"Oh, it's been too dreadful," said Nurse Davis. "We saw it all in the papers this morning. What a terrible business. You seem to be bearing up wonderfully, Miss Trefusis—really wonderfully."

There was a faint note of disapproval in the nurse's voice. Hospital nurses, she implied, were able to bear up owing to their force of character, but lesser mortals were expected to *give way*.

"Well, one mustn't sag at the knees," said Emily. "I hope you don't mind very much. I mean, it must be awkward for you to be associated with a family that has got a murder in it."

"It's very unpleasant, of course," said Nurse Davis, unbending at this proof of consideration. "But one's duty to one's patient comes before everything."

"How splendid," said Emily. "It must be wonderful for Aunt Jennifer to feel she has somebody upon whom she can rely."

"Oh, really," said the nurse, simpering, "you are too kind. But, of course, I have had curious experiences before this. Why, at the last case I attended—" Emily listened patiently to a long and scandalous anecdote comprising complicated divorce and paternity questions. After complimenting Nurse Davis on her tact, discretion, and *savoir faire,* Emily slid back to the topic of the Gardners.

"I don't know Aunt Jennifer's husband at all," she said. "I've never met him. He never goes away from home, does he?"

"No, poor fellow."

"What exactly is the matter with him?"

Nurse Davis embarked on the subject with professional gusto.

"So, really he might get well again any minute?" Emily murmured thoughtfully.

"He would be terribly weak," said the nurse.

"Oh, of course. But it makes it seem more hopeful, doesn't it?"

The nurse shook her head with firm professional despondency. "I don't suppose there will be any cure in his case."

Emily had copied down in her little notebook the timetable of what she called Aunt Jennifer's alibi. She now murmured tentatively, "How queer it seems to think that Aunt Jennifer was actually at the pictures when her brother was being killed."

"Very sad, isn't it?" said Nurse Davis. "Of course, she couldn't tell—but it gives one such a shock afterward."

Emily cast about in her mind to find out what she wanted to know without asking a direct question. "Didn't she have some queer kind of vision or premonition?" she inquired. "Wasn't it you who met her in the hall when she came in and exclaimed that she looked quite queer."

"Oh, no," said the nurse. "It wasn't me. I didn't see her until we were sitting down to dinner together, and she seemed quite her ordinary self then. How very interesting."

"I expect I am mixing it up with something else," said Emily.

"Perhaps it was some other relation," suggested Nurse Davis. "I came in rather late myself. I felt rather guilty about leaving my patient so long, but he himself had urged me to go." She suddenly looked at her watch. "Oh, dear. He asked me for another hot water bottle. I must see about it. Will you excuse me, Miss Trefusis?"

Emily excused her and going over to the fireplace she put her finger on the bell. The slipshod maid came with rather a frightened face.

"What's your name?" said Emily.

"Beatrice, Miss."

"Oh, Beatrice, I may not be able to wait to see my aunt after all. I wanted to ask her about some shopping she did on Friday. Do you know if she brought a big parcel back with her?"

"No, Miss, I didn't see her come in."

"I thought you said she came in at six o'clock."

"Yes, Miss, she did. I didn't see her come in, but when I went to take some hot water to her room at seven o'clock it gave me a shock to find her lying in the dark on the bed. 'Well, ma'am,' I said to her, 'you gave me quite a shock.' 'I came in quite a long time ago. At six o'clock,' she said. I didn't see a big parcel anywhere," said Beatrice trying her hardest to be helpful.

"That's all right, Beatrice, it doesn't matter."

Beatrice left the room. Emily took a small local time-table out of her handbag and consulted it.

"Leave Exeter, St. David's, three-ten," she murmured. "Arrive Exhampton, three forty-two. Time allowed for going to brother's house and murdering him—how beastly and cold-blooded it sounds—and such nonsense too—say half an hour to three quarters. What are the trains back? There's one at four twenty-five and there's one Mr. Dacres mentioned at six-ten, that gets in at twenty-three minutes to seven. Yes, it's actually possible either way. It's a pity there's nothing to suspect the nurse for. She was out all the afternoon and nobody knows where she was. But you can't have a murder without any motive at all. Of course, I don't really believe anybody in this house murdered Captain Trevelyan but in a way it's comforting to know that they could have. Hello—there's the front door."

There was a murmur of voices in the hall and the door opened and Jennifer Gardner came into the room. "I'm Emily Trefusis," said Emily. "You know—the one who is engaged to Jim Pearson."

"So you are Emily," said Mrs. Gardner, shaking hands. "Well, this is a surprise."

Suddenly Emily felt very weak and small. Rather like a little girl in the act of doing something very silly. An extraordinary person, Aunt Jennifer. Character—that was what it was. Aunt Jennifer had about enough character for two and three-quarter people instead of one. "Have you had tea, my dear? No? Then we'll have it here. Just a moment—I must go up and see Robert first."

A strange expression flitted over her face as she mentioned her husband's name. The hard, beautiful voice softened. It was like a light passing over dark ripples of water.

She does adore him, thought Emily, left alone in the drawing-room. *All the same, there's something frightening about Aunt Jennifer. I wonder if Uncle Robert likes being adored as much as that.*

When Jennifer Gardner returned, she had taken off her hat. "Do you want to talk about things, Emily, or don't you? If you don't, I shall quite understand."

"It isn't much good talking about them, is it?"

"We can only hope," said Mrs. Gardner, "that they will find the real murderer quickly. Just press the bell, will you, Emily? I'll send Nurse's tea up to her. I don't want her chattering down here. How I hate hospital nurses."

"Is she a good one?"

"I suppose she is. Robert says she is, anyway. I dislike her intensely and always have. But Robert says she's far and away the best nurse we've had."

"She's rather good-looking," said Emily.

"Nonsense. With her ugly, beefy hands?"

Emily watched her aunt's long white fingers as they touched the milk jug and the sugar tongs.

"Robert has been very upset over all this," said Mrs. Gardner. "He works himself into such curious states. I suppose it's all part of his illness really."

"He didn't know Captain Trevelyan well, did he?"

Jennifer Gardner shook her head. "He neither knew him nor cared about him. To be honest, I myself can't pretend any great sorrow over his death. He was a cruel, grasping man, Emily. He knew the struggle we have had. The poverty! He knew that a loan of money at the right time might have given Robert special treatment that would have made all the difference. Well, retribution has overtaken him." She spoke in a deep, brooding voice.

What a strange woman she is, thought Emily. *Beautiful and terrible, like something out of a Greek play.*

"It may still not be too late," said Mrs. Gardner. "I wrote to the lawyers at Exhampton today, to ask them if I could have a certain sum of money in advance. The treatment I am speaking of is in some respects what they would call a quack remedy, but it has been successful in a large number of cases. Emily—how wonderful it will be if Robert is able to walk again." Her face was glowing, lit up as though by a lamp.

Emily was tired. She had had a long day, little or nothing to eat, and she was worn out by suppressed emotion. The room kept going away and coming back.

"Aren't you feeling well, dear?"

"It's all right," gasped Emily, and to her own surprise, annoyance, and humiliation burst into tears.

Mrs. Gardner did not attempt to rise and console her, for which Emily was grateful. She just sat silently until Emily's tears should subside. She murmured in a thoughtful voice, "Poor child. It's very unlucky that Jim Pearson should have been arrested—very unlucky. I wish—something could be done about it."

CHAPTER TWENTY-ONE

CONVERSATIONS

LEFT TO HIS OWN DEVICES, Charles Enderby did not relax his efforts. To familiarize himself with life as lived in Sittaford village he had only to turn on Mrs. Curtis much as you would turn on the tap of a hydrant. Listening to a stream of anecdote, reminiscence, rumors, surmise, and meticulous detail, he endeavored valiantly to sift the grain from the chaff. He then mentioned another name and immediately the force of the water was directed in that direction. He heard all about Captain Wyatt, his tropical temper, his rudeness, his quarrels with his neighbors, his occasional amazing graciousness, usually to personable young women. The life he led his Indian servant, the peculiar times he had his meals and the exact diet that composed them. He heard about Mr. Rycroft's library, his hair tonics, his insistence on strict tidiness and punctuality, his inordinate curiosity over other people's doings, his recent selling of a few old prized personal possessions, his inexplicable fondness for birds, and the prevalent idea that Mrs. Willett was setting her cap at him. He heard about Miss Percehouse and her tongue and the way she bullied her nephew, and of the rumors of the gay life that same nephew led in London. He heard all over again of Major Burnaby's friendship with Captain Trevelyan, their reminiscences of the past, and their fondness for chess. He heard everything that was known about the Willetts, including the belief that Miss Violet Willett was leading Mr. Ronnie Garfield on and that she didn't really mean to have him. It was hinted that she made mysterious excursions to the moor and that she had been seen walking there with a young man. And it was doubtless for that reason, so Mrs. Curtis had surmised, that they had come to this desolate spot. Her mother had taken her right away, "to get right over it like." But there—"girls can be far more artful than ladies ever dream of." About Mr. Duke, there was curiously little to hear. He had been there only a short time and his activities seemed to be solely horticultural.

It was half-past three and with his head spinning from the effects of Mrs. Curtis's conversation, Mr. Enderby went out for a stroll. His intention was to cultivate the acquaintance of Miss Percehouse's nephew more closely. Prudent reconnaissance in the neighborhood of Miss Percehouse's cottage proved unavailing but by a stroke of good fortune he ran into that young man just as he was emerging disconsolately from the gates of Sittaford House. He had all the appearance of having been sent away with a flea in his ear.

"Hello," said Charles. "I say, isn't that Captain Trevelyan's house?"

"That's right," said Ronnie.

"I was hoping to get a snapshot of it this morning. For my paper, you know," he added. "But this weather is hopeless for photography."

Ronnie accepted this statement in all good faith without reflecting that if photography was only possible on days of brilliant sunshine, the pictures appearing in the daily papers would be few.

"It must be a very interesting job—yours," he said.

"A dog's life," said Charles, faithful to the convention of never showing enthusiasm about one's work. He looked over his shoulder at Sittaford House. "Rather a gloomy place, I should imagine."

"No end of a difference there since the Willetts moved in," said Ronnie. "I was down here last year about the same time and really you would hardly take it for the same place, and yet I don't know quite what they have done. Moved the furniture about a bit, I suppose, got cushions and things of that sort about. It's been a godsend to me their being here, I can tell you."

"Can't be a very jolly spot as a rule, I suppose," said Charles.

"Jolly? If I lived here a fortnight I should pass out altogether. How my aunt manages to cling on to life in the way she does beats me. You haven't seen her cats, have you? I had to comb one of them this morning and look at the way the brute scratched me." He held out a hand and an arm for inspection.

"Rather rough luck," said Charles.

"I should say it was. I say, are you doing any sleuthing? If so, can I help? Be the Watson to your Sherlock, or anything of that kind?"

"Any clues in Sittaford House?" inquired Charles casually. "I mean did Captain Trevelyan leave any of his things there?"

"I don't think so. My aunt was saying he moved lock, stock, and barrel. Took his elephant's trotters and his hippopotamus's toothy pegs and all the sporting rifles and whatnots."

"Almost as though he didn't mean to come back," said Charles.

"I say—that's an idea. You don't think it was suicide, do you?"

"A man who can hit himself correctly on the back of the head with a sandbag would be something of an artist in the suicide world," said Charles.

"Yes, I thought there wasn't much in that idea. Looks as if he had had a premonition though." Ronnie's face brightened. "Look here, what about this? Enemies on his track, he knows they're coming, so he clears out and passes the buck, as it were, to the Willetts."

"The Willetts were a bit of a miracle by themselves," said Charles.

"Yes, I can't make it out. Fancy planting yourself down here in the country like this. Violet doesn't seem to mind—actually says she likes it. I don't know what's the matter with her today, I suppose it's the domestic trouble. I can't think why women worry so about servants. If they cut up nasty, just push them out."

"That's just what they have done, isn't it?" said Charles.

"Yes, I know. But they are in a great stew about it all. Mother lying down with screaming hysterics or something and daughter snapping like a turtle. Fairly pushed me out just now."

"They haven't had the police there, have they?"

Ronnie stared. "The police, no, why would they?"

"Well, I wondered. Seeing Inspector Narracott in Sittaford this morning."

"Inspector Narracott?"

"Yes."

"Is he—is he the man in charge of the Trevelyan case?"

"That's right."

"What was he doing in Sittaford? Where did you see him?"

"Oh, I suppose he was just nosing about," said Charles, "checking up Captain Trevelyan's past life so to speak."

"You think that's all?"

"I suppose so."

"He doesn't think anyone in Sittaford had anything to do with it?"

"That would be very unlikely, wouldn't it?"

"Oh, frightfully. But then you know what the police are—always butting in on the wrong tack. At least that's what it says in detective novels."

"I think they are really rather an intelligent body of men," said Charles. "Of course, the press does a lot to help them," he added. "But if you really read a case carefully it's amazing the way they track down murderers with practically no evidence to go on."

"Oh—well—it's nice to know that, isn't it? They have certainly got on to this man Pearson pretty quick. It seems a pretty clear case."

"Crystal clear," said Charles. "A good thing it wasn't you or me, eh? Well, I must be sending off a few wires. They don't seem very used to telegrams in this place. If you send more than half a crown's worth at one go they seem to think you are an escaped lunatic."

Charles sent his telegrams. He then returned to the cottage, threw himself on his bed, and slept peacefully, blissfully unaware that he and his affairs, particularly Miss Emily Trefusis, were being discussed in various places all around him.

It is fairly safe to say that there were only three topics of conversation at present in Sittaford. One was the murder, one was the escape of the convict, and the other was Miss Emily Trefusis and her cousin. Indeed, at a certain moment, four separate conversations were going on with her as their main theme.

Conversation No. One was at Sittaford House, where Violet Willett and her mother had just washed up their own tea things owing to the domestic retreat.

"It was Mrs. Curtis who told me," said Violet. She still looked pale and wan.

"It's almost a disease the way that woman talks," said her mother.

"I know. It seems the girl is actually stopping there with a cousin or something. She did mention this morning that she was at Mrs. Curtis's, but I thought that that was simply because Miss Percehouse hadn't room for her. And now it seems that she'd never even seen Miss Percehouse till this morning!"

"I dislike that woman intensely," said Mrs. Willett.

"Mrs. Curtis?"

"No, no, the Percehouse woman. That kind of woman is dangerous. They live for what they can find out about other people. Sending that girl along here for a recipe for coffee cake! I'd like to have sent her a poisoned cake. That would have stopped her interfering for good and all!"

"I suppose I ought to have realized—" began Violet. But her mother interrupted her.

"How could you, my dear! And anyway what harm is done?"

"Why do you think she came here?"

"I don't suppose she had anything definite in mind. She was just spying out the land. Is Mrs. Curtis sure about her being engaged to Jim Pearson?"

"The girl told Mr. Rycroft so, I believe. Mrs. Curtis said she suspected it from the first."

"Well, then the whole thing's natural enough. She's just looking about aimlessly for something that might help."

"You didn't see her, mother," said Violet. "She isn't aimless."

"I wish I had seen her," said Mrs. Willett. "But my nerves were all to pieces this morning. Reaction, I suppose, after that interview with the police inspector yesterday."

"You were wonderful, mother. If only I hadn't been such an utter fool—to go and *faint*. Oh! I'm ashamed of myself for giving the whole show away. And there were you perfectly calm and collected—not turning a hair."

"I'm in pretty good training," said Mrs. Willett in a hard, dry voice. "If you'd been through what I've been through—but there, I hope you never will, my child. I trust and believe that you've got a happy, peaceful life ahead of you."

Violet shook her head. "I'm afraid—I'm afraid—"

"Nonsense—and as for saying you gave the show away by fainting yesterday—nothing of the kind. Don't worry."

"But that Inspector—he's bound to think—"

"That it was the mention of Jim Pearson made you faint? Yes—he'll think that all right. He's no fool, that Inspector Narracott. But what if he does? He'll suspect a connection—and he'll look for it—*and he won't find it.*"

"You think not?"

"Of course not! How can he? Trust me, Violet dear. That's cast-iron certainty and, in a way, perhaps that faint of yours was a lucky happening. We'll think so, anyway."

Conversation No. Two was in Major Burnaby's cottage. It was a somewhat one-sided one, the brunt of it being borne by Mrs. Curtis, who had been poised for departures for the last half-hour, having dropped in to collect Major Burnaby's laundry.

"Like my Great Aunt Sarah's Belinda, that's what I said to Curtis this morning," said Mrs. Curtis triumphantly. "A deep one—and one that can twist all the men round her little finger."

A great grunt from Major Burnaby.

"Engaged to one young man and carrying on with another," said Mrs. Curtis. "That's my Great Aunt Sarah's Belinda all over. And not for the fun of it, mark you. It's not just flightiness—she's a deep one. And now young Mr. Garfield—she'll have him roped in before you can say knife. Never have I seen a young gentleman look more like a sheep than he did this morning—and that's a sure sign." She paused for breath.

"Well, well," said Major Burnaby. "Don't let me keep you, Mrs. Curtis."

"Curtis will be wanting his tea and that's a fact," said Mrs. Curtis without moving. "I was never one to stand about gossiping. Get on with your job—that's what I say. And talking about jobs, what do you say, sir, to a good turn-out."

"No!" said Major Burnaby with force.

"It's a month since it's been done."

"No. I like to know where to lay my hand on everything. After one of these turn-outs nothing's ever put back in its place."

Mrs. Curtis sighed. She was an impassioned cleaner and turner out. "It's Captain Wyatt as could do with a spring cleaning," she observed. "That nasty native of his—what does he know about cleaning, I should like to know? Nasty black fellow."

"Nothing better than a native servant," said Major Burnaby. "They know their job and they don't talk."

Any hint the last sentence might have contained was lost upon Mrs. Curtis. Her mind had reverted to a former topic. "Two telegrams she got—two arriving in half an hour. Gave me quite a turn it did. But she read them as cool as anything. And then she told me she was going to Exeter and wouldn't be back till tomorrow."

"Did she take her young man with her?" inquired the Major with a gleam of hope.

"No, he's still here. A pleasant-spoken young gentleman. He and she'd make a nice pair."

Grunt from Major Burnaby.

"Well," said Mrs. Curtis. "I'll be getting along."

The Major hardly dared breathe for fear he might distract her from her purpose. But this time Mrs. Curtis was as good as her word. The door closed behind her.

With a sigh of relief the Major drew forth a pipe and began to peruse a prospectus of a certain mine which was couched in terms so blatantly optimistic that it would have aroused suspicion in any heart but that of a widow or a retired soldier. "Twelve percent," murmured Major Burnaby. "That sounds pretty good."

Next door Captain Wyatt was laying down the law to Mr. Rycroft. "Fellows like you," he said, "don't know anything of the world. You've never lived. You've never roughed it."

Mr. Rycroft said nothing. It was so difficult not to say the wrong thing to Captain Wyatt that it was usually safer not to reply at all.

The Captain leaned over the side of his chair. "Where has that bitch got to? Nice-looking girl," he added.

The association of ideas in his mind was quite natural. It was less so to Mr. Rycroft who looked at him in a scandalized fashion.

"What's she doing here? That's what I want to know?" demanded Captain Wyatt. "Abdul!"

"Sahib?"

"Where's Bully? Has she got out again?"

"She in kitchen, Sahib."

"Well, don't feed her." He sank back in his chair again and proceeded on his second tack. "What does she want here? Who's she going to talk to in a place like this? All you old fogies will bore her stiff. I had a word with her this morning. Expect she was surprised to find a man like me in a place like this."

He twisted his mustache.

"She's James Pearson's fiancée," said Mr. Rycroft. "You know—the man who has been arrested for Trevelyan's murder."

Wyatt dropped a glass of whisky he was just raising to his lips with a crash upon the floor. He immediately roared for Abdul and cursed him in no measured terms for not placing a table at a convenient angle to his chair. He then resumed the conversation.

"So that's who she is. Too good for a counter jumper like that. A girl like that wants a real man."

"Young Pearson is very good-looking," said Mr. Rycroft.

"Good-looking—good-looking—a girl doesn't want a barber's block. What does that sort of young man who works in an office every day know of life? What experience has he had of reality?"

"Perhaps the experience of being tried for murder will be sufficient reality to last him for some time," said Mr. Rycroft dryly.

"Police sure he did it, eh?"

"They must be fairly sure or they wouldn't have arrested him."

"Country bumpkins," said Captain Wyatt contemptuously.

"Not quite," said Mr. Rycroft. "Inspector Narracott struck me this morning as an able and efficient man."

"Where did you see him this morning?"

"He called at my house."

"He didn't call at mine," said Captain Wyatt in an injured fashion.

"Well, you weren't a close friend of Trevelyan's or anything like that."

"I don't know what you mean. Trevelyan was a skin-flint and I told him so to his face. He couldn't come bossing it over me. I didn't kowtow to him like the rest of the people here. Always dropping in—dropping in—

too much dropping in. If I don't choose to see anyone for a week, or a month, or a year, that's my business."

"You haven't seen anyone for a week now, have you?" said Mr. Rycroft.

"No, and why should I?" The irate invalid banged the table. Mr. Rycroft was aware, as usual, of having said the wrong thing. "Why the bloody hell should I? Tell me that?"

Mr. Rycroft was prudently silent. The Captain's wrath subsided. "All the same," he growled, "if the police want to know about Trevelyan, I'm the man they should have come to. I've knocked about the world, and I've got judgment. I can size a man up for what he's worth. What's the good of going to a lot of dodderers and old women. What they want is a *man's* judgment." He banged the table again.

"Well," said Mr. Rycroft, "I suppose they think they know themselves what they are after."

"They inquired about me?" said Captain Wyatt. "They would naturally."

"Well—er—I don't quite remember," said Mr. Rycroft cautiously.

"Why can't you remember? You're not in your dotage yet."

"I expect I was—er—rattled," said Mr. Rycroft soothingly.

"Rattled, were you? Afraid of the police? I'm not afraid of the police. Let 'em come here. That's what I say. I'll show them. Do you know I shot a cat at a hundred yards the other night?"

"Did you?" said Mr. Rycroft.

The Captain's habit of letting off a revolver at real or imaginary cats was a sore trial to his neighbors.

"Well, I'm tired," said Captain Wyatt suddenly. "Have another drink before you go?"

Rightly interpreting this hint, Mr. Rycroft rose to his feet. Captain Wyatt continued to urge a drink upon him. "You'd be twice the man if you drank a bit more. A man who can't enjoy a drink isn't a man at all."

But Mr. Rycroft continued to decline the offer. He had already consumed one whisky and soda of most unusual strength.

"What tea do you drink?" asked Wyatt. "I don't know anything about tea. Told Abdul to get some. Thought that girl might like to come in to tea one day. Darned pretty girl. Must do something for her. She must be bored to death in a place like this with no one to talk to."

"There's a young man with her," said Mr. Rycroft.

"The young men of the present day make me sick," said Captain Wyatt. "What's the good of them?"

This being a difficult query to answer suitably, Mr. Rycroft did not attempt it; he took his departure. The bull terrier bitch accompanied him to the gate and caused him acute alarm.

In No. 4 The Cottages, Miss Percehouse was speaking to her nephew, Ronald. "If you like to moon about after a girl who doesn't want you, that is your affair, Ronald," she was saying. "Better stick to the Willett girl. You may have a chance there, though I think it is extremely unlikely."

"Oh, I say," protested Ronnie.

"The other thing I have to say is, that if there was a police officer in Sittaford I should have been informed of it. Who knows, I might have been able to give him valuable information."

"I didn't know about it till after he had gone."

"That is so like you, Ronnie. Absolutely typical."

"Sorry, Aunt Caroline."

"And when you are painting the garden furniture, there is no need to paint your face as well. It doesn't improve it and it wastes the paint."

"Sorry, Aunt Caroline."

"And now," said Miss Percehouse, closing her eyes, "don't argue with me any more. I'm tired."

Ronnie shuffled his feet and looked uncomfortable.

"Well?" said Miss Percehouse sharply.

"Oh! nothing—only—"

"Yes?"

"Well, I was wondering if you'd mind if I blew in to Exeter tomorrow?"

"Why?"

"Well, I want to meet a fellow there."

"What kind of a fellow?"

"Oh! just a fellow."

"If a young man wishes to tell lies, he should do so well," said Miss Percehouse.

"Oh! I say—but—"

"Don't apologize."

"It's all right then? I can go?"

"I don't know what you mean by saying, 'I can go?' as though you were a small child. You are over twenty-one."

"Yes, but what I mean is, I don't want—"

Miss Percehouse closed her eyes again. "I have asked you once before not to argue. I am tired and wish to rest. If the 'fellow' you are meeting in Exeter wears skirts and is called Emily Trefusis, more fool you—that is all I have to say."

"But look here—"

"I am tired, Ronald. That's enough."

CHAPTER TWENTY-TWO

NOCTURNAL ADVENTURES

CHARLES WAS NOT LOOKING FORWARD with any relish to the prospect of his night's vigil. He privately considered that it was likely to be a wild goose chase. Emily, he considered, was possessed of a too vivid imagination. He was convinced that she had read into the few words she had overheard a meaning that had its origin in her own brain. Probably sheer weariness had induced Mrs. Willett to yearn for night to come.

Charles looked out of his window and shivered. It was a piercingly cold night, raw and foggy—the last night one would wish to spend in the open hanging about and waiting for something, very nebulous in nature, to happen.

Still he dared not yield to his intense desire to remain comfortably indoors. He recalled the liquid melodiousness of Emily's voice as she said, "It's wonderful to have someone you can really rely on."

She relied on him, Charles, and she should not rely in vain. What? Fail that beautiful, helpless girl? Never. Besides, he reflected as he donned all the spare underclothes he possessed before encasing himself in two pullovers and his overcoat, things were like to be deucedly unpleasant if Emily on her return found out that he had not carried out his promise.

She would probably say the most unpleasant things. No, he couldn't risk it. But as for anything happening— And anyway, when and how was it going to happen? He couldn't be everywhere at once. Probably whatever was going to happen would happen inside Sittaford House and he would never know a thing about it.

"Just like a girl," he grumbled, "waltzing off to Exeter and leaving me to do the dirty work."

And then he remembered once more the liquid tones of Emily's voice as she expressed her reliance on him, and he felt ashamed of his outburst.

He completed his toilet, rather after the model of Tweedledee, and effected a surreptitious exit from the cottage. The night was even colder and more unpleasant than he had thought. Did Emily realize all he was about to suffer on her behalf? He hoped so.

His hand went tenderly to a pocket and caressed a hidden flask concealed in a near pocket.

"The boy's best friend," he murmured. "It *would* be a night like this of course."

With suitable precautions he introduced himself into the grounds of Sittaford House. The Willetts kept no dog, so there was no fear of alarm from that quarter. A light in the gardener's cottage showed that it was inhabited. Sittaford House itself was in darkness save for one lighted window upstairs. *Those two women are alone in the house,* thought Charles. *I shouldn't care for that myself. A bit creepy!*

He supposed Emily had really overheard that sentence, *Will tonight never come?* What did it really mean? *I wonder,* he thought to himself, *if they mean to do a flit? Well, whatever happens, little Charles is going to be here to see it.*

He circled the house at a discreet distance. Owing to the foggy nature of the night he had no fears of being observed. Everything as far as he could see appeared to be as usual. A cautious visiting of the outbuildings showed them to be locked.

I hope something does happen, thought Charles as the hours passed. He took a prudent sip from his flask. *I've never known anything like this cold.*

He glanced at his watch and was surprised to find that it was still only twenty minutes to twelve. He had been convinced that it must be nearly dawn.

An unexpected sound made him prick up his ears excitedly. It was the sound of a bolt being very gently drawn back in its socket, and it came from the direction of the house. Charles made a noiseless sprint from bush to bush. Yes, he had been quite right, the small side door was slowly opening. A dark figure stood on the threshold. It was peering anxiously out into the night. *Mrs. or Miss Willett,* said Charles to himself. *The fair Violet, I think.*

After waiting a minute or two, the figure stepped out on the path and closed the door noiselessly behind her and started to walk away from the house in the opposite direction to the front drive. The path in question led up behind Sittaford House, passing through a small plantation of trees and so out on to the open moor.

The path wound quite near the bushes where Charles was concealed, so near that Charles was able to recognize the woman as she passed. He had been quite right; it was Violet Willett. She was wearing a long dark coat and had a beret on her head.

She went on up and as quietly as possible Charles followed her. He had no fears of being seen, but he was alive to the danger of being overheard. He was particularly anxious not to alarm the girl. Owing to his care in this respect, she outdistanced him. For a moment or two he was afraid lest he should lose her, but as he in his turn wound his way anxiously through the plantation of trees he saw her standing a little way ahead of him. Here the low wall which surrounded the estate was broken by a gate. Violet Willett was standing by this gate, leaning over it peering out into the night.

Charles crept up as near as he dared and waited. The time passed. The girl had a small pocket torch with her and once she switched it on for a moment or two, directing it, Charles thought, to see the time by the wrist watch she was wearing, then she leaned over the gate again in the same attitude of expectant interest. Suddenly Charles heard a low whistle twice repeated.

He saw the girl start to sudden attention. She leaned farther over the gate and from her lips came the same signal—a low whistle twice repeated.

Then with startling suddenness a man's figure loomed

out of the night. A low exclamation came from the girl. She moved back a pace or two, the gate swung inward, and the man joined her. She spoke to him in a low, hurried voice. Unable to catch what they said, Charles moved forward somewhat imprudently. A twig snapped beneath his feet. The man swung round instantly.

"What's that?" he said.

He caught sight of Charles's retreating figure.

"Hie, you stop! What are you doing here?"

With a bound he sprang after Charles. Charles turned and tackled him adroitly. The next moment they were rolling over and over together locked in a tight embrace.

The tussle was a short one. Charles's assailant was by far the heavier and stronger of the two. He rose to his feet, jerking his captive with him.

"Switch on that light, Violet," he said, "let's have a look at this fellow."

The girl, who had been standing terrified a few paces away, came forward and switched on the torch obediently. "It must be the man who is staying in the village," she said. "A journalist."

"A journalist, eh?" exclaimed the other. "I don't like the breed. What are you doing, you skunk, nosing round private grounds at this time of night?"

The torch wavered in Violet's hand. For the first time Charles was given a full view of his antagonist. For a few minutes he had entertained the wild idea that the visitor might have been the escaped convict. One look at the other dispelled any such fancy. This was a young man not more than twenty-four or -five years of age. Tall, good-looking, and determined, with none of the hunted criminal about him.

"Now then," he said sharply, "what's your name?"

"My name is Charles Enderby," said Charles. "You haven't told me yours," he continued.

"Confound your cheek!"

A sudden flash of inspiration came to Charles. An inspired guess had saved him more than once. It was a long shot but he believed that he was right. "I think, however," he said quietly, "that I can guess it."

"Eh?" The other was clearly taken aback.

"I think," said Charles, "that I have the pleasure of addressing Mr. Brian Pearson from Australia. Is that so?"

There was a silence—rather a long silence. Charles had a feeling that the tables were turned.

"How the devil you knew that I can't think," said the other at last, "but you're right. My name *is* Brian Pearson."

"In that case," said Charles, "supposing we adjourn to the house and talk things over!"

CHAPTER TWENTY-THREE

AT HAZELMOOR

MAJOR BUBNABY WAS DOING HIS ACCOUNTS or, to use a more Dickens-like phrase, he was looking into his affairs. The Major was an extremely methodical man. In a calf-bound book he kept a record of shares bought, shares sold, and the accompanying loss or profit—usually a loss, for in common with most retired army men the Major was attracted by a high rate of interest rather than a modest percentage coupled with safety.

"These oil wells looked all right," he was muttering. "Seems as though there ought to have been a fortune in it. Almost as bad as that diamond mine! Canadian land, that ought to be sound now."

His cogitations were interrupted as the head of Mr. Ronald Garfield appeared at the open window. "Hello," said Ronnie cheerfully, "I hope I'm not butting in?"

"If you are coming in go round to the front door," said Major Burnaby. "Mind the rock plants. I believe you are standing on them at the moment."

Ronnie retreated with an apology and presently presented himself at the front door.

"Wipe your feet on the mat, if you don't mind," cried the Major. He found young men extremely trying. Indeed, the only young man toward whom he had felt any kindliness for a long time was the journalist, Charles Enderby. Toward Ronnie Garfield the Major felt no such kindliness. Practically everything that the unfortunate Ronnie said or did managed to rub the Major up the wrong way. Still, hospitality is hospitality. "Have a drink?" said the Major, loyal to that tradition.

"No, thanks. As a matter of fact I just dropped in to see if we couldn't get together. I wanted to go to Exhampton today and I hear Elmer is booked to take you in."

Burnaby nodded. "Got to go over Trevelyan's things," he explained. "The police have done with the place now."

"Well, you see," said Ronnie rather awkwardly, "I particularly wanted to go into Exhampton today. I thought if we could get together and share and share alike as it were. Eh? What about it?"

"Certainly," said the Major. "I am agreeable. Do you a lot more good to walk. Exercise. None of you young chaps nowadays take any exercise. A brisk six miles there and a brisk six miles back would do you all the good in the world. If it weren't that I needed the car to bring some of Trevelyan's things back here, I should be walking myself. Getting soft—that's the curse of the present day."

"Oh, well," said Ronnie, "I don't believe in being strenuous myself. But I'm glad we've settled that all right. Elmer said you were starting at eleven o'clock. Is that right?"

"That's it."

"Good. I'll be there."

Ronnie was not quite so good as his word. His idea of being on the spot was to be ten minutes late and he found Major Burnaby fuming and fretting and not at all inclined to be placated by a careless apology. His mind played agreeably for a few minutes with the idea of a marriage between Major Burnaby and his aunt. Which, he wondered, would get the better of it? He thought his aunt every time. Rather amusing to think of her clapping her hands and uttering piercing cries to summon the Major to her side.

Banishing these reflections from his mind he proceeded to enter into cheerful conversation. "Sittaford has become a pretty gay spot—what? Miss Trefusis and this chap Enderby and the lad from Australia—by the way, when did he blow in? There he was as large as life this morning and nobody knew where he had come from. It's been worrying my aunt blue in the face."

"He is staying with the Willetts," said Major Burnaby tartly.

"Yes, but where did he blow in from? Even the Willetts haven't got a private airfield. You know, I think there's something deuced mysterious about this lad Pearson. He's got what I call a nasty gleam in his eye—a very nasty glint. It's my impression that he's the chap who did in poor old Trevelyan."

The Major made no reply.

"The way I look at it is this," continued Ronnie, "fellows that go off to the Colonies are usually bad hats. Their relations don't like them and push them out there for that reason. Very well then—there you are. The bad hat comes back, short of money, visits wealthy uncle in the neighborhood of Christmas time, wealthy relative won't cough up to impecunious nephew—and impecunious nephew bats him one. That's what I call a theory."

"You should mention it to the police," said Major Burnaby.

"I thought you might do that," said Mr. Garfield. "You're Narracott's little pal, aren't you? By the way, he hasn't been nosing about Sittaford again, has he?"

"Not that I know about."

"Not meeting you at the house today, is he?"

"No."

The shortness of the Major's answers seemed to strike Ronnie at last. "Well," he said vaguely, "that's that," and relapsed into a thoughtful silence.

At Exhampton the car drew up outside the Three Crowns. Ronnie alighted and after arranging with the Major that they would rendezvous there at half-past four for the return journey, he strode off in the direction of such shops as Exhampton offered.

The Major went first to see Mr. Kirkwood. After a brief conversation with him, he took the keys and started off for Hazelmoor. He had told Evans to meet him there at twelve o'clock and he found the faithful retainer waiting on the doorstep. With a rather grim face, Major

Burnaby inserted the key into the front door and passed into the empty house, Evans at his heels. He had not been in it since the night of the tragedy, and in spite of his iron determination to show no weakness, he gave a slight shiver as he passed the drawing-room.

Evans and the Major worked together in sympathy and silence. When either of them made a brief remark it was duly appreciated and understood by the other. "Unpleasant job this, but it has to be done," said Major Burnaby and Evans, sorting out socks into neat piles, and counting pajamas, responded.

"It seems rather unnatural like, but as you say, sir, it's got to be done."

Evans was deft and efficient at his work. Everything was neatly sorted and arranged and classified in heaps. At one o'clock they repaired to the Three Crowns for a short midday meal. When they returned to the house the Major suddenly caught Evans by the arm as the latter closed the front door behind him. "Hush," he said. "Do you hear that footstep overhead? It's—it's in Joe's bedroom."

"My Gawd, sir. So it is."

A kind of superstitious terror held them both for a minute and then breaking loose from it, and with an angry squaring of the shoulders, the Major strode to the foot of the stairs and shouted in a stentorian voice, "Who's that? Come out of there, I say."

To his intense surprise and annoyance and yet, be it confessed, to his slight relief, Ronnie Garfield appeared at the top of the stairs. He looked embarrassed and sheepish. "Hello," he said. "I have been looking for you."

"What do you mean, looking for me?"

"Well, I wanted to tell you that I shan't be ready at half-past four. I've got to go to Exeter. So don't wait for me. I'll have to get a car up from Exhampton."

"How did you get into this house?" asked the Major.

"The door was open," exclaimed Ronnie. "Naturally I thought you were here."

The Major turned to Evans sharply. "Didn't you lock it when you came out?"

"No, sir, I hadn't got the key."

"Stupid of me," muttered the Major.

"You don't mind, do you?" said Ronnie. "I couldn't see anyone downstairs so I went upstairs and had a look round."

"Of course, it doesn't matter," snapped the Major. "You startled me, that's all."

"Well," said Ronnie airily, "I shall be pushing along now. So long."

The Major grunted. Ronnie came down the stairs.

"I say," he said boyishly, "do you mind telling me er—er—where it happened?"

The Major jerked a thumb in the direction of the drawing-room.

"Oh, may I look inside?"

"If you like," growled the Major.

Ronnie opened the drawing-room door. He was absent a few minutes and then returned. The Major had gone up the stairs but Evans was in the hall. He had the air of a bulldog on guard; his small deep-set eyes watched Ronnie with a somewhat malicious scrutiny.

"I say," said Ronnie. "I thought you could never wash out bloodstains. I thought, however much you washed them, they always came back. Oh, of course—the old fellow was sandbagged, wasn't he? Stupid of me. It was one of these, wasn't it?" He took up a long narrow bolster that lay against one of the other doors. He weighed it thoughtfully and balanced it in his hand. "Nice little toy, eh?" He made a few tentative swings with it in the air.

Evans was silent.

"Well," said Ronnie, realizing that the silence was not a wholly appreciative one, "I'd better be getting along. I'm afraid I've been a bit tactless, eh?" He jerked his head toward the upper story. "I forgot about them being such pals and all that. Two of a kind, weren't they? Well, I'm really going now. Sorry if I've said all the wrong things."

He walked across the hall and out through the front door. Evans stayed impassively in the hall, and only when he had heard the latch of the gate close behind Mr. Garfield did he mount the stairs and rejoin Major Burnaby. Without any word or comment he resumed where he had left off, going straight across the room and kneeling down in front of the boot cupboard.

At half-past three their task was finished. One trunk of clothes and underclothes was allotted to Evans, and another was strapped up ready to be sent to the Seamen's Orphanage. Papers and bills were packed into an attaché case and Evans was given instructions to see a local firm of removers about the storage of the various sporting trophies and heads, as there was no room for them in Major Burnaby's cottage. Since Hazelmoor was rented furnished, no other questions arose.

When all this was settled Evans cleared his throat nervously once or twice and then said, "Beg pardon, sir, but—I'll be wanting a job to look after a gentleman, same as I did to look after the Capting."

"Yes, yes, you can tell anyone to apply to me for a recommendation. That will be quite all right."

"Begging your pardon, sir, that wasn't quite what I meant. Rebecca and me, sir, we've talked it over and we was wondering if, sir—if maybe you would give us a trial?"

"Oh! but—well—I look after myself as you know. That old what's-her-name comes in and cleans for me once a day and cooks a few things. That's—er—about all I can afford."

"It isn't the money that matters so much, sir," said Evans quickly. "You see, sir, I was very fond of the Capting and—well, if I could do for you, sir, the same as I did for him, well, it would be almost like the same thing, if you know what I mean."

The Major cleared his throat and averted his eyes. "Very decent of you, 'pon my word. I'll—I'll think about it." And escaping with alacrity, he almost bolted down the road. Evans stood looking after him, an understanding smile upon his face.

"Like as two peas, him and the Capting," he murmured.

And then a puzzled expression came over his face. "Where can they have got to?" he murmured. "It's a bit queer that. I must ask Rebecca what she thinks."

CHAPTER TWENTY-FOUR

NARRACOTT DISCUSSES THE CASE

"I AM NOT ENTIRELY HAPPY ABOUT IT, SIR," said Inspector Narracott.

The Chief Constable looked at him inquiringly.

"No," said Inspector Narracott. "I'm not nearly as happy about it as I was."

"You don't think we've got the right man?"

"I'm not satisfied. You see, to start with, everything pointed the one way, but now—it's different."

"The evidence against Pearson remains the same."

"Yes, but there's a good deal of further evidence come to light, sir. There's the other Pearson—Brian. Feeling that we had no farther to look, I accepted the statement that he was in Australia. Now, it turns out that he was in England all the time. It seems he arrived back in England two months ago—traveled on the same boat as these Willetts apparently. Looks as though he had got sweet on the girl on the voyage. Anyway, for whatever reason, he didn't communicate with any of his family. Neither his sister nor his brother had any idea he was in England. On Thursday of last week he left the Ormsby Hotel in Russell Square and drove to Paddington. From there until Tuesday night, when Enderby ran across him, he refuses to account for his movements in any way."

"You pointed out to him the gravity of such a course of action?"

"Said he didn't give a damn. He had had nothing to do with the murder and it was up to us to prove he had. The way he had employed his time was his own business and none of ours, and he declined definitely to state where he had been and what he had been doing."

"Most extraordinary," said the Chief Constable.

"Yes, sir. It's an extraordinary case. You see, there's no use getting away from the facts; this man's far more the type than the other. There's something incongruous about James Pearson hitting an old man on the head with a sandbag—but in a manner of speaking it might be all in the day's work to Brian Pearson. He's a hot-tempered, high-handed young man—and he profits to exactly the same extent, remember. Yes—he came over with Mr. Enderby this morning, very bright and breezy, quite square and above-board, that was his attitude. But it won't wash, sir, it won't wash."

"H'm—you mean—"

"It isn't borne out by the facts. Why didn't he come forward before? His uncle's death was in all the papers Saturday. His brother was arrested Monday. And he doesn't give a sign of life. And he wouldn't have, either, if that journalist hadn't run across him in the garden of Sittaford House at midnight last night."

"What was he doing there? Enderby, I mean?"

"You know what journalists are," said Narracott, "always nosing round. They're uncanny."

"They are a darned nuisance very often," said the Chief Constable. "Though they have their uses too."

"I fancy it was the young lady put him up to it," said Narracott.

"The young lady?"

"Miss Emily Trefusis."

"How did she know anything about it?"

"She was up at Sittaford nosing around. And she's what you'd call a sharp young lady. There's not much gets past her."

"What was Brian Pearson's own account of his movements?"

"Said he came to Sittaford House to see his young lady, Miss Willett, that is. She came out of the house to meet him when everyone was asleep because she didn't want her mother to know about it. That's their story." Inspector Narracott's voice expressed distinct disbelief. "It's my belief, sir, that if Enderby hadn't run him to earth, he never would have come forward. He'd have gone back to Australia and claimed his inheritance from there."

A faint smile crossed the Chief Constable's lips. "How he must have cursed these pestilential prying journalists," he murmured.

"There's something else come to light," continued the Inspector. "There are three Pearsons, you remember, and Sylvia Pearson is married to Martin Dering, the novelist. He told me that he lunched and spent the afternoon with an American publisher and went to a literary dinner in the evening, but it now seems that he wasn't at that dinner at all."

"Who says so?"

"Enderby again."

"I think I must meet Enderby," said the Chief Constable. "He appears to be one of the live wires of this investigation. No doubt about it the *Daily Wire* does have some bright young men on their staff."

"Well, of course, that may mean little or nothing," continued the Inspector. "Captain Trevelyan was killed before six o'clock, so where Dering spent his evening is really of no consequence—but why should he have deliberately lied about it? I don't like it, sir."

"No," agreed the Chief Constable. "It seems a little unnecessary."

"It makes one think that the whole thing may be false. It's a far-fetched supposition, I suppose, but Dering *might* have left Paddington by the twelve-ten train, arrived at Exhampton some time after five, have killed the old man, got the six-ten train, and been back home again before midnight. At any rate it's got to be looked into, sir. We've got to investigate his financial position, see if he was desperately hard up. Any money his wife came into he would have the handling of—you've only got to look at her to know that. We've got to make perfectly sure that the afternoon alibi holds water."

"The whole thing is extraordinary," commented the Chief Constable. "But I still think the evidence against

Pearson is pretty conclusive. I see that you don't agree with me—you've a feeling you've got hold of the wrong man."

"The evidence is all right," admitted Inspector Narracott, "circumstantial and all that, and any jury ought to convict on it. Still, what you say is true enough—I don't see him as a murderer."

"And his young lady is very active in the case," said the Chief Constable.

"Miss Trefusis, yes, she's a one and no mistake. A real fine young lady. And absolutely determined to get him off. She's got hold of that journalist, Enderby, and she's working him for all she's worth. She's a great deal too good for Mr. James Pearson. Beyond his good looks I wouldn't say there was much to him in the way of character."

"But if she's a managing young woman that's what she likes," said the Chief Constable.

"Ah, well," said Inspector Narracott, "there's no accounting for tastes. Well, you agree, sir, that I had better take up this alibi of Dering's without any more delay?"

"Yes, get on to it at once. What about the fourth interested party in the will? There's a fourth, isn't there?"

"Yes, the sister. That's perfectly all right. I have made inquiries there. She was at home at six o'clock all right, sir. I'll get right on with the Dering business."

It was about five hours later that Inspector Narracott found himself once more in the small sitting-room of The Nook. This time Mr. Dering was at home. He couldn't be disturbed, as he was writing, the maid had said at first, but the Inspector had produced an official card and bade her take it to her master without delay. While waiting, he strode up and down the room. His mind was working actively. Every now and then he picked up a small object from a table, looked at it almost unseeingly, and then replaced it. The cigarette box of Australian fiddleback—a present from Brian Pearson possibly. He picked up a rather battered old book, *Pride and Prejudice*. He opened the cover and saw scrawled on the flyleaf in rather faded ink the name, *Martha Rycroft.* Somehow the name of Rycroft seemed familiar, but he could not for the moment remember why. He was interrupted as the door opened and Martin Dering came into the room.

The novelist was a man of middle height with thick, rather heavy chestnut hair. He was good-looking in a somewhat heavy fashion, with lips that were rather full and red.

Inspector Narracott was not prepossessed by his appearance. "Good morning, Mr. Dering. Sorry to trouble you all here again."

"Oh, it doesn't matter, Inspector, but really I can't tell you any more than you've been told already."

"We were led to understand that your brother-in-law, Mr. Brian Pearson, was in Australia. Now we find that he has been in England for the last two months. I might have been given an inkling of that, I think. Your wife distinctly told me that he was in New South Wales."

"Brian in England!" Dering seemed genuinely astonished. "I can assure you, Inspector, that I had no knowledge of the fact—nor, I'm sure, had my wife."

"He has not communicated with you in any way?"

"No, indeed. I know for a fact that Sylvia has twice written him letters to Australia during that time."

"Oh, well, in that case I apologize, sir. But naturally I thought he would have communicated with his relations and I was a bit sore with you for holding out on me."

"Well, as I tell you, we knew nothing. Have a cigarette, Inspector? By the way, I see you've recaptured your escaped convict."

"Yes, got him late Tuesday night. Rather bad luck for him, the mist coming down. He walked right round in a circle. Did about twenty miles to find himself about half a mile from Princetown at the end of it."

"Extraordinary how everyone goes round in circles in a fog. Good thing he didn't escape on the Friday. I suppose he would have had this murder put down to him as a certainty."

"He's a dangerous man. Freemantle Freddy, they used to call him. Robbery with violence, assault—led the most extraordinary double life. Half the time he passed as an educated, respectable, wealthy man. I am not at all sure myself that Broadmoor wasn't the place for him. A kind of criminal mania used to come over him from time to time. He would disappear and consort with the lowest characters."

"I suppose many people don't escape from Prince-town?"

"It's well-nigh impossible, sir. But this particular escape was extraordinarily well planned and carried out. We haven't nearly got to the bottom of it yet."

"Well," Dering rose and glanced at his watch, "if there's nothing more, Inspector—I'm afraid I am rather a busy man—"

"Oh, but there *is* something more, Mr. Dering. I want to know why you told me that you were at a literary dinner at the Cecil Hotel on Friday night?"

"I—I don't understand you, Inspector."

"I think you do, sir. You weren't at that dinner, Mr. Dering."

Martin Dering hesitated. His eyes ran uncertainly from the Inspector's face, up to the ceiling, then to the door, and then to his feet.

The Inspector waited calm and stolid.

"Well," said Martin Dering at last, "supposing I wasn't. What the hell has that got to do with you? What have my movements, five hours after my uncle was murdered, got to do with you or anyone else?"

"You made a certain statement to us, Mr. Dering, and I want that statement verified. Part of it has already proved to be untrue. I've got to check up on the other half. You say you lunched and spent the afternoon with a friend."

"Yes—my American publisher."

"His name?"

"Rosenkraun, Edgar Rosenkraun."

"Ah, and his address?"

"He's left England. He left last Saturday."

"For New York?"

"Yes."

"Then he'll be on the sea at the present moment. What boat is he on?"

"I—I really can't remember."

"You know the line?"

"I—I really don't remember."

"Ah, well," said the Inspector, "we'll cable his firm in New York. They'll know."

"It was the *Gargantua*," said Dering sullenly.

"Thank you, Mr. Dering, I thought you could remember if you tried. Now, your statement is that you lunched with Mr. Rosenkraun and that you spent the afternoon with him. At what time did you leave him?"

"About five o'clock, I should say."

"And then?"

"I decline to state. It's no business of yours. That's all you want, surely."

Inspector Narracott nodded thoughtfully. If Rosenkraun confirmed Dering's statement then any case against Dering must fall to the ground. Whatever his mysterious activities had been that evening could not affect the case.

"What are you going to do?" demanded Dering uneasily.

"Wireless Mr. Rosenkraun on board the *Gargantua*."

"Damn it all," cried Dering, "you'll involve me in all sorts of publicity. Look here—"

He went across to his desk, scribbled a few words on a bit of paper, then took it to the Inspector.

"I suppose you've got to do what you're doing," he said ungraciously, "but at least you might do it in my way. It's not fair to run a chap in for a lot of trouble."

On the sheet of paper was written: *Rosenkraun S.S. "Gargantua." Please confirm my statement I was with you lunch-time until five o'clock Friday 14th. Martin Dering.*

"Have the reply sent straight to you—I don't mind. But don't have it sent to Scotland Yard or a Police Station. You don't know what these Americans are like. Any hint of me being mixed up in a police case and this new contract that I've been discussing will go to the winds. Keep it a private matter, Inspector."

"I've no objection to that, Mr. Dering. All I want is the truth. I'll send this reply paid, the reply to be sent to my private address in Exeter."

"Thank you. It's not such easy going earning your living by literature, Inspector. You'll see the answer will be all right. I did tell you a lie about the dinner, but as a matter of fact I had told my wife that that was where I had been, and I thought I might as well stick to the same story to you. Otherwise I would have let myself in for a lot of trouble."

"If Mr. Rosenkraun confirms your statement, Mr. Dering, you will have nothing else to fear."

An unpleasant character, the Inspector thought, as he left the house. *But he seems pretty certain that this American publisher will confirm the truth of his story.*

A sudden remembrance came to the Inspector as he hopped into the train which would take him back to Devon. *Rycroft, of course—that's the name of the old gentleman who lives in one of the cottages at Sittaford. A curious coincidence.*

CHAPTER TWENTY-FIVE

AT DELLER'S CAFÉ

EMILY TREFUSIS AND CHARLES ENDERBY were seated at a small table in Deller's Café in Exeter. It was half-past three and at that hour there was comparative peace and quiet. A few people were having a quiet cup of tea, but the restaurant on the whole was deserted.

"Well," said Charles, "what do you think of him?"

Emily frowned. "It's difficult," she said.

After his interview with the police, Brian Pearson had lunched with them. He had been extremely polite to Emily, rather too polite in her opinion. To that astute girl it seemed a shade unnatural. Here was a young man conducting a clandestine love affair and an officious stranger butts in.

Brian Pearson had taken it like a lamb, had fallen in with Charles's suggestion of having a car and driving over to see the police. Why this attitude of meek acquiescence? It seemed to Emily entirely untypical of the natural Brian Pearson as she read his character. *I'll see you in hell first!* would, she felt sure, have been far more his attitude. This lamb-like demeanor was suspicious. She tried to convey something of her feelings to Enderby.

"I get you," said Enderby. "Our Brian has got something to conceal; therefore he can't be his natural high-handed self."

"That's it exactly."

"Do you think he might possibly have killed old Trevelyan?"

"Brian," said Emily thoughtfully, "is—well, a person to be reckoned with. He is rather unscrupulous, I should think, and if he wanted anything, I don't think he would let ordinary conventional standards stand in his way. He's not plain tame English."

"Putting all personal considerations on one side, he's a more likely starter than Jim," said Enderby.

Emily nodded. "Much more likely. He would carry a thing through well—because he would never lose his nerve."

"Honestly, Emily, do you think he did it?"

"I—I don't know. He fulfills the conditions—the only person who does."

"What do you mean by fulfills the conditions?"

"Well, One: *Motive*." She ticked off the items on her fingers. "The same motive. Twenty thousand pounds. Two: *Opportunity*. Nobody knows where he was on Friday afternoon, and if he was anywhere that he could say—well—surely he would say it. So we assume that he was actually in the neighborhood of Hazelmoor on Friday."

"They haven't found anyone who saw him in Exhampton," Charles pointed out, "and he's a fairly noticeable person."

Emily shook her head scornfully. "He wasn't in Exhampton. Don't you see, Charles, if he committed the murder, he planned it beforehand. It's only poor innocent Jim who came down like a mug and stayed there. There's Lydford and Chagford or perhaps Exeter. He might have walked over from Lydford—that's a main road and the snow wouldn't have been impassable. It would have been pretty good going."

"I suppose we ought to make inquiries all round."

"The police are doing that," said Emily, "and they'll do it a lot better than we could. All public things are much better done by the police. It's private and personal things like listening to Mrs. Curtis and picking up a hint from Miss Percehouse and watching the Willetts—that's where we score."

"Or don't, as the case may be," said Charles.

"To go back to Brian Pearson fulfilling the conditions," said Emily. "We've done two, motive and opportunity, and there's the third—the one that in a way I think is the most important of all."

"What's that?"

"Well, I have felt from the beginning that we couldn't ignore that queer business of the table turning. I have tried to look at it as logically and clear-sightedly as possible. There are just three solutions of it. *One:* That it was supernatural. Well, of course, that may be so, but personally I am ruling it out. *Two:* That it was deliberate—someone did it on purpose, but as one can't arrive at any conceivable reason, we can rule that out also. *Three:* Accidental. Someone gave himself away without meaning to do so—indeed quite against his will. An unconscious piece of self-revelation. If so, someone among those six people either knew definitely that Captain Trevelyan was going to be killed at a certain time that afternoon, or that someone was having an interview with him from which violence might result. None of those six people could have been the actual murderer, but one of them must have been in collusion with the murderer. There's no link between Major Burnaby and anybody else, or Mr. Rycroft and anybody else, or Ronald Garfield and anyone else, but when we come to the Willetts, it's different. There's a link between Violet Willett and Brian Pearson. Those two are on very intimate terms and that girl was all on the jump after the murder."

"You think she knew?" said Charles.

"She or her mother—one or other of them."

"There's one person you haven't mentioned," said Charles. "Mr. Duke."

"I know," said Emily. "It's queer. He's the one person we know absolutely nothing about. I've tried to see him twice and failed. There seems no connection between him and Captain Trevelyan, or between him and any of Captain Trevelyan's relations. There's absolutely nothing to connect him with the case in any way, and yet—"

"Well?" said Charles Enderby as Emily paused.

"And yet we met Inspector Narracott coming out of his cottage. What does Inspector Narracott know about him that we don't? I wish I knew."

"You think—"

"Supposing Duke is a suspicious character and the police know it. Supposing Captain Trevelyan had found out something about Duke. He was particular about his tenants, remember, and supposing he was going to tell the police what he knew. And Duke arranges with an accomplice to have him killed. Oh, I know it all sounds dreadfully melodramatic put like that, and yet, after all, something of the kind might be possible."

"It's an idea certainly," said Charles slowly.

They were both silent, each one deep in thought. Suddenly Emily said, "Do you know that queer feeling you get when somebody is looking at you. I feel now as though someone's eyes were burning the back of my neck. Is it all fancy or is there really someone staring at me now?"

Charles moved his chair an inch or two and looked round the café in a casual manner. "There's a woman at a table in the window," he reported. "Tall, dark, and handsome. She's staring at you."

"Young?"

"No, not very young. Hello!"

"What is it?"

"Ronnie Garfield. He has just come in and he's shaking hands with her and he's sitting down at her table. I think she's saying something about us."

Emily opened her handbag. Rather ostentatiously she powdered her nose, adjusting the small pocket mirror to a convenient angle. "It's Aunt Jennifer," she said softly. "They are getting up."

"They are going," said Charles. "Do you want to speak to her?"

"No," said Emily. "I think it's better for me to pretend that I haven't seen her."

"After all," said Charles, "why shouldn't Aunt Jennifer know Ronnie Garfield and ask him to tea?"

"Why should she?" said Emily.

"Why shouldn't she?"

"Oh, for goodness sake, Charles, don't let's go on and on like this, *should—shouldn't—should—shouldn't*. Of course it's all nonsense, and it doesn't mean anything! But we *were* just saying that nobody else at that séance had any relation with the family, and not five minutes later we see Ronnie Garfield having tea with Captain Trevelyan's sister."

"It shows," said Charles, "that you never know."

"It shows," said Emily, "that you are always having to begin again."

"In more ways than one," said Charles.

Emily looked at him. "What do you mean?"

"Nothing at present," said Charles.

He put his hand over hers. She did not draw it away. "We've got to put this through," said Charles. "Afterward—"

"Afterward?" said Emily softly.

"I'd do anything for you, Emily," said Charles. "Simply anything—"

"Would you?" said Emily. "That's rather nice of you, Charles dear."

CHAPTER TWENTY-SIX

ROBERT GARDNER

IT WAS JUST TWENTY MINUTES LATER when Emily rang the front door bell of the Laurels. It had been a sudden impulse. She smiled beamingly on Beatrice when the latter opened the door to her. "It's me again," said Emily. "Mrs. Gardner's out, I know, but can I see Mr. Gardner?"

Such a request was clearly unusual. Beatrice seemed doubtful. "Well, I don't know. I'll go up and see, shall I?"

"Yes, do," said Emily.

Beatrice went upstairs and returned in a few minutes to ask the young lady to please step this way.

Robert Gardner was lying on a couch by the window in a big room. He was a big man, blue-eyed and fair-haired. He looked, Emily thought, as Tristan ought to look in the third act of *Tristan and Isolde* and as no Wagnerian tenor has ever looked yet. "Hello," he said. "You are the criminal's spouse to be, aren't you?"

"That's right, Uncle Robert," said Emily. "I suppose I *do* call you Uncle Robert, don't I?" she asked.

"If Jennifer will allow it. What's it like having a young man languishing in prison?"

A cruel man, Emily decided. A man who would take a malicious joy in giving you sharp digs in painful places. But she was a match for him. She said smilingly, "Very thrilling."

"Not so thrilling for Master Jim, eh?"

"Oh, well," said Emily, "it's an experience, isn't it?"

"Teach him life can't be all beer and skittles," said Robert Gardner maliciously.

He looked at her curiously. "What did you want to come and see me for, eh?" There was a tinge of something like suspicion in his voice.

"If you are going to marry into a family it's just as well to see all your relations-in-law beforehand."

"Know the worst before it's too late. So you really think you are going to marry young Jim, eh?"

"Why not?"

"In spite of this murder charge?"

"In spite of this murder charge."

"Well," said Robert Gardner, "I have never seen anybody less cast down. Anyone would think you were enjoying yourself."

"I am. Tracking down a murderer is frightfully thrilling."

"Eh?"

"I said tracking down a murderer is frightfully thrilling," said Emily.

Robert Gardner stared at her, then he threw himself back on his pillows. "I am tired," he said in a fretful voice. "I can't talk any more. Nurse, where's Nurse? Nurse, I'm tired."

Nurse Davis had come swiftly at his call from an adjoining room. "Mr. Gardner gets tired very easily. I think you had better go now if you don't mind, Miss Trefusis."

Emily rose to her feet. She nodded brightly and said, "Good-by, Uncle Robert. Perhaps I'll come back some day."

"What do you mean?"

"*Au revoir,*" said Emily.

She was going out of the front door when she stopped. "Oh!" she said to Beatrice. "I have left my gloves."

"I will get them, Miss."

"Oh, no," said Emily. "I'll do it." She ran lightly up the stairs and entered without knocking.

"Oh," said Emily, "I beg your pardon. I am so sorry. It was my gloves." She took them up ostentatiously and smiling sweetly at the two occupants of the room who were sitting hand in hand ran down the stairs and out of the house.

This glove-leaving is a terrific scheme, said Emily to herself. *This is the second time it's come off. Poor Jennifer, does she know, I wonder? Probably not. I must hurry or I'll keep Charles waiting.*

Enderby was waiting in Elmer's Ford at the agreed rendezvous. "Any luck?" he asked.

"In a way, yes. I'm not sure."

Enderby looked at her inquiringly. "No," said Emily in answer to his glance, "I'm not going to tell you about it. You see, it may have nothing whatever to do with it— and if so, it wouldn't be fair."

Enderby sighed. "I call that hard," he observed.

"I'm sorry," said Emily firmly. "But there it is."

"Have it your own way," said Charles coldly.

They drove on in silence—an offended silence on Charles's part—an oblivious one on Emily's.

They were nearly at Exhampton when she broke the silence by a totally unexpected remark. "Charles," she said, "are you a bridge player?"

"Yes, I am. Why?"

"I was thinking. You know what they tell you to do when you're assessing the value of your hand? If you're defending—count the winners—but if you're attacking, count the losers. Now, we're attacking in this business of ours—but perhaps we have been doing it the wrong way."

"How do you mean?"

"Well, we've been counting the winners, haven't we? I mean going over the people who *could* have killed Captain Trevelyan, however improbable it seems. And that's perhaps why we've got so terribly muddled."

"I haven't got muddled," said Charles.

"Well, I have then. I'm so muddled I can't think at all. Let's look at it the other way round. Let's count the losers—the people who can't possibly have killed Captain Trevelyan."

"Well, let's see—" Enderby reflected. "To begin with there's the Willetts and Burnaby and Rycroft and Ronnie— Oh! and Duke."

"Yes," agreed Emily. "We know none of them can have killed him. Because at the time he was killed they were all at Sittaford House and they all saw each other and they can't all be lying. Yes, they're all out of it."

"As a matter of fact everyone in Sittaford is out of it," said Enderby. "Even Elmer." He lowered his voice in deference to the possibility of the driver hearing him. "Because the road to Sittaford was impassable for cars on Friday."

"He could have walked," said Emily in an equally low voice. "If Major Burnaby could have got there that evening, Elmer could have started at lunch time—got to Exhampton at five, murdered him, and walked back again."

Enderby shook his head. "I don't think he could have walked back again. Remember the snow started to fall about half-past six. Anyway, you're not accusing Elmer, are you?"

"No," said Emily, "though, of course, he might be a homicidal maniac."

"Hush," said Charles. "You'll hurt his feelings if he hears you."

"At any rate," said Emily, "you can't say definitely that he couldn't have murdered Captain Trevelyan."

"Almost," said Charles. "He couldn't walk to Exhampton and back without all Sittaford knowing about it and saying it was queer."

"It certainly is a place where everyone knows everything," agreed Emily.

"Exactly," said Charles, "and that's why I say that everyone in Sittaford is out of it. The only ones that weren't at the Willetts'—Miss Percehouse and Captain Wyatt—are invalids. They couldn't go plowing through snowstorms. And dear old Curtis and Mrs. C. If any of them did it, they must have gone comfortably to Exhampton for the week-end and come back when it was all over."

Emily laughed. "You couldn't be absent from Sittaford for the week-end without its being noticed, certainly," she said.

"Curtis would notice the silence if Mrs. C. was," said Enderby.

"I know," he said suddenly.

"What?" said Emily eagerly.

"The blacksmith's wife. The one who's expecting her eighth. The intrepid woman despite her condition walked all the way to Sittaford and batted him one with the sandbag."

"And why, pray?"

"Because, of course, although the blacksmith was the father of the preceding seven, Captain Trevelyan was the father of her coming che-ild."

"Charles," said Emily, "don't be indelicate. And anyway, it would be the blacksmith who did it, not her. A really good case there. Think how that brawny arm could wield a sandbag! And his wife would never notice his absence with seven children to look after. She wouldn't have time to notice a mere man."

"This is degenerating into mere idiocy," said Charles.

"It is rather," agreed Emily. "Counting losers hasn't been a great success."

"What about you?" said Charles.

"Me?"

"Where were you when the crime was committed?"

"How extraordinary! I never thought of that. I was in London, of course. But I don't know that I could prove it. I was alone in my flat."

"There you are," said Charles. "Motive and everything. Your young man coming into twenty thousand pounds. What more do you want?"

"You are clever, Charles," said Emily. "I can see that really I'm a most suspicious character. I never thought of it before."

CHAPTER TWENTY-SEVEN

NARRACOTT ACTS

Two MORNINGS LATER, Emily was seated in Inspector Narracott's office. She had come over from Sittaford that morning. Inspector Narracott looked at her appraisingly. He admired Emily's pluck, her courageous determination not to give in, and her resolute cheerfulness. She was a fighter and Inspector Narracott admired fighters. It was his private opinion that she was a great deal too good for Jim Pearson, even if that young man was innocent of the murder.

"It's generally understood in books," he said, "that the police are intent on having a victim and don't in the least care if that victim is innocent or not as long as they have enough evidence to convict him. That's not the truth, Miss Trefusis; it's only the guilty man we want."

"Do you honestly believe Jim to be guilty, Inspector Narracott?"

"I can't give you an official answer to that, Miss Trefusis. But I'll tell you this—that we are examining not only the evidence against him but the evidence against other people very carefully."

"You mean against his brother—Brian?"

"A very unsatisfactory gentleman, Mr. Brian Pearson. Refused to answer questions or to give any information about himself, but I think—" Inspector Narracott's slow Devonshire smile widened. "I think I can make a pretty good guess at some of his activities. If I am right, I shall know in another half hour. Then there's Mr. Dering."

"You've seen him?" asked Emily curiously.

Inspector Narracott looked at her vivid face, and felt tempted to relax official caution. Leaning back in his chair, he recounted his interview with Mr. Dering; then from a file at his elbow he took out a copy of the wireless message he had dispatched to Mr. Rosenkraun. "That's what I sent," he said. "And here's the reply."

Emily read it: *Narracott 2 Drysdale Road Exeter. Certainly confirm Mr. Dering's statement. He was in my company all Friday afternoon. Rosenkraun.*

"Oh—bother!" said Emily.

"Ye-es," said Inspector Narracott reflectively. "It's annoying, isn't it?" And his slow Devonshire smile broke out again. "But I am a suspicious man, Miss Trefusis. Mr. Dering's reasons sounded very plausible—but I thought it a pity to play into his hands too completely. So I sent another wireless message."

Again he handed her two pieces of paper.

The first ran: *Information wanted re murder of Captain Trevelyan. Do you support Martin Dering's statement of alibi for Friday afternoon. Divisional Inspector Narracott Exeter.*

The return message showed agitation and a reckless disregard for expense: *Had no idea it was criminal case. Did not see Martin Dering Friday. Agreed support his statement as one friend to another. Believed his wife was having him watched for divorce proceedings.*

"Oh," said Emily. "Oh!—you *are* clever, Inspector."

The Inspector evidently thought that he *had* been rather clever. His smile was gentle and contented.

"How men do stick together," went on Emily, looking over the telegrams. "Poor Sylvia. In some ways I really think that men are beasts. That's why," she added, "it's so nice when one finds a man on whom one can really rely." And she smiled admiringly at the Inspector.

"Now, all this is very confidential, Miss Trefusis," the Inspector warned her. "I have gone further than I should in letting you know about this."

"I think it's adorable of you," said Emily. "I shall never, *never* forget it."

"Well, mind," the Inspector warned her. "Not a word to *anybody*."

"You mean that I am not to tell Charles—Mr. Enderby."

"Journalists will be journalists," said Inspector Narra-cott. "However well you have got him tamed, Miss Trefusis—well, news is news, isn't it?"

"I won't tell him then," said Emily. "I think I've got him muzzled all right, but as you say, newspaper men will be newspaper men."

"Never part with information unnecessarily. That's my rule," said Inspector Narracott.

A faint twinkle appeared in Emily's eyes, her un-spoken thought being that Inspector Narracott had in-fringed this rule rather badly during the last half hour. A sudden recollection came into her mind, not of course that it probably mattered now. Everything seemed to be pointing in a totally different direction. But still it would be nice to know. "Inspector Narracott," she said suddenly, "who is Mr. Duke?"

"Mr. Duke?"

She thought the Inspector was rather taken aback by her questions. "You remember," said Emily, "we met you coming out of his cottage in Sittaford."

"Ah, yes, yes, I remember. To tell you the truth, Miss Trefusis, I thought I would like to have an independent account of that table-turning business. Major Burnaby is not a first-rate hand at description."

"And yet," said Emily thoughtfully, "if I had been you, I should have gone to somebody like Mr. Rycroft for it. Why Mr. Duke?"

There was a silence and then the Inspector said, "Just a matter of opinion."

"I wonder. I wonder if the police know something about Mr. Duke."

Inspector Narracott didn't answer. He had got his eyes fixed very steadily on the blotting-paper.

"The man who leads a blameless life!" said Emily, "that seems to describe Mr. Duke awfully accurately, but perhaps he hasn't always led a blameless life? Per-haps the police know that?"

She saw a faint quiver on Inspector Narracott's face as he tried to conceal a smile. "You like guessing, don't you, Miss Trefusis?" he said amiably.

"When people don't tell you things you have to guess!" retaliated Emily.

"If a man, as you say, is leading a blameless life," Inspector Narracott said, "and if it would be an annoyance and an inconvenience for him to have his past life raked up, well, the police are capable of keeping their own counsel. We have no wish to give a man away."

"I see," said Emily, "but all the same—you went to see him, didn't you? That looks as though you thought, to begin with at any rate, that he might have had a hand in it. I wish—I wish I knew who Mr. Duke really was? And what particular branch of criminology he indulged in in the past?"

She looked appealingly at Inspector Narracott but the latter preserved a wooden face, and realizing that on this point she could not hope to move him, Emily sighed and took her departure.

When she had gone the Inspector sat staring at the blotting-pad, a trace of a smile still lingering on his lips. Then he rang the bell and one of his underlings entered. "Well?" demanded Inspector Narracott.

"Quite right, sir. But it wasn't the Duchy at Princetown, it was the hotel at Two Bridges."

"Ah!" The Inspector took the papers the other handed to him. "Well," he said, "that settles that all right. Have you followed up the other young chap's movements on Friday?"

"He certainly arrived at Exhampton by the last train, but I haven't found out yet what time he left London. Inquiries are being made."

Narracott nodded.

"Here is the entry from Somerset House, sir."

Narracott unfolded it. It was the record of a marriage between William Martin Dering and Martha Elizabeth Rycroft.

"Ah!" said the Inspector, "anything else?"

"Yes, sir. Mr. Brian Pearson sailed from Australia on a Blue Funnel Boat, the *Phidias*. She touched at Cape

Town but no passengers of the name of Willett were aboard. No mother and daughter at all from South Africa. There was a Mrs. and Miss Evans and a Mrs. and Miss Johnson from Melbourne. The latter answer the description of the Willetts."

"H'm," said the Inspector—"Johnson. Probably neither Johnson nor Willett is the right name. I think I've got them taped out all right. Anything more?" There was nothing else, it seemed. "Well," said Narracott, "I think we have got enough to go on with."

CHAPTER TWENTY-EIGHT

BOOTS

"BUT, MY DEAR YOUNG LADY," said Mr. Kirkwood, "what can you possibly expect to find at Hazelmoor. All Captain Trevelyan's effects have been removed. The police have made a thorough search of the house. I quite understand your position and your anxiety that Mr. Pearson shall be—er—cleared if possible. But what can you do?"

"I don't expect to find anything," Emily replied, "or to notice anything that the police have overlooked. I can't explain to you, Mr. Kirkwood. I want—I want to get the *atmosphere* of the place. Please let me have the key. There's no harm in it."

"Certainly there's no harm in it," said Mr. Kirkwood with dignity.

"Then please be kind," said Emily.

So Mr. Kirkwood was kind and handed over the key with an indulgent smile.

That morning Emily had received a letter. It was couched in the following terms:

DEAR MISS TREFUSIS (wrote Mrs. Belling) : *You said as how you would like to hear if anything at all should happen that was in any way out of the common even if not important, and as this is peculiar, though not in any way important, I thought it my duty Miss to let you know at once, hoping this will catch you by the last post tonight or by the first post tomorrow. My niece she come round and said it wasn't of any importance but peculiar which I agreed with her. The police said, and it was generally thought that nothing was taken from Captain Trevelyan's house and nothing was in a manner of speaking nothing that is of any value, but something*

*there is missing though not noticed at the time being
unimportant. But it seems Miss that a pair of the Captain's boots is missing which Evans noticed when he
went over the things with Major Burnaby. Though I
don't suppose it is of any importance Miss I thought you
would like to know. It was a pair of boots Miss the thick
kind you rubs oil into and which the Captain would
have worn if he had gone out in the snow but as he
didn't go out in the snow it doesn't seem to make sense.
But missing they are and who took them nobody knows
and though I well know it's of no importance I felt it
my duty to write and hoping this finds you as it leaves
me at present and hoping you are not worrying too
much about the young gentleman I remain Miss Yours
truly—*Mrs. J. Belling.

Emily had read and reread this letter. She had discussed it with Charles.

"Boots," said Charles thoughtfully. "It doesn't seem
to make sense."

"It must mean something," Emily pointed out. "I
mean—why should a pair of boots be missing?"

"You don't think Evans is inventing?"

"Why should he? And after all, if people do invent,
they invent something sensible. Not a silly, pointless
thing like this."

"Boots suggests something to do with footprints,"
said Charles thoughtfully.

"I know. But footprints don't seem to enter into this
case at all. Perhaps if it hadn't come on to snow again—"

"Yes, perhaps, but even then. Could he have given
them to some tramp," suggested Charles, "and then the
tramp did him in?"

"I suppose that's possible," said Emily, "but it doesn't
sound very like Captain Trevelyan. He might perhaps
have found a man some work to do or given him a
shilling, but he wouldn't have pressed his best winter
boots on him."

"Well, I give it up," said Charles.

"I'm not going to give it up," said Emily. "By hook or by crook I'm going to get to the bottom of it."

Accordingly she came to Exhampton and went first to the Three Crowns, where Mrs. Belling received her with great enthusiasm.

"And your young gentleman still in prison, Miss! Well, it's a cruel shame and none of us don't believe it was him at least I would like to hear them say so when I am about. So you got my letter? You'd like to see Evans? Well, he lives right round the corner, 85 Fore Street it is. I wish I could come with you, but I can't leave the place, but you can't mistake it."

Emily did not mistake it. Evans himself was out, but Mrs. Evans received her and invited her in. Emily sat down and induced Mrs. Evans to do so also and plunged straight into the matter on hand. "I've come to talk about what your husband told Mrs. Belling. I mean about a pair of Captain Trevelyan's boots being missing."

"It's an odd thing, to be sure," said the girl.

"Your husband is quite certain about it?"

"Oh, yes. Wore these boots most of the time in winter, the Captain did. Big ones they were, and he wore a couple of pairs of socks inside them."

Emily nodded.

"They can't have gone to be mended or anything like that?" she suggested.

"Not without Evans knowing, they couldn't," said his wife boastfully.

"No, I suppose not."

"It's queer like," said Mrs. Evans, "but I don't suppose it had anything to do with the murder, do you, Miss?"

"It doesn't seem likely," agreed Emily.

"Have they found out anything new, Miss?" The girl's voice was eager.

"Yes, one or two things—nothing very important."

"Seeing as that the Inspector from Exeter was here again today, I thought as though they might."

"Inspector Narracott?"

"Yes, that's the one, Miss."

"Did he come by train?"

"No, he came by car. He went to the Three Crowns first and asked about the young gentleman's luggage."

"What young gentleman's luggage?"

"The gentleman you go about with, Miss."

Emily stared.

"They asked Tom," went on the girl. "I was passing by just after and he told me about it. He's a one for noticing, is Tom. He remembered there were two labels on the young gentleman's luggage, one to Exeter and one to Exhampton."

A sudden smile illuminated Emily's face as she pictured the crime being committed by Charles in order to provide a scoop for himself. One could, she decided, write a gruesome little story on that theme. But she admired Inspector Narracott's thoroughness in checking every detail to do with anyone, however remote his connection with the crime. He must have left Exeter almost immediately after his interview with her. A fast car would easily beat the train and in any case she had lunched in Exeter.

"Where did the Inspector go afterward?" she asked.

"To Sittaford, Miss. Tom heard him tell the driver."

"To Sittaford House?"

Brian Pearson was, she knew, still staying at Sittaford House with the Willetts.

"No, Miss, to Mr. Duke's."

Duke again. Emily felt irritated and baffled. Always Duke—the unknown factor. She ought, she felt, to be able to deduce him from the evidence, but he seemed to have produced the same effect on everyone—a normal, ordinary, pleasant man.

I've got to see him, said Emily to herself. *I'll go straight there as soon as I get back to Sittaford.*

Then she had thanked Mrs. Evans, gone on to Mr. Kirkwood's and obtained the key, and was now standing in the hall of Hazelmoor and wondering how and what she had expected to feel there.

She mounted the stairs slowly and went into the first room at the top of the stairs. This was quite clearly Captain Trevelyan's bedroom. It had, as Mr. Kirkwood had said, been emptied of personal effects. Blankets were folded in a neat pile, the drawers were empty, there was not so much as a hanger left in the cupboard. The boot cupboard showed a row of bare shelves.

Emily sighed and then turned and went downstairs. Here was the sitting-room where the dead man had lain, the snow blowing in from the open window.

She tried to visualize the scene. Whose hand had struck Captain Trevelyan down, and why? Had he been killed at five-and-twenty past five as everyone believed—or had Jim really lost his nerve and lied? Had he failed to make anyone hear at the front door and gone round to the window, looked in and seen his dead uncle's body, and dashed away in an agony of fear? If only she knew. According to Mr. Dacres, Jim stuck to his story. Yes—but Jim might have lost his nerve. She couldn't be sure.

Had there been, as Mr. Rycroft had suggested, someone else in the house—someone who had overheard the quarrel and seized his chance?

If so—did that throw any light on the boot problem? Had someone been upstairs—perhaps in Captain Trevelyan's bedroom? Emily passed through the hall again. She took a quick look into the dining-room; there were a couple of trunks there neatly strapped and labeled. The sideboard was bare. The silver cups were at Major Burnaby's bungalow.

She noticed, however, that the prize of three new novels, an account of which Charles had had from Evans and had reported with amusing embellishments to her, had been forgotten and lay dejectedly on a chair. She looked round the room and shook her head. There was nothing here.

She went up the stairs again and once more entered the bedroom. She *must* know why these boots were missing! Until she could concoct some theory reasonably

satisfactory to herself which would account for their
disappearance, she felt powerless to put them out of
her mind. They were soaring to ridiculous proportions,
dwarfing everything else to do with the case. Was there
nothing to help her?

She took each drawer out and felt behind it. She felt
for loose boards; she felt round the edge of the carpet
with her fingers. She investigated the spring mattress.
What she expected to find in all these places she hardly
knew, but she went on looking with dogged persever-
ance. And then, as she straightened her back and stood
upright, her eye was caught by the one incongruous
touch in this room of apple-pie order, a little pile of soot
in the grate.

Emily looked at it with the fascinated gaze of a bird
for a snake. She drew nearer, eyeing it. It was no logical
deduction, no reasoning of cause and effect; it was simply that the sight of soot as such suggested a certain
possibility. Emily rolled up her sleeves and thrust both
arms up the chimney.

A moment later she was staring with incredulous de-
light at a parcel wrapped loosely in newspaper. One
shake detached the newspaper and there, before her,
were the missing pair of boots.

"But why?" said Emily. "Here they are. But why?
Why? Why? Why?"

She stared at them. She turned them over. She examined them outside and inside and same question beat
monotonously in her brain. Why?

Granted that someone had removed Captain Trevelyan's boots and hidden them up the chimney. Why had
they done so? "Oh!" cried Emily desperately, "I shall
go mad!"

She put the boots carefully in the middle of the floor
and drawing up a chair opposite them she sat down.
And then deliberately she set herself to think out things
from the beginning, going over every detail that she
knew herself or had learned by hearsay from other peo-

ple. She considered every actor in the drama and outside the drama.

And suddenly a queer, nebulous idea began to take shape—an idea suggested by that pair of innocent boots that stood there dumbly on the floor. "But if so," said Emily—"if so—"

She picked up the boots in her hand and hurried downstairs. She pushed open the dining-room door and went to the cupboard in the corner. Here was Captain Trevelyan's motley array of sporting trophies and sporting outfits, all the things he had not trusted within reach of the female tenants. The skis, the sculls, the elephant's foot, the tusks, the fishing-rods—everything still waiting for Messrs. Young and Peabody to pack them expertly for storage.

Emily bent down, boots in hand. In a minute or two she stood upright, flushed, incredulous.

"So that was it," said Emily. "So that was it."

She sank into a chair. There was still much that she did not understand.

After some minutes she rose to her feet. She spoke aloud: "I know who killed Captain Trevelyan," she said. "But I don't know *why*. I still can't think *why*. But I mustn't lose time."

She hurried out of Hazelmoor. To find a car to drive her to Sittaford was the work of a few minutes. She ordered it to take her to Mr. Duke's bungalow. Here she paid the man and then walked up the path as the car drove away.

She lifted the knocker and gave a loud rat-tat. After a moment or two's interval the door was opened by a big burly man with a rather impassive face. For the first time, Emily met Mr. Duke face to face. "Mr. Duke?" she asked.

"Yes."

"I am Miss Trefusis. May I come in, please?"

There was a momentary hesitation. Then he stood aside to let her pass. Emily walked into the living-room. He closed the front door and followed her.

"I want to see Inspector Narracott," said Emily. "Is he here?"

Again there was a pause. Mr. Duke seemed uncertain how to answer. At last he appeared to make up his mind. He smiled—a rather curious smile. "Inspector Narracott is here," he said. "What do you want to see him about?"

Emily took the parcel she was carrying and unwrapped it. She took out a pair of boots and placed them on the table in front of him. "I want," she said, "to see him about those boots."

CHAPTER TWENTY-NINE

THE SECOND SÉANCE

"HULLO, HULLO, HULLO," said Ronnie Garfield.

Mr. Rycroft, slowly ascending the steep slope of the lane from the post office, paused till Ronnie overtook him.

"Been to the local Harrods, eh?" said Ronnie. "Old Mother Hibbert."

"No," said Mr. Rycroft. "I have been for a short walk along past the forge. Very delightful weather today."

Ronnie looked up at the blue sky. "Yes, a bit of a difference from last week. By the way, you're going to the Willetts, I suppose?"

"I am. You also?"

"Yes. Our bright spot in Sittaford—the Willetts. Mustn't let yourself get downhearted, that's their motto. Carry on as usual. My aunt says it is unfeeling of them to ask people to tea so soon after the funeral and all that, but that's all bunkum. She just says that because she's feeling rattled about the Emperor of Peru."

"The Emperor of Peru?" said Mr. Rycroft, surprised.

"One of the blinking cats. It's turned out to be an Empress instead and Aunt Caroline's naturally annoyed about it. She doesn't like these sex problems—so, as I say, she got her feelings off her chest by making catty remarks about the Willetts. Why shouldn't they ask people to tea? Trevelyan wasn't a relation, or anything like that."

"Very true," said Mr. Rycroft, turning his head and examining a bird which flew past and in which he thought he recognized a rare species.

"How annoying," he murmured. "I haven't got my glasses with me."

"Eh! I say, talking of Trevelyan, do you think Mrs.

Willett can have known the old boy better than she says?"

"Why do you ask that?"

"Because of the change in her. Have you ever seen anything like it? She's aged about twenty years in the last week. You must have noticed it."

"Yes," said Mr. Rycroft, "I have noticed it."

"Well, there you are. Trevelyan's death must have been the most frightful shock to her in some way or other. Queer if she turned out to be the old man's long lost wife whom he deserted in his youth and didn't recognize."

"I hardly think that likely, Mr. Garfield."

"Bit too much of a movie stunt, eh? All the same very odd things happen. I've read some really amazing things in the *Daily Wire*—things you wouldn't credit if a newspaper didn't print them."

"Are they any more to be credited on that account?" inquired Mr. Rycroft acidly.

"You have got a down on young Enderby, haven't you?" said Ronnie.

"I dislike ill-bred nosing into affairs that do not concern you," said Mr. Rycroft.

"Yes, but then they do concern him," Ronnie persisted. "I mean nosing about is the poor chap's job. He seems to have tamed old Burnaby all right. Funny, the old boy can hardly bear the sight of me. I'm like a red rag to a bull to him."

Mr. Rycroft did not reply.

"By Jove," said Ronnie, again glancing up at the sky. "Do you realize it's Friday? Just a week ago today at about this time we were trudging up to the Willetts just as we are now. But a bit of a change in the weather."

"A week ago," said Mr. Rycroft. "It seems infinitely longer."

"More like a bally year, doesn't it? Hullo, Abdul."

They were passing Captain Wyatt's gate over which the melancholy Indian was leaning.

"Good afternoon, Abdul," said Mr. Rycroft. "How's your master?"

The native shook his head. "Master bad today, Sahib. Not see anyone. Not see anyone for long time."

"You know," said Ronnie as they passed on, "that chap could murder Wyatt quite easily and no one would know. He could go on for weeks shaking his head and saying the master wouldn't see anyone and no one would think it the least odd."

Mr. Rycroft admitted the truth of the statement. "But there would still be the problem of the disposal of the body," he pointed out.

"Yes, that's always the snag, isn't it? Inconvenient thing, a human body."

They passed Major Burnaby's cottage. The Major was in his garden looking sternly at a weed which was growing where no weed should be.

"Good afternoon, Major," said Mr. Rycroft. "Are you also coming to Sittaford House?"

Burnaby rubbed his nose. "Don't think so. They sent me a note asking me. But—well—I don't feel like it. Expect you'll understand."

Mr. Rycroft bowed his head in token of understanding. "All the same," he said, "I wish you'd come. I've got a reason."

"A reason. What sort of a reason?"

Mr. Rycroft hesitated. It was clear that the presence of Ronnie Garfield constrained him. But Ronnie, completely oblivious of the fact, stood his ground listening with ingenuous interest.

"I'd like to try an experiment," Mr. Rycroft said at last slowly.

"What sort of experiment?" demanded Burnaby.

Mr. Rycroft hesitated. "I'd rather not tell you beforehand. But if you come, I'll ask you to back me up in anything I suggest."

Burnaby's curiosity was aroused. "All right," he said. "I'll come. You can count on me. Where's my hat?"

He rejoined them in a minute, and all three turned in

at the gates of Sittaford House.

"Hear you are expecting company, Rycroft," said Burnaby conversationally.

A shade of vexation passed over the older man's face. "Who told you that?"

"That chattering magpie of a woman, Mrs. Curtis. She's clean and she's honest, but her tongue never stops, and she pays no attention to whether you listen or whether you don't."

"It's quite true," admitted Mr. Rycroft. "I am expecting my niece, Mrs. Dering, and her husband, tomorrow."

They had arrived at the front door by now, and on pressing the bell it was opened to them by Brian Pearson. As they removed their overcoats in the hall, Mr. Rycroft observed the tall broad-shouldered young man with an interested eye. *Fine specimen,* he thought. *Very fine specimen. Strong temper. Curious angle of the jaw. Might be a nasty customer to tackle in certain circumstances. What you might call a dangerous young man.*

A queer feeling of unreality stole over Major Burnaby as he entered the drawing-room, and Mrs. Willett rose to greet him.

"Splendid of you to turn out."

The same words as last week. The same blazing fire on the hearth. He fancied, but was not sure, the same gowns on the two women.

It did give one a queer feeling. As though it were last week again—as though Joe Trevelyan hadn't died—as though nothing had happened or were changed. Stop, that was wrong. The Willett woman had changed. A wreck, that was the only way of describing her. No longer the prosperous, determined woman of the world, but a broken, nervy creature making an obvious and pathetic effort to appear as usual. *But I'm hanged if I can see what Joe's death meant to her,* thought the Major.

For the hundredth time he registered the impression that there was something deuced odd about the Willetts.

As usual, he awoke to the realization that he was being silent and that someone was speaking to him.

"Our last little gathering, I am afraid," Mrs. Willett was saying.

"What's that?" Ronnie Garfield looked up suddenly.

"Yes." Mrs. Willett shook her head with a would-be smile. "We have to forego the rest of the winter in Sittaford. Personally, of course, I love it—the snow and the tors and the wildness of it all. But the domestic problem! The domestic problem is too difficult—it defeats me!"

"I thought you were going to get a chauffeur-butler and a handy man," said Major Burnaby.

A sudden shiver shook Mrs. Willett's frame. "No," she said, "I—I have had to give up that idea."

"Dear, dear," said Mr. Rycroft. "This is a great blow to us all. Very sad indeed. We will sink back into our little rut after you have gone. When do you go, by the way?"

"On Monday, I expect," said Mrs. Willett. "Unless I can get away tomorrow. It's so very awkward with no servants. Of course, I must arrange things with Mr. Kirkwood. I took the house for four months."

"You are going to London?" inquired Mr. Rycroft.

"Yes, probably, to start with anyway. Then I expect we shall go abroad to the Riviera."

"A great loss," said Mr. Rycroft bowing gallantly.

Mrs. Willett gave a queer aimless little titter. "Too kind of you, Mr. Rycroft. Well, shall we have tea?"

Tea was laid ready. Mrs. Willett poured out. Ronnie and Brian handed things. A queer kind of embarrassment lay over the party.

"What about you?" said Burnaby abruptly to Brian Pearson. "You off too?"

"To London, yes. Naturally I shan't go abroad till this business is over."

"This business?"

"I mean until my brother is cleared of this ridiculous charge." He flung the words at them defiantly in such a challenging manner that nobody knew quite what to say.

Major Burnaby relieved the situation. "Never have believed he did it. Not for a moment," he said.

"*None* of us think so," said Violet, flinging him a grateful glance.

The tinkle of a bell broke the ensuing pause. "That's Mr. Duke," said Mrs. Willett. "Let him in, Brian."

Young Pearson had gone to the window. "It's not Duke," he said. "It's that damned journalist."

"Oh! dear," said Mrs. Willett. "Well, I suppose we must let him in all the same."

Brian nodded and reappeared in a few minutes with Charles Enderby.

Enderby entered with his usual ingenuous air of beaming satisfaction. The idea that he might not be welcome did not seem to occur to him. "Hullo, Mrs. Willett. How are you? Thought I'd just drop in and see how things were. I wondered where everyone in Sittaford had got to. Now I see."

"Have some tea, Mr. Enderby?"

"Awfully kind of you. I will. I see Emily isn't here. I suppose she's with your aunt, Mr. Garfield."

"Not that I know of," said Ronnie, staring. "I thought she'd gone to Exhampton."

"Ah! but she's back from there. How do I know? A little bird told me. The Curtis bird, to be accurate. Saw the car pass the post office and go up the lane and come back empty. She is not in Number Five and she's not in Sittaford House. Puzzle—where is she? Failing Miss Percehouse, she must be sipping tea with that determined lady killer, Captain Wyatt."

"She may have gone up Sittaford Beacon to see the sunset," suggested Mr. Rycroft.

"Don't think so," said Burnaby. "Should have seen her pass. I've been in the garden for the last hour."

"Well, I don't think it's a very vital problem," said Charles cheerfully. "I mean I don't think she's been kidnaped or murdered or anything."

"That's a pity from the point of view of your paper, isn't it?" sneered Brian.

"Even for copy, I wouldn't sacrifice Emily," said Charles. "Emily," he added thoughtfully, "is unique."

"Very charming," said Mr. Rycroft. "Very charming. We are—er—collaborators, she and I."

"Has everyone finished?" said Mrs. Willett. "What about some bridge?"

"Er—one moment," said Mr. Rycroft.

He cleared his throat importantly. Everyone looked at him. "Mrs. Willett, I am, as you know, deeply interested in psychic phenomena. A week ago today, in this very room, we had an amazing, indeed an awe-inspiring experience."

There was a faint sound from Violet Willett. He turned to her. "I know, my dear Miss Willett, I know. The experience upset you; it was upsetting. I do not deny it. Now, ever since the crime the police force have been seeking the murderer of Captain Trevelyan. They have made an arrest. But some of us, at least, in this room do not believe that Mr. James Pearson is the guilty party. What I propose is this, that we repeat the experiment of last Friday, though approaching it this time in a rather different spirit."

"No," cried Violet.

"Oh, I say!" said Ronnie. "That's a bit too thick. I'm not going to join in anyway."

Mr. Rycroft took no notice of him. "Mrs. Willett, what do you say?"

She hesitated. "Frankly, Mr. Rycroft, I do not like the idea. I don't like it at all. That miserable business last week made a most disagreeable impression on me. It will take me a long time to forget it."

"What are you getting at exactly?" asked Enderby interestedly. "Do you propose that the spirits should tell us the name of Captain Trevelyan's murderer? That seems a pretty tall order."

"It was a pretty tall order, as you call it, when last

week a message came through saying that Captain Trevelyan was dead."

"That's true," agreed Enderby. "But—well—you know this idea of yours might have consequences you haven't considered."

"Such as?"

"Supposing a name was mentioned? Could you be sure that someone present did not deliberately—"

He paused and Ronnie Garfield tendered the word. "Shove. That's what he means. Supposing somebody goes and shoves."

"This is a serious experiment, sir," said Mr. Rycroft warmly. "Nobody would do such a thing."

"I don't know," said Ronnie dubiously. "I wouldn't put it past them. I don't mean myself. I swear I wouldn't, but suppose everyone turns on me and says I have. Jolly awkward, you know."

"Mrs. Willett, I am in earnest." The little old gentleman disregarded Ronnie. "I beg of you, let us make the experiment."

She wavered. "I don't like it. I really don't. I—" She looked round her uneasily, as though for a way of escape. "Major Burnaby, you were Captain Trevelyan's friend. What do you say?"

The Major's eyes met those of Mr. Rycroft. This, he understood, was the contingency which the latter had foreshadowed. "Why not?" he said gruffly.

It had all the decision of a casting vote.

Ronnie went into the adjoining room and brought the small table which had been used before. He set it in the middle of the floor and chairs were drawn up round it. No one spoke. The experiment was clearly not popular.

"That is correct, I think," said Mr. Rycroft. "We are about to repeat the experiment of last Friday under precisely similar conditions."

"Not precisely similar," objected Mrs. Willett. "Mr. Duke is missing."

"True," said Mr. Rycroft. "A pity he is not here. A

great pity. Well—er—we must consider him as replaced by Mr. Pearson."

"Don't take part in it, Brian. I beg of you. Please don't," cried Violet.

"What does it matter? It's all nonsense anyway."

"That is quite the wrong spirit," said Mr. Rycroft severely.

Brian Pearson did not reply but took his place beside Violet.

"Mr. Enderby—" began Mr. Rycroft, but Charles interrupted him.

"I was not in on this. I'm a journalist and you mistrust me. I'll take notes in shorthand of any phenomena—that's the word isn't it?—that occur."

Matters were settled like that. The other six took their places round the table. Charles turned off the lights and sat down on the fender.

"One minute," he said. "What's the time?" He peered at his wrist watch in the firelight. "That's odd," he said.

"What's odd?"

"It's just twenty-five minutes past five."

Violet uttered a little cry.

Mr. Rycroft said severely, "Silence."

The minutes passed. A very different atmosphere this to the one a week ago. There was no muffled laughter, no whispered comments—only silence, broken at last by a slight crack from the table.

Mr. Rycroft's voice rose. "Is there anyone there?"

Another faint crack—somehow an eerie sound in that darkened room. "Is there anyone there?'

Not a crack this time but a deafening tremendous rap. Violet screamed and Mrs. Willett gave a cry.

Brian Pearson's voice rose reassuringly. "It's all right. That's a knock at the front door. I'll go and open it." He strode from the room.

Still nobody spoke.

Suddenly the door flew open, the lights were switched on. In the doorway stood Inspector Narracott. Behind him were Emily Trefusis and Mr. Duke.

Narracott took a step into the room and spoke. "John Burnaby, I charge you with the murder of Joseph Trevelyan on Friday the 14th instant, and I hereby warn you that anything you may say will be taken down and may be used in evidence."

CHAPTER THIRTY

EMILY EXPLAINS

IT WAS A CROWD OF PEOPLE almost too surprised for words that crowded round Emily Trefusis. Inspector Narracott had led his prisoner from the room.

Charles Enderby found his voice first. "For heaven's sake, cough it up, Emily," he said. "I want to get to the telegraph office. Every moment's vital."

"It was Major Burnaby who killed Captain Trevelyan."

"Well, I saw Narracott arrest him. And I suppose Narracott's sane—hasn't gone off his nut suddenly. But how *can* Burnaby have killed Trevelyan? I mean how is it humanly possible? If Trevelyan was killed at five-and-twenty past five—"

"He wasn't. He was killed at about a quarter to six."

"Well, but even then—"

"I know. You'd never guess unless you just happened to think of it. *Skis*—that's the explanation—*skis.*"

"Skis?" repeated everyone.

Emily nodded. "Yes. He deliberately engineered that table turning. It wasn't accident and done unconsciously as we thought, Charles. It was the second alternative that we rejected—done on purpose. He saw it was going to snow before very long. That would make it perfectly safe and wipe out all tracks. He created the impression that Captain Trevelyan was dead—got everyone all worked up. Then he pretended to be very upset and insisted on starting off for Exhampton.

"He went home, buckled on his skis (they were kept in a shed in the garden with a lot of other tackle), and started. He was an expert on skis. It's all down hill to Exhampton—a wonderful run. It would only take about ten minutes.

"He arrived at the window and rapped. Captain Trevelyan let him in, all unsuspecting. Then, when Captain Trevelyan's back was turned, he seized his opportunity, picked up that sandbag thing, and—and killed him. Ugh! It makes me sick to think of it."

She shuddered. "It was all quite easy. He had plenty of time. He must have wiped and cleaned the skis and then put them into the cupboard in the dining-room, pushed in among all the other things. Then I suppose he forced the window and pulled out all the drawers and things—to make it look as though someone had broken in.

"Then, just before eight o'clock, all he had to do was to go out, make a detour on to the road higher up and come puffing and panting into Exhampton as though he'd walked all the way from Sittaford. So long as no one suspected about the skis, he'd be perfectly safe. The doctor couldn't fail to say that Captain Trevelyan had been dead at least two hours. And, as I say, so long as no one thought of skis, Major Burnaby would have a perfect alibi."

"But they were friends—Burnaby and Trevelyan," said Mr. Rycroft. "Old friends—they've always been friends. It's incredible."

"I know," said Emily. "That's what I thought. I couldn't see *why*. I puzzled and I puzzled and at last I had to come to Inspector Narracott and Mr. Duke."

She paused and looked at the impassive Mr. Duke.

"May I tell them?" she said.

Mr. Duke smiled. "If you like, Miss Trefusis."

"Anyway—no, perhaps you'd rather I didn't. I went to them, and we got the thing clear. Do you remember telling me, Charles, that Evans mentioned that Captain Trevelyan used to send in solutions of competitions in his name? He thought Sittaford House was too grand an address. Well—that's what he did in that football competition that you gave Major Burnaby five thousand pounds for. It was Captain Trevelyan's solution really, and he sent it in in Burnaby's name. *No. 1, The Cottages, Sittaford,* sounded much better, he thought. Well, you see what happened? On Friday morning Major Burnaby got the letter saying he'd won five thousand pounds, and by the way, that ought to have made us suspicious. He told you he never got the letter—that nothing had come through on Friday owing to the weather. That was a lie. Friday morning was the last day things did come through. Where was I? Oh!—Major Burnaby getting the letter. He wanted that five thousand—wanted it badly. He'd been investing in some rotten shares or other and had lost a terrible lot of money.

"The idea must have come into his head quite suddenly, I should think. Perhaps when he realized it was going to snow that evening. *If Trevelyan were dead*—he could keep that money and no one would ever know."

"Amazing," murmured Mr. Rycroft. "Quite amazing. I never dreamed— But my dear young lady, how did you learn all this? What put you on the right track?"

For answer, Emily explained Mrs. Belling's letter, and told how she had discovered the boots in the chimney. "It was looking at them that put it into my mind. They were ski boots, you see, and it made me think of skis. And suddenly I wondered if perhaps— I rushed downstairs to the cupboard, and sure enough there were *two* pairs of skis there. One pair was longer than the other. And the boots fitted the long pair—*but they didn't fit the other.* The toe-clip things were adjusted for a much smaller pair of boots. The shorter pair of skis belonged to a different person."

"He ought to have hidden the skis somewhere else," said Mr. Rycroft with artistic disapproval.

"No—no," said Emily. "Where else could he hide them? It was a very good place really. In a day or two the whole collection would have been stored, and in the meantime it wasn't likely that the police would bother whether Captain Trevelyan had had one or two pairs of skis."

"But why did he hide the boots?"

"I suppose," said Emily, "that he was afraid the police might do exactly what I did—the sight of ski boots might have suggested skis to them. So he stuffed them up the chimney. And that's really, of course, where he made his mistake, because Evans noticed that they'd gone and I got to know of it."

"Did he deliberately mean to fasten the crime on Jim?" demanded Brian Pearson angrily.

"Oh! no. That was just Jim's usual idiotic luck. He *was* an idiot, poor lamb."

"He's all right now," said Charles. "You needn't worry about him. Have you told me everything, Emily, because if so, I want to rush to the telegraph office. You'll excuse me, everybody."

He dashed out of the room.

"The live wire," said Emily.

Mr. Duke spoke in his deep voice. "You've been rather a live wire yourself, Miss Trefusis."

"You have," said Ronnie admiringly.

"Oh, dear!" said Emily suddenly and dropped limply on a chair.

"What you need is a pick-me-up," said Ronnie. "A cocktail, eh?"

Emily shook her head.

"A little brandy," suggested Mr. Rycroft solicitously.

"A cup of tea," suggested Violet.

"I'd like a spot of face powder," said Emily wistfully. "I've left my powder puff in the car. And I know I'm simply shining with excitement."

Violet led her upstairs in search of this sedative to the nerves.

"That's better," said Emily, dabbing her nose firmly. "What a nice kind. I feel much better now. Have you got any lipstick? I feel almost human."

"You've been wonderful," said Violet. "So brave."

"Not really," said Emily. "Underneath this camouflage I've been as wobbly as a jelly, with a sort of sick feeling in my middle."

"I know," said Violet. "I've felt much the same myself. I have been so terrified this last few days—about Brian, you know. They couldn't hang him for murdering Captain Trevelyan, of course, but if once he had said where he was during that time, they would soon have ferreted out that it was he who engineered father's escape."

"What's that?" said Emily, pausing in her facial repairs.

"Father was the convict who escaped. That's why we came here. Mother and I. Poor father, he's always—been queer at times. Then he does these dreadful things. We met Brian on the way over from Australia, and he and I—well—he and I—"

"I see," said Emily helpfully. "Of course you did."

"I told him everything and between us we concocted a plan. Brian was wonderful. We had got plenty of money fortunately, and Brian made all the plans. It's awfully hard to get away from Princetown, you know, but Brian engineered it. Really it was a kind of miracle. The arrangement was that after father got away he was to go straight across country here and hide in the Pixie's Cave and then later he and Brian were to be our two menservants. You see, with our arriving so long beforehand we imagined we would be quite free from suspicion. It was Brian who told us about this place, and suggested us offering a big rent to Captain Trevelyan."

"I'm awfully sorry," said Emily—"I mean that it all went wrong."

"It's broken mother up completely," said Violet. "I think Brian's wonderful. It isn't everybody who would want to marry a convict's daughter. But I don't think it's really father's fault. He had an awful kick on the head from a horse about fifteen years ago, and since then he has been a bit queer. Brian says if he had had a good counsel he would have got off. But don't let's talk about me any more."

"Can't anything be done?"

Violet shook her head. "He's very ill—the exposure, you know. That awful cold. It's pneumonia. I can't help feeling that if he dies—well—it may be the best for him really. It sounds dreadful to say so, but you know what I mean."

"Poor Violet," said Emily. "It *is* a rotten shame."

The girl shook her head. "I've got Brian," she said. "And you've got—"

She stopped, embarrassed.

"Ye-es," said Emily thoughtfully, "that's just it."

CHAPTER THIRTY-ONE

THE LUCKY MAN

TEN MINUTES LATER Emily was hurrying down the lane. Captain Wyatt, leaning over his gate, tried to arrest her progress. "Hie, Miss Trefusis. What's all this I hear?"

"It's all true," said Emily, hurrying on.

"Yes, but look here. Come in—have a glass of wine or a cup of tea. There's plenty of time. No need to hurry. That's the worst of you civilized people."

"We're awful, I know," said Emily and sped on.

She burst in on Miss Percehouse with the explosive force of a bomb. "I've come to tell you all about it."

And straightway she poured forth the complete story. It was punctuated by various ejaculations of "Bless us," "You don't say so?" "Well, I declare," from Miss Percehouse.

When Emily had finished her narrative, Miss Percehouse raised herself on her elbow and wagged a finger portentously. "What did I say?" she demanded. "I told you Burnaby was a jealous man. Friends indeed! For more than twenty years Trevelyan had done everything a bit better than Burnaby. He skied better, and he climbed better and he shot better and he did cross word puzzles better. Burnaby wasn't a big enough man to stand it. Trevelyan was rich and he was poor.

"It's been going on a long time. I can tell you it's a difficult thing to go on really liking a man who can do everything just a little better than you can. Burnaby was a narrow-minded, small-natured man. He let it get on his nerves."

"I expect you're right," said Emily. "Well, I had to come and tell you. It seemed so unfair you should be out of everything. By the way, did you know that your nephew knew my Aunt Jennifer? They were having tea together at Deller's on Wednesday."

"She's his godmother," said Miss Percehouse. "So that's the 'fellow' he wanted to see in Exeter. Borrowing money, if I know Ronnie. I'll speak to him."

"I forbid you to bite anyone on a joyful day like this," said Emily. "Good-by. I must fly. I've got a lot to do."

"What have you got to do, young woman? I should say you'd done your bit."

"Not quite. I must go up to London and see Jim's insurance company people and persuade them not to prosecute him over that little matter of the borrowed money."

"H'm," said Miss Percehouse.

"It's all right," said Emily. "Jim will keep straight enough in future. He's had his lesson."

"Perhaps. And you think you'll be able to persuade them?"

"Yes," said Emily firmly.

"Well," said Miss Percehouse, "perhaps you will. And after that?"

"After that," said Emily, "I've finished. I'll have done all I can for Jim."

"Then suppose we say—what next?" said Miss Percehouse.

"You mean?"

"What next? Or if you want it put clearer: *Which of them?*"

"Oh!" said Emily.

"Exactly. That's what I want to know. Which of them is to be the unfortunate man?"

Emily laughed. Bending over, she kissed the old lady. "Don't pretend to be an idiot," she said. "You know perfectly well which it is."

Miss Percehouse chuckled.

Emily ran lightly out of the house and down to the gate just as Charles came racing up the lane. He caught her by both hands. "Emily darling!"

"Charles! Isn't everything marvelous?"

"I shall kiss you," said Mr. Enderby and did.

"I'm a made man, Emily," he said. "Now look here, darling, what about it?"

"What about what?"

"Well—I mean—well, of course, it wouldn't have been playing the game with poor old Pearson in prison and all the rest of it. But he's cleared now and—well, he has got to take his medicine just like anybody else."

"What *are* you talking about?" said Emily.

"You know well enough I am crazy about you," said Mr. Enderby, "and you like me. Pearson was just a mistake. What I mean is—well—you and I, we are made for each other. All this time, we have known it, both of us, haven't we? Do you like a registry office or a church, or what?"

"If you are referring to marriage," said Emily, "there's nothing doing."

"What—but I say—"

"No," said Emily.

"But—Emily—"

"If you will have it," said Emily, "I love Jim. Passionately!"

Charles stared at her in speechless bewilderment. "You can't!"

"I can! And I do! And I always have! And I always shall!"

"You—you made me think—"

"I said," said Emily demurely, "that it was wonderful to have someone one could rely on."

"Yes, but I thought—"

"I can't help what you thought."

"You *are* an unscrupulous devil, Emily."

"I know, Charles darling. I know. I'm everything you like to call me. But never mind. Think how great you are going to be. You've got your scoop! Exclusive news for the *Daily Wire*. You're a made man. What's a woman anyway? Less than the dust. No really strong man needs a woman. She only hampers him by clinging to him like the ivy. Every great man is one who is independent of women. A career—there's nothing so fine, so absolutely satisfying to a man, as a great career. You are a strong man, Charles, one who can stand alone—"

"Will you stop talking, Emily? It's like a talk to young men on the wireless! You've broken my heart. You don't know how lovely you looked as you came into that room with Narracott. Just like something triumphant and avenging off an arch."

A footstep crunched on the lane, and Mr. Duke appeared.

"Oh! there you are, Mr. Duke," said Emily. "Charles, I want to tell you. This is Ex-Chief Inspector Duke of Scotland Yard."

"What?" cried Charles, recognizing the famous name. "Not *the* Inspector Duke?"

"Yes," said Emily. "When he retired, he came here to live, and being nice and modest he didn't want his renown to get about. I see now why Inspector Narracott twinkled so when I wanted him to tell me what kind of crimes Mr. Duke had committed."

Mr. Duke laughed.

Charles wavered. There was a short tussle between the lover and the journalist. The journalist won.

"I'm delighted to meet you, Inspector," he said. "Now I wonder if we could persuade you to do us a short article, say eight hundred words, on the Trevelyan Case."

Emily stepped quickly up the lane and into Mrs. Curtis's cottage. She ran up to her bedroom and pulled out her suitcase. Mrs. Curtis had followed her up. "You're not going, Miss?"

"I am. I've got a lot to do—London, and my young man."

Mrs. Curtis drew nearer. "Just tell me, Miss, which of 'em is it?"

Emily was throwing clothes haphazardly into the suitcase. "The one in prison, of course. There's never been any other."

"Ah! You don't think, Miss, that maybe you're making a mistake. You're sure the other young gentleman is worth as much as this one?"

"Oh! no," said Emily. "He isn't. This one will get on." She glanced out of the window where Charles was still holding Ex-Chief Inspector Duke in earnest parley. "He's the kind of young man who's simply born to get on—but I don't know what would happen to the other one if I weren't there to look after him. Look where he would be now if it weren't for me!"

"And you can't say more than that, Miss," said Mrs. Curtis. She retreated downstairs to where her lawful spouse was sitting and staring into vacancy.

"The living image of my Great Aunt Sarah's Belinda she is," said Mrs. Curtis. "Threw herself away she did on that miserable George Plunket down at the Three Cows. Mortgaged and all it was. And in two years she had the mortgage paid off and the place a going concern."

"Ah!" said Mr. Curtis and shifted his pipe slightly.

"He was a handsome fellow, George Plunket," said Mrs. Curtis reminiscently.

"Ah!" said Mr. Curtis.

"But after he married Belinda he never so much as looked at another woman."

"Ah!" said Mr. Curtis.

"She never gave him the chance," said Mrs. Curtis.

"Ah!" said Mr. Curtis.